# LEFT FOR DEAD

Detective Laura Warburton Series

Book One

**JAY DARKMOORE**

# Copyright ©

Jay Darkmoore 2023

Also by Jay Darkmoore –
*Horror*

The Space Between Heaven and Hell
The Space Between Heaven and Hell – The Shadow
Man

*Dark Fantasy*

The Everlife Chronicles – Hunted
The Everlife Chronicles – Conquest
The Everlife Chronicles – Ruin (Coming Soon)

*Thrillers*

Detective Laura Warburton Series: Book One – Left for
Dead
Detective Laura Warburton Series: Book Two –
Breaking Point (Coming Soon)

*Short Story Collections*

Tales From the Inferno Volume One
Tales From the Inferno Volume Two

*Novellas*

Lorna – A Dark Romance
The Night Shift

"People sleep peacefully in their beds at night only because rough men stand ready to do violence on their behalf." —George Orwell.

**From the Author –**

In my years working in crime and investigation, I have seen some of the worst things human beings can do to each other, intent on plunging the world into darkness. This book is dedicated to those that hold the light to that darkness each day, no matter the cost.

For my brothers and sisters in blue, that keep the dark away. Without you, this world would be a much worse place.

-    Jay Darkmoore

Charlotte,

Thank you for the Support,!

Enjoy -

- Jay Darkmoore

April 2023.

Support the author by signing up for his newsletter at https://www.jaydarkmooreauthor.com/ for a free novella and exclusive content.

# LEFT FOR DEAD

# XXX

I clean the knife dripping with the fresh cut on the rag. She was sobbing. I like it when they cry.

I look upon her. She is *filthy*. A Whore. A filthy, filthy whore. Her blue denim jeans ripped. A dark patch in the centre between her legs. "You pissed yourself." I smile. "You pissed yourself, you dirty girl."

I move closer, the blade handle still nestled in my hand. I feel myself getting hard. My dirty part in my pants. That's what my mother always said. *Don't touch your dirty part, or it will fall off you bad boy!* But it throbbed and ached at the sight of her. But what I do isn't for sex. No. It was for a much greater purpose. And that is what really got my blood flowing.

She tried to kick out as I got closer, but the ropes held her to the chair legs. Her false nails dug into the wood that I had just varnished. I should have taken her fingers first. The scratching rattled through the air. She had no respect for other people's things, which is precisely why she had found herself here with me.

She was crying now. Not like before, but a lower, longer whimper that kept on going, like a vinyl disk held down with fat greasy fingers and pulled under the needle. The rag in her mouth was tucked behind her teeth. I was getting good at this. Too far in, and they would suffocate. Not far enough, and they could shout. I got it just right. Like Goldilocks.

Before I got as good as I am now, I had to cut out a few tongues when their shouting got too loud. This whore had some spirit. She had tried to bite me like a feral rat, but I crushed one of her teeth with my pliers when I put her back in the room. After that, she didn't try it again.

"Please…" She muffled behind the rag. I bit my lip. The throbbing grew more intense. They always begged. She tried to say something else, gagging, mouthing something behind that thick ball of rope.

I stand before her, eyeing those blue eyes and olive skin. Her hair was pitch black, sticking to her face like a spider's web drenched in ink. She was such a wonderful sack of meat, and she had wasted every day of her life, filling her body with filth. I made her pure. Now I will make her perfect. She didn't like the straw at the start. They never do. But they all have it in the end. I lean into her.

"Don't bite." She nodded, her eyes widening. I pull the rag away and remove strands of straw from between her teeth. I dance the edge of the blade around her exposed chest. The blood from her cuts fell like a red river around her nipples. She eyed me. Primal terror in those eyes. I could untie her right now, and she wouldn't move. Wouldn't run. Wouldn't fight. That's when I knew it was time. When they had truly surrendered to their fate, like a deer trapped in the headlights of an oncoming truck. It's their time, and they accept it in a shattering of bone and twisted metal. "Talk."

"What do you want?" She whimpered, spit falling onto her chin like long, melted slugs. Her nose was running, thick and green.

"Perfection," I say. She looks into my eyes through the sagging mask. Her eyes flick to my erection.

"You can do anything. You can fuck me. I'll suck your…"

The back of my hand connects with her mouth. "Dirty girl." She spits blood onto the floor. My. Fucking. Floor. In the house my father built. A flare of rage bubbles, and I squeeze the knife tighter. I grip her face. "Don't do that. Don't ever defile my home."

She shakes her head quickly, terror running over her face. "I'm sorry. I don't… I don't think you're a monster." I lock eyes with her.

"That's right." I move away, leaving her whimpering under that dim light, her shadow stretching, desperately clinging to my feet. "I am not a monster," I say, my back to her. I can hear her nails scratching again, like a cheese grater on my bones. *Next time,* I think. *I'll take the nails first.* "Monsters are amongst men." I turn to her, the mask in my hands, before placing it over my head. "And I am so much worse than that."

Her face turned vacant; all hope had left those puffy blue eyes. She screamed when I began to remove her fingers, and that was when I put the gag back in.

# Chapter One
# Laura

A blanket of dark grey covered the skyline of Wigtown. The heavy, swollen raindrops attacked the bus window that broke through the macabre hum.

"Wigtown Centre," the tannoy said. Laura studied the people around her: Two teenagers with blue hair recording a TikTok. An elderly lady with a Tesco bag and a miniature Yorkie lying on her lap. A middle-aged man reading a novel with a flaming skull on the front. A detective for over ten years, it was something she did instinctively. Especially when your job was to catch killers. She pressed the bell and got off the bus, thanking the driver on her way out.

"Must be a Northern thing," she said to herself, tying the buttons to her thick winter coat and throwing her hood over her copper hair. She moved through the streets, which given the weather, were much busier than she would have ever thought. Back in London, the slightest hint of bad weather and everyone either worked from home or waited for the sun to break before converging onto the streets. But people passed her through the busy streets with their heads hiding under umbrellas like she was invisible. Which was just the way she wanted it to be. She didn't need anyone to recognise her from the papers. A fresh start.

Following the rain-splattered Google Map on her phone, Laura made her way up the street as cars flew by her, splashing pools of water toward her that nearly, oh so very nearly, made for a much wetter walk indeed. Laura moved through the alien streets. Accents different. The spelling on chalkboards outside of the café's written in slang. What the hell was a *Babbies Yed?* And why was it only £1.99?

Not once had she seen a sign for the station, and she wasn't asking anyone. Screw that. She didn't need to stumble to the local crack dealer and ask where the *po po* hung out. She was already piss wet through. She didn't want to add *dead in a ditch with her purse missing* to the list. That was the reason she was up here, after all. She didn't want to become part of the spiralling body count.

After what seemed like going in circles, she found the old brick building of the station that looked like it had been built over one hundred years ago and had since been left to rot. Laura eyed the ancient-looking monument that carved into the darkening sky.

"Here we go." She pushed the heavy blue reception door open. The walls were lined with blue plastic chairs that were bolted to the floor. Behind the counter of thick glass, a constable: young looking with only a slither of facial hair, was typing away on his computer that looked older than he was. Laura approached the glass. "Hello," she said. The constable didn't hear her; if he did, he was just being rude. "Excuse me," she said again, tapping on the glass which made a buffered knock. The constable looked up, eyeing her with distaste.

"Can I help you?"

"I'm looking for the staff entrance," she said. "It's my first day, and I don't know where I am going." He eyed Laura up and down like she was a stray dog.

"You don't look like a police officer?" He said, eyeing her wet coat and tied back hair, her umbrella hanging, leaking the rain onto the carpet.

"My details should be on your system."

"Do you have any ID?" He said, looking back to his computer and typing on the keyboard.

"No," she said sharply. "It was a rushed transfer. I haven't been given my new ID card. Everything should have been emailed over. I'm here to see –"

"I can't let you in without ID," he said, not taking his eyes off the screen. Laura eyed him, taking note of his collar number, the eyes of the waiting room on her and feeling a bubbling of anger fill her veins. She tapped on the glass again. The constable exhaled before peeling his eyes from the monitor, folding his arms and meeting her eyes.

"Is there someone I can talk to?" Laura snapped impatiently.

"Like?"

"Your superintendent." The constable laughed. Another member of the public not taking *no* for an answer.

"It doesn't work that way. You can fill in a complaint form on –" Laura slammed her hand on the desk.

"I am here to see Superintendent Mary Dutton. Now you either drop the attitude and get her for me, or I will make sure you're on every rural night-time badger watch or whatever the hell you lot do around here for the rest of the year." She eyed him fiercely. She could see the sweat gathering on his brow. *Call my bluff. I dare you.* The cop laughed nervously, then put his hands up. He picked up the phone and pressed a single number before sitting back in his swivel chair, eyeing Laura. A slight smile from him as the phone rang. The sound of the ticking clock above the reception desk. The dripping from her coat. A cough from behind her. The officer spoke into the phone.

"I have a…." He raised his brow at her.

"Laura Warburton."

"Laura Warburton, here to see Ma'am Mary Dutton. Okay. Yes, I'll tell her." The phone hung up. "She'll be with you shortly. Take a seat please."

"I'll stand thanks." Neither said anything else. After what seemed like a lifetime in wet heels with eyes staring at her, someone finally came to the door.

"Laura?" She was an older woman dressed in a white shirt with a black chequered cravat with crowns on her shoulders. She stood like she was summoning Laura to the head teacher's office.

Laura moved through the door and into the corridor, taking hold of her umbrella and bag. Mary Dutton had an aroma of cinnamon. Only then did Laura spot the camomile tea in her hand, in a mug that said *I don't give a Fox*. Laura smiled.

"Nice mug."

"It was a Christmas present," Mary said, closing the door. Both women smiled at each other politely. She leant into the reception office. "Darren." The constable turned in his chair. "Get Detective Inspector Warburton a coffee. She must be freezing." Darren's eyes went wide.

"Inspector?" He said, his mouth turning dry.

"Detective Inspector," Mary corrected. "Of the Major Investigation Unit." Laura felt her insides curl.

"I'll have a black coffee, no sugar," Laura said before following Mary through the corridor.

"I'll be in my office," Mary told Darren before they left him to contemplate his career choices. When they had gone, Darren took his phone out of his pocket. He knew he had heard that name before. He typed her name into Google, and the results came up. His heart picked up its pace.

"Yeah," he said to himself, eyeing the news article. "No wonder she transferred in a hurry."

# Chapter Two
# Sheree

Sheree eyed the brown bubbling liquid on the spoon hungrily. The flicker of the lighter broke through the darkness around her. She needed to get the bedroom light fixed, but that cost money. Money she could spend better elsewhere. It had been most of the day since she had had a hit, and she could feel the turkey skin settling in. Mark had helped her get some cash. He didn't give rocks to her for free anymore. That was just the taster to get her on the line. He helped her find new spots. More discreet for clients. Drunks and crackheads had overtaken her usual places. This meant more police were patrolling, and on a suspended sentence already, she didn't want to take another trip to Stile for having some brown on her.

She was trying to cut back. Her probation worker had told her that her teeth were looking better since she had stopped smoking it, but as she pulled the needle from between her teeth and sucked up the melted liquid love, she knew she would have to wear the long sleeves to her meetings for a little longer.

It was winter, so it didn't draw too much attention. In the summer, she would have to start injecting into her feet again. She didn't like doing that. She knew someone from the estate that did that too much and lost their leg from infection. Punters don't want to fuck brass in wheelchairs. So it was her arms in the winter and then feet in the summer, and that was the jolly merry-go-round she rode on. Thankfully, this was England, and it wasn't warm very often.

She bit the belt and tied it around her arm. Blue veins, thick and pulsing, pushed through her thin pale skin. She felt the needle bite like an old friend and depressed the plunger. A release of the belt, and she felt that blanket of warmth envelope her.

Her head met the pillow of the dirtied bed. Old takeaway and microwave meals littered around her that were writhing with maggots and rat shit, as well as a pouch of tobacco and a little skunk to stave off the rattle when business was slow.

Her world melted away into the dark, chipped walls. The shape appeared in the doorway. Tall, broad. Uninvited into her home. She tried to tell him to fuck off, but she fell further into that sea of euphoria before the shape climbed atop her.

# Chapter Three
# Laura

The station was open plan with officers walking around the place. Laura could tell who had been in the job the longest by the degree of dried blood and mud that clung to their high-vis stab vests.

Someone liked the AC turned right down, and Laura rubbed her hands together like trying to start a fire with two damp twigs. She was led through the office past officers on the phones with victims, whispering condolences to them and then asking if they were still there. Other officers were offloading what they had dealt with, with a little dark humour.

"So, the husband comes home and finds his wife dead upstairs," an officer said. "But she's meant to be at work, and he's planned on shagging a brass, right? So, he closes the bedroom door and nails the prostitute in the spare bedroom." A roar of laughter. Another cop pipes up.

"Well, I mean, if you have an evening planned...." Another ruckus of laughter. Laura felt a smile creep along her face. It reminded her of her days on the detective unit in the Met. Before it all went to shit. Before she found the house of the dead.

Before she met *him*.

She shook the thoughts away. She could still taste the salt water when those thoughts came. She hadn't been to the sea since.

Laura moved past the Sargent's desk that sat three abreast. They dipped their head to Mary as she moved by.

"Ma'am," one said.

"Gentlemen. Make sure that *missing from home* gets found. You can't have another one go rogue. Get the dogs on it." She said before they moved past them. Laura caught a glimpse of the Sargent's incident log screen.

"Olivia Murray - Female, missing time – 82 hours."

"You think she's been taken?" Laura asked the superintendent as they walked. Mary stopped at the door, placing her hand on the frame.

"I don't want to jump to conclusions," she said. "But it doesn't look good. Which is why you're here." She moved again through the door, and Laura followed like a lap dog. "But Olivia is a frequent missing person. Drug user. No doubt holding up somewhere and has forgotten to charge her graft phone," she said, laughing. Laura, however, didn't share the joke.

"Have we completed telecoms work yet?" Mary's smile faltered.

"On a drug addict using a burner phone? We wouldn't get any subscriber info."

"But we would get cell site data?" Dutton brushed the comment off.

"Until I know she's in trouble, I won't be authorising anything of the kind. Do you know how much money running someone's phone through the masts costs? I must justify each ping for triangulation. And frankly, I have better things to spend the taxpayer's money on than finding someone who would rather fill their veins with shit than want to contribute to society." Laura felt the venom in Dutton's voice. She wanted to press but thought it best not to poke the bear when you're new in its honey pot.

They continued down another myriad of hallways, passing officers who gave a long smile and a nod as they walked. Finally, they slipped through a double door with 'Major Investigation Unit' over the top.

"I don't know what resources you have down south," Dutton said unprompted. "But up here, we don't have a pot to piss in. Resources are stretched enough, and a recurring missing person who is a substance user isn't at the top of our priorities. You'll do well to remember that." Laura felt the walls closing in around her. What had she gotten herself into? She was to run the Major Investigation Unit, but not ask for money to be spent on investigating them?

"Well, what about the murders?" Laura blurted. Mary stopped in her tracks and turned slowly on a dial. Her eyes were hard, and Laura felt her throat run dry.

*Don't poke the bear!*

"You get me a suspect, and I'll give you the budget. But until you have a suspect, find me a victim worth looking for." With that, Dutton turned, continued walking through another set of doors, and passed a kitchen that made Laura's toes curl at the stench. Next, the two of them entered a smaller room with one window. "Here is your office," Mary said. Upon entering, she saw four detectives. A blonde woman was painting her nails. Another younger guy with his head in a monitor, a man with thick-rimmed glasses that was rattling on a keyboard, and another larger man with grey hair was sitting behind two large monitors in the corner next to a busted fan that had a piece of paper taped to it saying, 'OUT OF ORDER.' It didn't take a genius to realise this, either. The fan had no fins.

"Ma'am," they all said in unison like well-trained dogs. They went to stand, but Dutton batted her hand.

"Come on now," she said. "You know I don't like formalities like that," she said gently with a smile that stretched her face like a barbie doll. "Sit down, all of you."

So they did, and the rattling of keyboards resumed. Laura was led to a desk which had a man, easily in his fifties, staring at a computer screen with hair as white as the first snow of January and a face as red as the Indian summer before it. "Jeremy," Dutton said.

Jeremey jolted to his feet, knocking the desk and his cup of cold black coffee. He tried to hide his embarrassment as the coffee filled the stale air.

"Ma'am," he said, smiling awkwardly, trying to both shake her hand and mop up the mess with a role of conveniently placed blue paper towels at his desk. They shook hands, and he turned to Laura who met his smile. "You must be Inspector Warburton?" Jeremy said, extending the invitation to her. Laura nodded, trying not to look at the stain on his dark blue pants.

"The pleasure is all mine," she said, taking his hand. She nearly recoiled at his cold palms, like shaking hands with a corpse.

"She's from the Met," Dutton said, enunciating the last word. "I'll leave you to it." Dutton bowed a goodbye at the hip before leaving the room. Laura felt the room get a little less cramped. Jeremy eyed Laura.

"You get used to her," he said, laughing. "Did she talk to you about her Gin collection?"

"No, actually," Laura said with a furrowed brow. "Should she have done?" Jeremy scoffed.

"If she starts with her Gin collection, you know you're in the shit."

"Good job I didn't get the low down then." Jeremy sat down and pulled another wad of paper towels out from his desk.

"So," he said, soaking up the liquid. "I'm Detective Sargent Jeremy Marriot. I was the head of the Major

Investigation Unit whilst our last DI went off with stress. I've been holding the fort since then." He sighed. "It's been a long few months. I wasn't always this grey." The two laughed again, and Laura felt herself grow a little warmer in the cold room.

"Well, being part of the team is a pleasure." She looked around her. There were three other detectives around her rattling away on their keyboards. He led her to the blonde woman with thick-rimmed glasses, fair skin and a flowery black and white blouse that puffed up around the shoulders. She painted her nails a vermillion red and smoked an e-cigarette between coats. "That's Detective Catherine Morris," he said. Catherine looked up from her nails and grunted a slight smile. She was missing a bottom tooth. She was obviously self-conscious about it, as she wore a lot of make-up and no lipstick to draw attention away. Laura didn't think many people noticed, but she did. She noticed a lot of the more minor details.

"Nice to meet you, ma'am," she said. She caught a look at Laura's ankle bracelet that was shining in the light, peeking out between her pants and socks. "I like your bracelet. Didn't think we could wear jewellery in the office."

"It's just a cheap little thing," Laura said. "Nothing too fancy. And I don't know what the policy is. And less of the Ma'am shit," she said. "Not in here. Out there, maybe, but not in here. We are all one team here. It's Laura. That's what my old team called me down south."

"Dern seeerth," one of the other detectives blurted. Her eyes fell on him. The younger one. Way too young to be a detective. Less a wrinkle on his face. He was built like a tree with short dark hair and a speckling of stubble creeping along his square jaw.

"That's Craig Sinick," Jeremy said. "He's fresh out of the box to the detective world and the biggest prick I have worked with in a long time." Jeremy laughed. Craig let out a snigger.

"Thanks, Sarge," Craig said, leaning back in his chair. Laura eyed him curiously, cocking her head.

"Have we met?" She said. Craig narrowed his gaze, then shook his head.

"Not that I can recall," he said. Laura focused her mind but then drew a blank and shook the thought away. With the number of people she dealt with, it's natural to confuse some of them. Mixing the living with ghosts of the dead wasn't a good thing. But yet, something about him was definitely familiar.

Jeremy continued to talk, sounding far away like he was in a dream. Laura was still eyeing Craig as he continued working on his computer. "Ma'am?" Jeremy said. Laura snapped her attention back to him, running her hand through her hair. Jeremy was pointing to a smaller man, frailer, with thick-rimmed glasses and hair that was running away from his face. His shirt was creased, and his pants were held up by braces.

"That's Dennis. Our data head. You won't get much out of him. He's dealing with a banking fraud case, and he sits at that computer most of the day, clicking away at his files and going through spreadsheets."

"Sometimes we have to nudge him to ensure he's alive," Catherine said from behind them. "Even at the Christmas parties. Just sits there, don't you Dennis?" Dennis was absorbed in his work. Focused. Catherine blew on her drying nails. "See? Like speaking to a statue."

"Nice to meet you, Dennis," Laura said. Dennis didn't answer. She felt a flare of anger running through her. Laura eyed Jeremy with a pained look. He shook the heat off like melting snow.

"He's a good detective," Jeremy said in a hushed whisper. "A little odd, but anyone who does this kind of work must have a screw loose somewhere, am I right?" Laura didn't answer.

"Where is my desk?" She said, changing the subject. Jeremy led her to the corner of the room behind Jeremy's desk. On the wall was the outstanding incident list. She reviewed the stats and the number of unsolved murders, rapes, frauds, robberies and missing people. Jeremy was talking, but his voice sounded miles away. Laura's attention was on the utterly failing unit she had taken over. "Jesus fucking Christ," Laura mouthed. Jeremy sat back down, and Laura surveyed her new team. She eyed the Sargent's screen. He was playing some game. Catherine was on a fresh coat of nail polish, and Dennis hadn't so much as looked at her. The only one who avoided eye contact and looked like they were working was Craig. She felt that flare of anger bubble even more. This was meant to be a fresh start, and she was already knee-deep in shit.

# Chapter Four
# Laura

Laura made a face of war as she scraped the mould from the bottom of the coffee cup, which looked like it had more time in the job than she did. She rinsed it out, letting the putrid coagulated liquid slop into the plug hole and washed it away.

Next was the pile of dishes that had food practically glued to them. Laura opened the fridge by the sink and nearly hurled right there on the spot. She saw old plastic containers that resembled forgotten science experiments. She didn't bother opening them, but instead threw them straight in the bin which erupted with a mist of buzzing flies.

"Want a coffee, ma'am?" Craig said from behind her, standing in the doorway. He slipped past her and flicked on the kettle that looked more stained than a hooker's bedsheet. Laura didn't answer. She was staring at the massacre that was the inside of the microwave.

"Don't think Dennis is being rude," Craig continued. He's going through some family stuff right now." Laura turned her attention to the bins, covering her nose from the smell of rot.

"Who the hell let this get so bad?" She said. Craig laughed awkwardly.

"Hey, I come to clean the streets, not dishes." He lifted and pointed to the kettle. "Now, about that coffee?" There is nothing Laura wanted less in the world right now than to drink anything from this kitchen. With the number of foodstuffs laying around and old discarded tea bags, she was surprised they didn't have a severe rat problem. Craig opened up the cupboard below the sink and fingered the assortment of chipped mugs. He took one out, then opened another drawer to find a teaspoon and one of the hinges came loose, making the door droop. On the verge of seeing a cutlery massacre on the floor, Craig shot his hand under the failing drawer and caught the catastrophe before it happened. "You gotta be careful with that drawer," he said laughing. "It's a little worn out."

"Estates?" Laura said.

"What?"

"Estates? Maintenance? Won't they fix the drawers? Or put something in to make it, you know, less terrible?" Laura had a bitter tone to her voice. Craig closed the drawer quickly, batting the corners with his palm.

"The constabulary is broke ma'am," he said. "They can't afford to give cops new boots, never mind new drawers. Dennis tried to fix it a while ago, but he made it so much worse, so now we just pull and hope."

"Pull and hope?"

"Yeah," Craig said, placing his own personal coffee mug on the stained worktop. The mug read, '*I'd rather be in bed than in this place.*' Craig smirked at Laura. "Pull and hope. Just like my love life." Laura felt her skin prickle. She didn't know if it was the stench or the way his eye just winked at the comment, but she was close to the steam train of bile reaching mouth town.

The kitchen walls were spreading with damp, and the mountain of unwashed dishes was piling high, thick with grime and soaking in dirtied dishwater. The light overhead buzzed and blinked loudly. At least the clock on the wall was busted. She didn't mind that.

Craig turned to the kettle as it *clicked*. He took hold of it and poured his own cup, before taking a long slurp.

"The Superintendent in charge of the budget said that due to high demand of what's going on, we have to cut costs in other areas." He eyed the pile of dishes. "I'm not a cleaner. I'm a detective. I don't wash dishes."

"That's a very bad attitude," Laura bit. Craig leant back on the counter and slurped his coffee loudly. "So, what do you know of the cases then, the missing girls? Any confirmed dead?" Craig shook his head.

"Two dead. Two women. Found in a warehouse a long way out near the edge of town. Both drug addicts. Pathology is being done now but neither have been deemed suspicious. Other than that, just a whole lot of missing people. If more bodies were showing up, we would have the press all over us. The home office won't pay for a missing person, so until we start finding corpses, we get no funding. Which is good, because when bodies do start turning up, we'll be getting asked questions."

"And what is the team doing about it right now?" Laura said, her tone hard, eyeing the nonchalant way Craig was standing speaking to someone three times his rank and more service than he'd had birthdays.

"We're exploring leads. Dennis is trying to put something together for a pattern but nothing is coming together. Not with his workload coming out of his ears. Then Catherine is on the lead for the sexual stuff but, you know." He shrugged. "Sadly, victims don't always like speaking to the police."

"And what about you?" Laura scalded. "What are you doing on this team to find these missing girls?" Craig placed his cup down with a loud rattle.

"I'm doing my best. I have a workload too. I'm drowning myself. I have robberies and other shit going on." He took another drink of his coffee as Laura continued to bag up the overflowing bins. "So," "What brings you to the North? Transfer? Or did you piss someone off?" A red rag to a bull. She turned and furrowed her brow.

"Excuse me?" Laura spat, the cursing cutting her nerves. Craig smiled.

"Sorry," he laughed. "I –"

"Wipe that fucking smile off your face right now." Craig's smile wavered, and then he stood straight and dipped his head, reducing eye contact.

"Just a question."

"It's a hell of an assumption. You're assuming I don't want to be up here."

"Well, do you?" Craig said, eyeing her. Laura chewed the inside of her lip.

"You have two bodies and a lot of unaccounted-for people. Your force is on the verge of special measures. You have a staggering crime rate and your detection rates are down the toilet. More missing people than any other force in the Northwest. So yes Craig. I am fucking thrilled to be here." Laura eyed him with fire. She took the drink out of Craig's hand and put the mug on the table. In her pocket, she dug out a five-pound note and placed it in his hand. "Go and buy some cleaning products and clean this kitchen." Craig's face went all kinds of crazy.

"Excuse me?"

"Am I not speaking English?" Laura said. "You told me that they won't clean in here, and you work in here. You told me that you're not a cleaner, which means you're happy to let other people clean up after you. Now I'm guessing by your lack of wrinkles and grey hair, you're not much older than say, twenty-three, twenty-four?" Craig's mouth curled inwards.

"I'm twenty-five."

"Okay, and you joined the Major Investigation Unit at such a young age? You can't have gone through the proper channels, meaning you either know someone high up, or you're good with your mouth."

"What does that mean?"

"I'll let you think about it." Laura said, holding his gaze. "I want team players on my team. And if you are going to be on *my* team, then you will act as part of *my* team. And as part of *my* team, you will make the place where *my* team makes drinks and eats food less of a shit hole." Laura put the rest of the chipped mugs into the sink. "Now go and get some cleaning stuff. I saw a mini market on my walk-in. Let me know when you're done." With that, she left the kitchen and left Craig staring at her both confused and vexed, holding the five-pound note in his hand.

"Bitch," he whispered, as he moved to get his coat from the locker room.


"Where's *soft lad*?" Jeremy said, looking over his desk.

"Who?" Laura said, pulling her hair from her face.

"Craig?" Jeremy said. "His file on the fraud job needs approval. I need to go over it with him."

"Is it urgent?" Laura said. Jeremy pursed his lips and shook his head. "Good, because I sent him to get some cleaning products for the kitchen. A silence filled the air then as fingers stopped tapping on keyboards.

"You're taking the piss aren't you ma'am?" Jeremy said with his mouth about to hit the floor. Laura shook her head.

"It needs cleaning, and the cleaners won't do it, so I made him do it." Jeremy's eyes went wide, and he shared a look of astonishment with Catherine who sat halfway through a sudoku puzzle. Dennis didn't even seem to notice anything was being said, tapping away on his computer furiously. "What?" Laura said, feeling like she wasn't privy to a big secret.

"She's not gonna be happy," Catherine squeaked from behind her desk. "The Superintendent who showed you around. It's his mother." Laura's blood went cold.

*You got to this position because you know someone high up,* the voice in her head repeated. Made perfect sense, hence why he never had to worry about a damn thing going wrong. Probably still wipes his arse for him.

"I don't care," she said defiantly, moving to her desk. "I'm in charge of this unit, not her, and I don't want to be making food and drinks for my team in that kitchen." The rest shared another look of bemusement and dropped their heads back to their monitors. Laura sat down and pulled out her phone to check her messages.

*Nothing.* She did it out of reflex. Like telling an alcoholic to guard my vodka. Sure, she had notifications and messages from friends, but nothing from *him.* She closed her screen and pinched the bridge of her nose. *It's been a year. It would be impossible.*

*Is it though?* The voice she tries to ignore scratched against her brain. *They never did find his body…*

Laura eyed them, and then she eyed the broken fan and touched the radiators that hadn't gotten warm all day. "Stop what you're doing," she said to the team. "I have a few tasks for the lot of you as well."

# Chapter Five
# Sheree

"Get the fuck off me, Mark!" Sheree yelped. Mark, whose relationship status was constantly marked as *it's complicated* on Facebook, rolled off of her with a hard-on poking through his tracksuit pants.

"You didn't call me back," he said, annoyed. He took a pack of smokes from his jacket and sparked one up, flicking the ash onto the floor, which was made of a carpet of discarded clothes.

"I was working," Sheree said, still half gone by the effects of the brown. "But I'm not working tonight. The last client, the fat client, the one who drives the Mondeo...." Sheree looked off into the dark. She pulled her hair behind her head, her loose vest top draping and showing her ribcage. "Tonight, I'm getting high. I'll text you in the morning." She stood from the bed. Naked from the waist down. Her legs were littered with swollen bruises of fingers that wouldn't take *no* for an answer. Sheree peered through the dirtied windows of the high-story apartment she called home. "What are you doing here anyway? Thought you got nicked?" Mark let out a laugh.

"Who told you that?"

"Olivia."

"Cunt," Mark spat. "Can't hold her piss, that girl." He scowled. "Yeah, they nicked me for having a wrap on me. Searched me on Bagot Avenue. Plain clothes."

"Told you not to go around there anymore, Mark. You want to go down again?"

"Better than this shit hole," he said with venom. Sheree felt the stab through the heart. Something she had gotten used to. "But," Mark continued. "I'm not gonna go down for it. Went '*no comment*' in the interview. The case got dropped because they couldn't prove it was crack cocaine. Gonna start keeping it in my mouth for when the cops turn up. I can swallow it if they search me then."

"That's disgusting," Sheree said. "Was it a rock?"

"No comment." He laughed again, lying back on the sheetless mattress, cigarette dimps and ash littering the bed covers, staring at the ceiling that was chipped and covered with mould. "Come here," he said, staring at her in that setting sunlight. Olive skin. Her ass like a snow globe. Sheree either didn't hear him or chose to ignore him. Either way, she stared out into the encroaching night as daylight descended over the city skyline. The world beneath her bustling, blackened windows lined the opposite buildings.

"Is this all we have?" She said, almost speaking to herself. Condensation gathered on the glass, and she ran her finger through it. She eyed the bleeding evening sky and felt like she was drifting away on a horse made of clouds.

"What you on about?" Mark said, turning onto his stomach, his teeth, what was left of them, clenching the cigarette butt, hands dirtied and yellowed, hanging over the edge of the bed.

"Never mind," Sheree said, tracing lines across the steamy window in the shape of a love heart, then quickly etching it out.

"Nah, come on, *Ree*," Mark said. "Come here and talk to me. You in a *deep* again?" Sheree smiled. A *Deep*. That's what they called it when the heroin was good and *really* took hold, and the thoughts that lay under the surface could sprout and float out of their mouths. The best and deepest conversations they ever had were when they were lying on the bed in a *deep* talking about the world, their hopes and dreams of getting clean, starting a family, and getting the fuck out of Wigtown. It never lasted though, and the next day the recollection was like listening to a conversation through a thick wall. She moved and lay next to him.

"We're gonna get clean," she said, looking into his eyes. "We'll do it properly this time." He held her gaze in that twilight. No bulb in the ceiling. She had sold that to buy bandages for her arms. She didn't want to go to the hospital and have everyone looking at her. Not like last time. Last time she got sectioned, she had to get through a rattle alone. The memories of her bones aching and her stomach expelling anything she had inside it. The memories of her screams through the night kept her awake even now. When she wasn't on the vodka at least. But a rock of brown was cheaper than a 75cl of poison.

"They're getting better," Mark said, tracing his fingers along Sheree's forearms, running over the bumpy scar tissue, wondering if it was a picture of some kind.

"I can't do this anymore," Sheree said, tears gathering on her eyelids. "I don't want to do this anymore." She closed her eyes and shook her head. The *deep* was first, but that always led to the *pit*. And when she was in the *pit*, all she could do was ride it out and try to stop herself from opening the window and taking a one-way trip down.

"I know baby," he said in a low whisper. "I know, and I want that too. I want us to be a family. To get out of this shit hole forever. And we will, I promise." She opened her reddening eyes, like burning emeralds. "I need you to keep helping me." Her eyes began to burn again.

"I don't want to go out tonight," Sheree whispered. "It's cold and wet. I look a mess; I still have the black eye." Mark squeezed her hips a little tighter.

"I know baby," he said, but I'm there to look after you remember?"

"You weren't there last night," she said, trying to pull away. He pulled her back into him, holding her face between his fingers, scrunching her cheeks up like a bad bunny rabbit.

"I was selling. I was trying to make us some cash so we can ditch this place. You gotta learn to look after yourself. I can't be your fucking babysitter all the time." She tried to pull away again, but his fingers wrapped tightly around her wrist. She made a face of war.

"You're hurting me!" She cried out, wining like a music disk dragging slowly under a rusty needle. "Let go!" Mark squeezed tighter, and when she tried to pull away again, he grabbed a fistful of her hair and buried her face into the pillow.

"You just said you want to leave but you won't work for it? Stop thinking about yourself all the time you selfish bitch!" He held her there until she stopped crying, then let her go, bouncing off of the bed. He picked up an empty vodka bottle and threw it against the wall where it smashed like an explosion of sharp marbles. "I do everything for you, and you can't do shit for me?" Sheree didn't answer, her face still in the pillow. Mark lit another cigarette and began pacing around the room, his hands running over his shaven head and over the half-finished tattoo on his neck of a British bulldog that looked like an infant did it in the dark. "Get cleaned up. We're going out working." Sheree didn't move. A steam train of rage exploded in Mark's chest. Before he could stop himself, he had a fist full of Sheree's hair and was pulling her head back, those emerald eyes now turned bloodshot and cracked, while his brown turned an abyssal black.

"You want to end up being some smack whore forever? Sucking dick in the rain for the rest of your life?"

"No," Sheree coughed through her tears. He looked at her with disgust like she was a writhing maggot he found on his food.

"You don't love me."

"I do…" He shook his head.

"If you did, then you wouldn't make me do this to you."

"I'm sorry…" she dithered, "I'll do it, just let go of me." Mark held her gaze for a moment and then threw her back down on the bed. Moving away, he took out a small bag of green and placed his ass on a chair with a weary *thump*. Sheree sobbed as she climbed out of bed, searching the forsaken clothes on the floor, trying to find something that was worth putting on. She settled for a vest and a pair of jeans.

"Not them," Mark barked, licking the paper of the rollup and sprinkling crushed weed into the paper. "Something sexier. Let them see those gorgeous legs baby." Sheree went to protest, but Mark met her eye. Sheree relinquished her gaze, again stripping off. She found a short denim skirt and pulled it up. Then, a small jacket that barely covered her. She held it in her hands.

"It's cold," she said quietly. Mark stood and moved to her, the stench of booze and smokes emanating from his breath, his large frame shadowing over her, muting out the dying light of dusk. He held up the joint.

"This will make it easier," he said, and sparked it up, exhaling a long noxious stream of smoke into her face. "Finish getting ready, and you can have some before we go out."

Sheree did as instructed: she cleaned herself downstairs with a dirtied flannel in the sink. The bathtub was filled with drenched clothes and her razors were dull and coated in hair and blood. But still, she used them anyway, wincing as they nicked her legs and underarms. She tied her hair back with a bobble, took a handful of paracetamol that she kept behind the dirtied medicine cabinet, and washed them down with a mouthful of wine that she stored next to the sink basin. Finally, she applied some concealer to her eyes, a dash of red lipstick and brushed her hair.

Mark moved behind her and wrapped his hands around her waist.

"You look beautiful, babe," he said. The words were both sweet and sour in Sheree's ears, landing like a warm bombshell on an iceberg, melting all the pain away but drowning what little chance she had of surfacing above the cascading water. "I love you." He held her tighter and then after a moment, led her to the front door and took her keys and phone from the bedside. "Here you go," he said, handing her half of the remaining joint. He put his hand in his pocket, pulled out his flick knife, held it up to the dull light, and then put it back into his pocket. "Let's go. It'll be a busy one."

# Chapter Six
# Laura

"Goodnight, everyone," Laura said as she turned the lights off in the office. All passed her with their heads low; not a single utterance of farewell or go fuck yourself left their lips as they moved down the corridor and out into the dark car park.

Laura listened to the silence envelope her. The night shift response unit was on duty now, and as she moved through the main office, she watched the constables drink strong coffee and tap furiously on their keyboards as their radios chattered in their ears.

A call came in, and it must have been urgent, because at once like some unheard call to action, they ran for the exit and dove out into the freezing night. She caught a glimpse at the radio of a passing bobby. It was flashing bright red. *Code zero,* she thought, remembering her days in uniform. When someone pressed that red button, you stopped what you were doing and made for wherever you were required. It meant someone needed help, and they needed it five minutes ago.

Laura moved to her locker and stopped. She was staring at the piece of A4 paper taped to the front of it. A word etched in crude writing.

*'Murderer'*

Laura's blood ran cold. She snatched the paper off quickly and crumpled it up. Laura looked around the locker room. Just ghosts stood with her.

*News travels fast,* her mind chattered in her ear. *How long before they found out what happened?* Laura could taste sea salt again. Then the voice changed to another, and she felt the prickle of spiders on her skin.

*Hey baby. How about a boat ride?*

The lights around her muted. Fear gripped her. Her heart beat in her head in that blackness. Seconds dragged by over broken glass. The sound of footsteps drawing closer. Laura felt cemented to the ground.

*Louder… Louder… He's coming back for you.*

*Kiss kiss…*

The lights came back on.

"Ma'am…"

"Jesus fucking…." She turned. Dennis was standing behind her, his thick glasses steamed up and hair a mess.

"You ok?" He said, looking more to the floor than at her. "You were just standing there in the dark. The lights are motion activated." Laura stood eyeing him.

"Did you write this?" She barked, clutching the crumpled paper. Dennis eyed her like a confused dog being scalded.

"Write what?" Silence between them. Laura stuffed the paper in her pocket.

"Nothing," she closed her eyes and let out a small laugh. She pointed to the ceiling. "The lights. Yeah. Right. I must have been daydreaming. Long day. I don't think the unit likes me very much."

"I think you were good," Dennis said, hands in his pockets. He was balding a little and had a serious dandruff issue. "The last Inspector wasn't excellent. Workloads were too high. Investigations falling by the wayside. Kitchen a mess. You fixed that part, and you've been here a day." That spouted a little warmth into her heart.

"Thanks," she said. "It's tough coming to a new unit. I'm used to all pistons firing in unison," she lowered her voice. "Look, I know it's nothing to do with me. But I heard you have things going on at home. I'm here if you need anything." Dennis squirmed in his stance.

"Thanks," he said coolly. "But I work it out in my own way."

"You look like you have your head in the game," Laura said quickly. "All considering. But the rest of the team?" She shook her head. "You not going home?"

"I like to stay a little after hours to finish some work. It's just me at home, so I can stay as long as I like." He laughed at that. "I was thinking of getting a sleeping bag and sticking it under my desk."

"Don't expect overtime," Laura laughed. Dennis reciprocated. She moved to the locker and pulled out her umbrella which was still wet through. "Brilliant."

"So why did you move up here?" He said. Laura felt like she was being questioned by a kid at a park.

"You know," she shook the umbrella off. "A new start." She staggered her breath. "How about you? Why did you become a detective?"

"I like fixing things. My mother always made sure things were perfect in the house. I like trying to put people back together. Some childhood trauma no doubt. Fix things that are *really* broken."

"I get you with that one," she said, pulling on her wet coat. "Anyway," Laura said, taking in a deep breath, "I better be going. I'll have to order a cab. My car should have been dropped off today. It was either drive up in a removal van from London and have no car for a week, or drive in my car and not have a bed so…" She smiled at Dennis with tired eyes. His thin frame drowned under his blue and white striped shirt. She moved past him. "Well, goodnight. See you tomorrow." He didn't respond, only stood and watched her leave, before heading back to the office.

Laura walked out of the back entrance and pulled out her mobile. A quick Google and she found the closest taxi firm. She dialled the number but was told it would be at least an hour before another cab was available. She tried a couple more and, to no surprise, they were the same. Disgruntled, she put her phone back into her bag and pulled out her pack of cigarettes.

Laura sparked up the smoke, inhaling the noxious gas deeply and felt the nicotine numb her stress. She checked her phone while she smoked. No Messages. *Good,* she thought. No one was checking in on her. It would only make the move more painful. She had blocked every old contact she had.

Laura leaned on the wall and listened to the passing cars push from the busy intersections. She Googled train times and bus times. She would be walking home at this rate. *At least it isn't raining,* she thought. But the thick clouds above her promised that that would change.

A flash of light pushed her out of her thoughts. In the car park, a black BMW was flashing at her. Someone behind the wheel waved. Laura looked around her and moved to the car.

"Hey," Craig said, winding down the window. "You look lost? You lose your car?"

"Hi," she said, perplexed. "I thought you were…"

"Mad at you?" He shrugged. "I won't lie, yeah, a little. But hey. At least we have a working fan and a clean office now. Crazy how things can go to shit when you aren't being whipped into shape." He laughed. He eyed Laura's cigarette. "You need a ride?"

"I'm okay thank you," she said politely but with an undertone of restraint.

"You sure? Where are you living?"

"South End."

"That's a hell of a walk from here, ma'am," Craig said. He pushed the centre console, and the doors unlocked. "Come on in," he said. "I'm heading near there. I don't mind. My way of apologising for being a brat earlier." Laura toyed this over. She had promised to leave work and friendship separate, even something as innocent as a lift home, in the past. But it was only a lift home, and she was back in early in the morning anyway. So what harm could it do?

*What harm could it do?*

"Just this once," she said like she was doing *him* the favour. She threw the cigarette onto the ground and got in. The car reeked of stale fast food. Craig fired up the engine. He tapped his lanyard on the gate, and it opened slowly before joining the busy streets towards home.

"What brought you to the North?" He said, after a few minutes of awkward silence.

"To be a *nursery teacher*," Laura bit.

"Fuck," Craig said, "shots fired. I was only –"

"You deliberately undermined me and cast doubt into my abilities as your new supervisor in front of my new team," she said, trying to hold back her viper tongue from strangling that slight smile from his face. "You won't do that again or you're off the murder investigation. I don't give a shit who your mother is. I am in charge. Do you understand?" Craig squirmed a little.

"Yes ma'am," he said. "Sorry."

"Right," Laura said, cracking the window for some air. "Now that's the end of it." She pulled out a cigarette and turned to Craig. "Mind if I?"

"Only if you give me one," he laughed. Laura passed him one. He held it between his teeth and smothered the butt with his lips, then using the lighter, breathed in and coughed sharply before wiping his mouth.

"You don't smoke, do you?" Laura said. Craig shook his head.

"I vape. Never smoked properly. But I try every now and then. Makes me look less of a bell end." They continued for a moment in silence, smoke filling the cab of the car.

"So, tell me about the murders," Laura said. "Haven't had a chance to look at them yet."

"We don't know if they're murders yet," Craig said sharply. "Two drug addicts found dead in a warehouse. All of the missing people are drug users. Probably just some new gear going around. Dennis is looking into if there is a connection, and Mary Dutton is overseeing the whole thing."

"Any leads?"

"At the minute, nothing major. Could be a drug dealer collecting cheques and they skipped town. But that's a hunch at best."

"So, a drug dealer is killing his customers?" Laura said, shaking her head. "Not the best business plan I've ever heard."

"Exactly," Craig laughed. They continued, and Laura directed him a little further until they stopped and idled at the bottom of a cul-de-sac. A large house with a white garage and high roofs stood to the right.

"This is me," Laura said, unclipping her seatbelt. Craig whistled at the sight of the house.

"Nice," he said. "Inspector's salary must be good." Laura stopped as she cracked the door open, holding off stepping out into the cold for just a moment.

"I didn't buy it with the salary," she said, her eyes beginning to burn, that old scar opening again.

"You win something then?" He said, not noticing the pain in her voice. She shook her head again, then locked eyes with him.

"Lost something," she said sombrely. "The bereavement fund paid for the house." She stepped out of the car. Craig tried to utter an apology before she shut the door. Then, without looking back, Laura marched to her house, took her keys out, and stepped through her front door into the dark hallway inside.

# Chapter Seven
# Laura

She closed the door and listened to the sound of tyres against gravel before they disappeared into the night. She stood there, dropping her bag and umbrella onto the ground, resting her head against the door with her eyes closed. What a first day.

Anxiety began to rise in her chest, and she pressed her hand where it hurt the most.

"Please, not again," she said, the fear in her chest building like a snake coiling around her lungs. Her hand came to her throat, and she fingered the wall. The light switch wasn't there.

*Welcome to the night, Laura,* her mind whispered. It was *His* voice again. *Come back to me, my love.* Her fingers found the switch, and her hall lit up – golden light drenching her. The voice melted away. Her breathing began to ease as she told herself things she could see, hear, feel and smell.

"*Grounding,*" the therapist had told her. "*You won't remember at first, but you must try. Then, when they strike, you have to push them away with logic and reason. It's the only way you will ever be normal again after what happened.*" Laura's chest slowed. She was drenched in sweat, her eyes catching her reflection in the hallway mirror. She looked like emaciated dog shit.

After a few moments, Laura moved through the house and threw off her coat onto the kitchen table and poured a tall glass of red wine. She knew she shouldn't be drinking, as it would interfere with her medication. The medication she no longer took, but still had to keep collecting anyway. They helped a little, like the yoga and meditation she had been prescribed. But nothing kept those intrusive thoughts away more than loud music and disturbing books washed down with red wine. It only worked for a while, like trying to keep the tide from coming in with sandcastles.

She sank the glass, poured another, and moved into the front room.

"Hey, Bagpipe," she said, eyeing her cat on the chair. She parked her ass next to him. "How have you been today?" He watched her with those sleepy spheres of hazel, then stretched out his paws, sticking the claws along her legs before climbing onto her lap and falling back asleep.

"Lazy boy," she smiled, nuzzling her face into his fur. Laura took another sip of her wine and placed it on the counter. She reached over to the nightstand, flicked on the side lamp, and took her hardcover book, '*The Winds of Which We Fly.*' She asked her Alexa to kill the main lights, and the shadows around her stretched their arms against the walls.

The book wasn't her usual read. She generally liked crime thrillers, despite the cliché of her profession. But this… this was Ron's, and she'd never finished reading it before he passed away. Her therapist had told her to immerse herself in it, to get it completed, as a symbol of moving on. After a few hours of reading, Laura could hardly keep her eyes open. The book was okay. It was about a young boy who goes to Asia to find himself and join a group of spies.

She turned the night light off and let her torch on her iPhone illuminate the stairs. The dark scratched at her nerves, and despite all her will and best intentions not to, she raced to her bedroom before the imagined jaws of death gripped her around the ankle and dragged her down into that dark abyss where monsters lived. She stabbed the bedroom light on.

"Get a hold of yourself," she whispered, shaking her head, the wine numbing her gums. She hadn't meant to drink the whole bottle but got through it anyway. She got into her nightwear and caught herself in her en suite mirror.

Her back was exposed at the shoulders from the drooping vest she was wearing over her small shorts.

*It's raised again,* she thought, running her fingers over her left shoulder just behind her neck.

*You leave me,* she heard *his* voice once more. *If you ever leave me, I'll kill you.*

Laura slept with the light on that night.

# Chapter Eight
# Sheree

The air was heavy and damp on Sheree's legs. The fishnets she wore didn't give much warmth, but the quarter of vodka she was sipping on from inside her handbag was doing the job just fine. Mark stood in the shadows behind her, just like he always did. Sheree took another gulp of Absolut as a car crawled down the road and parked by the curb. She felt Mark's eyes boring into her back as she approached the idling vehicle. A buzz of a window. A stretching smile along Sheree's puffy face.

"Hey baby," she said. He was older. They all usually were. He pulled out a twenty, and she got in. The drive was short. She knew the best spots to go, away from the cameras and the police. He was a tentative lover, not an arsehole like the others. He wasn't too pushy, and she went at his pace. Not all of her clients were creeps. Only some of them. Some are just lonely. Maybe their wife died, and they just wanted someone to talk to. Sheree didn't mind that. She preferred it. But if they were like this guy, tentative and hungry for much more than simple physical touch, she didn't mind that either. It was her job, and as she took his length out of his pants and locked lips with him over the driver's seat, she let the numbing hug of the vodka do the rest of the work.

He dropped her off a half hour later. Any longer than that, for just a twenty, and Mark would come looking. It had happened before, but Mark ensured they never touched her again. That was his job – both her saviour and her devil. Both her blessing and her curse.

Another car pulled up, and Sheree recognised it. She felt the vodka bubble in her stomach. The window went down, and that familiar smile came out. It was the guy in the Mondeo.

"Hey, beautiful," he said. His hair was greased back and balding like he had watched too many 80s movies. "Fancy another ride?" He grabbed his bulge. Sheree shot Mark a look of worry, and he stepped out of the alley.

"No sale for you tonight fuck face," Mark yelled through the window, flashing his blade. "Now fuck off." The sleazeball held Mark's gaze. Then finally, he rolled up the window and crept away. Sheree released her tight breath, but then it froze again in her lungs as she saw his brake lights flash and the car crept back. Mark moved to the opening window. "Are you fucking –" The wad of notes in the guy's hand stopped Mark's incoming tirade.

"I was drunk last night," he said. "Sober tonight. I'll pay extra." Mark looked at the notes in between his fingers. Easily five hundred right there for the taking. He turned to Sheree who eyed him with terror.

"I don't want to." Mark stepped towards her, his breath hot on her face.

"Look, if you do this, then you don't have to work the rest of tonight or tomorrow. We can go grab some food somewhere nice. Maybe take a ride to a beach somewhere." Mark looked over his shoulder, the sleazeball was rapping his fingers on the steering wheel. "Plus," he continued in a harsh whisper. "If he's willing to pay *that* much, then the guys loaded. That's a new car, and the watch on his hand?" He was practically salivating. "Take him where you normally go, get him all happy like, then I'll rob him."

"Maybe you should fuck him instead?" Sheree spat. Mark slapped her across the cheek. Sheree felt the pain push through the numb.

"Do it."

She felt a wave of fear crawl along her skin as he moved out of the way and returned to the alley.

"You getting in or what?" The guy called from the car. Sheree turned to Mark. He nodded for her to go ahead, flashing the knife in his jacket pocket. Reluctantly, she painted that smile back on and slipped inside.

A short ride to a car park by the local reservoir and not a second after the engine died were his grubby hands all over her flesh. His lips were fat, wet and stinking of whisky and cigarettes.

"You said you were sober!" She winced.

"Shut the fuck up."

"Slow down," she said, trying to pull away.

"Fuck you, cunt." He bit, grabbing hold of her wrists, his hands fumbling under her skirt, pulling at her fishnets.

"I said get off!" She burst out, screaming. She saw his teeth – Yellowed and stretched into a fat grin. The darkness shadowed his face, his eyes glimmering like gemstones at the bottom of the abyss. Her eyes darted out the window onto the empty lot.

"I like it when you fight back," he slobbered. His face came in again, his slobbering jaws falling over her face. *Where are you, Mark?* She thought, closing her eyes as he entered her. He wasn't big, far from it. His stomach pressed on her and she felt his fingers digging into her wrists. He grunted as he took her, his voice rattling in his throat, chest heaving and straining. She tried to push him away, tried to slip her fingers in his pants and pull out his wallet, but she couldn't move. He was so heavy, like an elephant lying atop her.

"Please…." She whimpered, tears gathering on her lip. He sniggered once more.

"That's right," he heaved. "Get daddy goin'." The driver's door flew open and the huge lump was pulled off her, his dick still hard and scraping along the gravel. He fumbled on all fours, coughing into the asphalt. Sheree erected, pulling her underwear back over herself, checking her wrists that were already beginning to bruise, and wiping the slobber from her face.

"Get him, Mark!" She said, pushing through the tears. She watched Mark move to the fat bastard and kick him in the ribs. Sheree heard him let out a furious rattle of breath. "Kick his ass baby!" She screamed. Mark stood tall, proud, his long black leather trench coat swaying in the breeze. Mark dug into his belt line and pulled out the knife. Sheree felt the blood drain from her body. "Mark, wait! Leave it! Let's just go!" He didn't listen, and Mark crouched down with the blade in hand and took hold of the back of the pig's head. He dragged the blade across his throat, opening him up on the floor like a bursting balloon. Sheree felt horror wrap her and the night air settling into her bones. She watched as the punter tried to crawl away, his shirt riding up his back, his pants still wrapped around his ankles. He got a few feet, coughing and spluttering before he stopped, still twitching, lying on the ground as life poured out of him. Sheree crawled to the edge of the driver's seat, mouth hung in terror. "Mark, what have you…." She whispered. Mark turned, and Sheree began to scream.

*It wasn't Mark.*

# Chapter Nine
# Laura

In the morning, Laura walked into the office feeling like she had been hit by a truck. Hell, that would be an improvement. Her hair she could take care of, throwing her red locks into a bobble. But she needed to fix the puffiness in her eyes. A couple of drops and a splash of concealer, and she looked a little more human. It would help a little, but she couldn't look like she had been crying all night. Not here. Not in this new place. She had left all that behind.

She strode through the double doors into the MIU office with a large drinks carrier filled with four cups of Starbucks in one hand and her vanilla skinny latte in the other.

"Morning, team," she said, moving to her desk and setting the coffee down.

"Morning, Ma'am," Jeremy said, tucking into a croissant. Given the number of crumbs on his jacket, he was already two pastries deep and picking his final victim. Another round of good mornings, followed by the clatter of keyboards.

Laura fired up the computer and opened up her emails. She saw one from the superintendent highlighted as *PRIORITY*. Laura opened it and read it.

"Fuck," she whispered. Her stomach both bubbling with bile and jumping with glee.

"Anyone doing the fun run on Tuesday with the Hidden Harm Team?" Jeremy said. Catherine, who was actually doing *work,* shook her head. Jeremy laughed, finishing off his final croissant. Laura stared at the screen reading the email, jotting notes down in her daybook. "Ma'am?"

"What?" She said, her mind miles away.

"Fun run, Tuesday. Hidden Harm Team. You fancy it?" Laura looked at him like he was speaking a foreign language. "Erm, yeah sure." She got back to her reading, then noticed the distinct lack of bravado in her ear. She turned and saw two empty desks. "Where are Dennis and Craig?"

"Running late," Jeremy said, wiping his mouth.

"What? Both of them?" Laura questioned, eyes beginning to strain once more. *I don't need this shit today. I should have called in sick.* "They travel in together?"

"No," Catherine said in that long, stretching tone that everyone up north seemed to have. "Craig's running late because of traffic. Dennis has got the shits."

Laura felt a flush of embarrassment. The thought of someone being glued to their toilet shouldn't be embarrassing but there are some things you just never outgrow, no matter how much shit you have seen in your life. Literally.

"Can you look at his file?" Laura said. "The fraud file? Make sure it's all in order for when he gets back?" Catherine eyed her with venom, waving her wet nails in the air.

"I would, ma'am," she began. "But I don't really know what I'm doing." She smiled and continued typing away slowly, fake nails rattling the keyboard. Catherine side-eyed Jeremy who had already buried his head into his mobile phone. The beating in Laura's head grew stronger.

"Okay," she snapped. "What's going on?"

"What do you mean?" Catherine said befuddled. Laura scoffed, putting her coffee on the table, a small volcano erupting from the lid onto the wooden tabletop.

"I get it. I'm new here. I don't know you. You don't know me. I come in cracking the whip telling you to clean up the shit hole of a kitchen and now, I have one staff ill, one staff late, and you two sniggering between each other and you're telling me you don't know what you're doing? Maybe I should run this fucking unit myself?" Laura spat, trying, but failing, to keep a lid on it.

"Ma'am, it's not like that," Jeremy piped up from behind his desk. "Catherine has a lot of work on, and she just –" Laura stood up, snatched her coat and grabbed her coffee.

"She'll do what her supervisor says." She turned, eyes burrowing into Catherine's wide spheres. "Or you can go on a new unit. Now open up the fraud file and see what needs doing." She left the room, feeling the glare of eyes stabbing into her back.

Coming down the hallway, Craig was walking quickly, a McDonald's coffee in his hand, his gym bag thrown over his shoulder and his shirt half-buttoned up. He saw Laura coming and his face flashed with panic.

"Running late?" Laura eyed him from head to toe.

"Uughhh," his voice croaked, brain not computing, sirens blaring in his head *Abort. Abort.* "I didn't think you started this early?"

"Get your shit together and come with me." She said, storming past him.

"Where are we going?" He said, turning on his heel to follow. She didn't answer, only carried on walking.

Outside in the car park, Laura stood by the unmarked cop car with her second cigarette of the day. Craig walked out, his shirt loosely buttoned up and a navy blue tie swinging in the wind. He hadn't even put a coat on. The smoke caught in her throat as he approached.

*Those shoulders are like two boulders flanking a mountain. Those arms. He's strong. I wonder if he could…* Laura snapped herself out of it. *Not up here.* She scalded herself again. *Not up here. Not after Ron.*

"Where are we off to then?" Craig said, walking with his coat folded over his arm and his bag containing statement paper and his laptop.

"You gave me a lift last night. It was really good of you," she said, finishing her cigarette. "So, rather than give you the shit I've given the rest of the team for happily leaving me stranded, I thought you could come with me on a job."

"Sounds good," he said, cracking the driver-side door open. Laura cleared her throat as Craig went to slip inside. "You okay?"

"I'm driving." She smiled, and Craig handed the keys over.

"Adjust the seat," Craig said. "I like to stretch out." Laura slipped into the driver's seat and fell backwards. Craig reached over and pulled the seat adjuster. Their eyes met a moment. "Just like that," he said, clicking her into place. She eyed him, the corner of her mouth curling into a smile.

"You're still not off the hook for being late," she said curtly and fired up the engine. It was a slick grey Peugeot with not a scratch on it. Good old CID fashion. She knew that the uniformed cops would sneer and jib at them as they drove through the car park. No matter.

"You sure you can still drive this Ma'am?" Craig joked. The comment flared her temper again. It didn't take much. She knew she hadn't been herself since leaving the Met. Laura turned to him with venom lingering in her eyes. She pulled up the centre console, flicked on the blue lights, and tested the siren with Zen-like efficiency.

"I may not have been in uniform for a while, but I still know how to drive like a mother fucking cop when some shit bag decides to get on his toes. The question is Craig, can you run after them if they decide to decamp and go off-road?" Craig sat back, scratching the stubble on his chin.

"Point taken," he said. "So, where are we heading?" Laura set the sat nav to their destination. A small car park just outside the city centre flanked a local park and reservoir.

"Hope you didn't eat this morning," she said. "We're heading to a murder scene."

# XXX

You smell like sweat and piss. Filthy girl. Why do you waste your life yet beg me to keep you alive?

Don't mind the rats. I feed them. They won't hurt you. Unless I leave you in here. But I won't do that. I'm not a monster. I lived in this room for years as a boy. I know what it's like. But I made myself *good* and *pure.* Unlike the rest of the vermin on the streets.

I like the way you look, like a broken plaything. Like the dolls I used to have. I couldn't have boys' toys like the other kids. Action men and superheroes weren't allowed in my home. But now I'm a superhero. I make the bad ones go away. But you aren't good. You aren't pure, so you will go with the others, and you will lead her to me. Lead *her back to me.*

My daddy was a drinker. Mother was a punching bag.

I don't like being sad. But I am sad a lot. Looking through his eyes, always just below the surface like a shark in still water. When I get too sad, I come above the surface, and then I get my playthings. I get them and they make me happy. Like I made dolls when I was younger, made a perfect mother and father. Made a happy home.

Mummy knows, of course – *A mother knows her children as she knows herself.* That is what she would say when I would be bad. *Oh, you shouldn't have done that. But I did know you weren't feeling well, which is why I got the bin bags ready just in case.* She always had the bin bags ready. Certainly, as I got older and better at catching the animals.

It was when I brought the stray cat home because it was filthy and eating things it shouldn't, I wasn't allowed to go outside again. I just had to watch them through my filthy room as my daddy disappeared and my mother cried all day. So, I took to playing with mice and rats that I found in the walls instead. They never left. I never let them. I didn't start with rats though. I started with burning bugs with a magnifying glass on our holidays to sunny places. I can never remember the names of where we went, but I can remember how the ants smelt as their bodies crinkled and turned black. It got bigger from there. The *blur* got worse, and I couldn't always remember what I had done, just the smell of bin bags and the sight of blood.

"Where? …"

I stood up and moved to your new home. You cracked your eyes open. How silly of me not to notice. I get too caught up in my own head sometimes.

You're shaking now. I love this part – When the prey finds out it's stuck in a cage. It's okay little plaything. I'll let you out soon enough. As soon as I'm done with the others, it will be your turn. Then you won't ever leave.

# Chapter Ten
# Laura

"We're here," Laura said, as they pulled up the dirt track. The car park was deserted, except for a single officer standing by a patrol vehicle. He raised his hand, and they stopped before he peered into the driver's side window. Laura and Craig held up their warrant cards, and the officer produced a scene log which they both scribbled on, before letting them through.

Pennington Flash was a place of natural beauty teaming with wildlife. One would usually find joggers and dog walkers enjoying the meandering of ducks and the sound of the tide lapping against the riverbank under a cloudless sky of ice blue.

Today however the frost that crunched under the tyres was undisturbed. Yesterday it was a place to come and observe natural beauty. Today, it was a place for horrors. The officer lifted the police tape as they drove under and moved into the car park. In the distance, sunlight bounced off the pop-up forensics tent.

Laura pulled the handbrake and killed the engine. She cracked the door and stepped out into the cool morning air, nestling her hands into her pockets. Craig followed.

"What a beautiful place," Laura said, hot breath like smoke. "Fuckers."

A huge open car park with a vast lake to one side and to the other, a deep forest thick with trees and shrubs. It was a short walk down to the CSI tents, and the bite of the cold was already nipping at Craig's flesh. He cupped his hands and heaved heavy breaths between his fingers.

CSI workers in full white suits were hanging out of the front of a silver Ford Mondeo, the clicking of cameras rattling through the air. Another worker was crouched over a large bloodstain and was taking samples. Mary Dutton spotted them coming down, she sipped her Costa coffee and moved towards them wrapped in a thick plush coat. Her white hair poked from under her black bowler cap like ash-covered snow.

"Ma'am," Laura said. Superintendent Dutton nodded, her nose turning a plum red.

"Inspector Warburton," Dutton said, then looked at Craig. Her expression was like staring at an insect needing to be crushed immediately. "Craig."

"Ma'am," he said, his voice firm, the cold vanishing from his vocal cords.

"Mother is fine."

"Ma'am is better." The air seemed to grow a thick skin, and Laura felt it gathering in her throat.

"So, what do we have then?" Laura said quickly, cutting the tension. Dutton flitted her eyes to her, her expression that of curiosity.

"Follow me."

More officers came into view as they got closer to the tents – dog handlers searching the encroaching woodland, other cops holding notepads, pointing to the vehicle and the bloodstains, discussing lines of enquiry of CCTV or possible witnesses. Laura knew this kind of killing was usually planned. They picked their location wisely. No ANPR. No witnesses. No cameras. A real *who done it.* And with all the unknown killers – Zodiac, and The Ripper, the body count must start tallying up before connections are formed, and that made the air bite Laura that little sharper.

Dutton passed Craig and Laura rubber gloves and a facemask before they stepped into the tent.

He was lying face down on the floor. His hairy arse and legs were exposed; pants tangled around his ankles. He was around his mid-fifties, with thinning black hair and overweight. Livor Mortis had set in, making his stomach and face look swollen. His eyes were open, stuck in a gaze of death as he stared into the void. Laura winced at the smell. She had never been good around dead bodies. She could ID them, look at photos and even touch them when needed. Speak to them when she felt the need to. But she never got used to that smell. Not since the *barn*. Not since *Alex Thompson*. Death had its own aroma. One that crawled in your nostrils and latched onto your brain. You can't ever describe it, but you can always remember it.

"How long has he been dead?" Laura asked. A CSI investigator that was taking snaps with a Canon camera looked at her with pitch-black eyes.

"It was cold last night so decay has been slow. Despite the pooling and the smell, it's actually quite fresh," she laughed. "Livor Mortis has kicked in, but it's more the cold than decay that has made him stiff. Given the discolouration and pooling of the stomach and face, the lack of insects and the consistency of the blood pooling, I would say he's been dead for around 4 hours."

"Very thorough," Laura said, trying to not breathe in the death.

"I'm a nerd, what can I say." She shrugged. "Dead things interest me." She extended a hand. "Celine Burrows."

"Laura Warburton."

"Haven't seen you before," Celine said, cheeks crinkling under the mask. Laura looked back at the body.

"I'm sure you'll be seeing plenty of me."

"Hope so." Laura let go of Celine's hand.

"So…" Laura cleared her throat, fingering her fringe. "Who called it in?"

"Dog walker around forty minutes ago," Superintendent Mary Dutton responded quickly, moving the conversation along, eyeing the body with the emotion of a rock. "He's back at the station now giving a statement. A local patrol was sent to investigate and confirmed it. The scene was set up around twenty minutes ago." Dutton took another sip of her coffee. "The media haven't gotten hold of the story yet, but it won't take long. If any of them ask you questions, we have a team to direct them to. Don't say shit." Craig and Laura nodded.

"Any identification?" Laura said.

"Nothing. No wallet, money. Anything. We're doing enquires. But right now, we've got a *John Doe.*"

"Have we run the car through?"

"Comes back to someone on the other end of the country. Reported stolen a week ago. False plates."

"Why was he here?" Craig said.

"You're the detective," Mary bit. "You tell me?" Craig turned with a look of fire in his eyes.

"If I had to say, I would say we're looking for a female, maybe around age 25." Laura eyed him.

"What makes you say that?"

"Isolated location in a rough part of the city. The male was found with his pants down with a laceration to his throat. No ID, money or wallet. I'm thinking this guy is a punter and picked someone up for some midnight action and it turned into a robbery gone wrong."

"Very good," Mary smiled. "I'll send someone out to the community and ask the questions. They went to move away from the tent, but then a voice crept into their ears.

"Ma'am," Celine said. Mary turned.

"Yes." She was crouched by the body. Her gloved hands were flat under his bulking swollen stomach. "What is it?" Mary said, drawing in.

"I think… there's…." Celine was trying to push her hand under the bulk. "Do you mind?" Craig looked around the tent, hoping for a volunteer, but Laura was already gloved up and moving. Mary eyed her son with disgust, then gestured for him to get to it. He did with a huff, taking off his jacket and letting the cold cut in a little deeper. He joined Laura and Celine by the hulk of the body. Those dead eyes stared at them, tongue swollen and blue falling limply out of his mouth.

Celine coiled her finger around what seemed to be a piece of wire stuck under the body like the end of a fishing line. Laura saw it too. *What is that?*

"Lift on three. Are you ready? One, two, three!" The group pushed that hulk of dead meat away from them. Laura saw it first, then Celine and Craig. Horror wrapped them. The corpse's chest had been roughly sewn shut. A long snaking line from the base of his neck stretched right down to his exposed genitals bulging with fat and leaking organ juices onto the ground.

"What in the world?" Laura gasped. Celine pulled the string. It went taut, but then began to pop away and come loose, unwrapping the stitching one nook at a time. The fleshy mouth of the wound vomited putrid insides onto the floor. The stench was eye-watering. Dutton evacuated the tent, and the group could hear her insides painting the car park. Withered intestines, blood like thick paint and other juicy bits slopped onto the ground like the inside of a butcher's shop. They dropped the body back onto the soup of fleshy delights.

Laura tried hard to hold back the stream train of bile that was hurtling for her throat but she couldn't. She dove out of the tent and hurled her insides onto the car park next to Dutton.

Craig appeared behind her, placing his hand on her back.

"You okay?"

Laura gasped at the air, pulling a wad of tissue from her coat and wiping the stringy phlegm from her mouth like a wriggling worm. "What the fuck…" She turned to Craig. "How the hell are you not puking?"

"Dad worked with animals. I don't mind the sight of blood." He looked at Dutton who was pacing, putting her face to the wind. "Mum on the other hand. Never quite got used to it." Laura reached for her cigarettes.

"Woah," Craig said, "You can't here." Laura lit the cigarette anyway. She had already thrown up at a crime scene. A little ash won't do much else. "That stitching? I've never seen anything like that in my life," Craig continued. Laura took a long, satisfying drag off her smoke. She wanted to speak, but the words wouldn't come, so she stood, and let the wind stroke her hair and the smoke fill her lungs.

The tent door pushed open. Celine emerged in her overalls like she had just helped a cow give birth, her hands and chest coated in thick blood. She stripped them off and threw them into a disposal bin by the side of Laura and Craig. Pulling out a pack of smokes from her Jeans, Laura offered her a light.

"Thanks," she said. Her skin the colour of caramel, her hair shaved at the side and longer on top. She was slim and a little shorter than Laura and so thin you could cup her hips with both hands. She found her voice again.

"What the fuck was that?" Laura said.

"Been doing this for five years and I've never seen that before." She stared at the ground at her feet. "His heart is missing."

"What?" Laura said, trying to make sense of what she had just heard. Celine stared at the ground, the smoke inches from her lips.

"He has everything else, but his heart is missing."

"Someone took his heart?" Celine held her gaze to the floor. A voice broke in the distance.

"I've found something!" Urgency struck Laura's legs and she moved quickly, flicking her cigarette into a flock of geese. Craig and Celine followed behind her. Up ahead, in a thicket, a dog handler was being pulled by his land shark which was frantically pushing its head through a thick bush of brambles. "Easy Cerberus!" The handler said, pulling at the reigns of his Alsatian. They stepped into the bush, following the dog that pulled until eventually, the handler let go and Cerberus dove through the leaves and trees.

Laura's feet cracked under twigs as she moved. Through the space, it opened up inside. Her eyes fell on it, and like stepping on a trap door, her world fell from under her feet.

"What the fuck is that?" Craig said, putting his hand to his mouth. Laura knew what it was, and she hoped she would never see it again. Then, eyes fell onto her, and the blood drained from her face.

There, sat on top of a stump of wood. The sight of it shattered her mind like a falling hammer on glass.

A candle placed atop a human heart. And next to it, a photo of Laura Warburton.

# Chapter Eleven
# Sheree

Sheree awoke with a headache worse than the hangover she got from a four-day coke and vodka bender. The ground below her was hard, and the blur of her vision began to focus.

*A room.*

Cream walls were completely consumed by mould, like skin devoured by cancer. A single window a little bigger than a letterbox marred with dirt. Reluctant daylight cast speckled shadows that resembled cheetah's coat. She sat up, wincing at the dull knives that scraped against her skull. Fear began to creep into her bones as she looked at the mattress she lay upon. Filthy, with more stains and blotches of all different colours. Shit stains, piss stains, and…

*Blood. Blood stains.*

*Hi there! I'm your mind about to fracture. But don't worry. We'll have so much fun in this room together!*

"W…w..wha…" She began, trying to string a sentence together. A bucket stained with shit and grime sat at the base of the wall. A single door with rusted hinges stood to the back of her. A dangling wire where a lightbulb used to be, and dirtied straw matted into the ground.

The silence was deafening, less for her heartbeat hammering in her ears. Terrified to breathe louder than a whisper, Sheree climbed off the sodden mattress and put her ear to the metal door. Silence met her ear. Everything in her body resisted her hand that was reaching for the handle. Sheree felt the cold brass inside her palm.

*Click.*

The door unlocked and she pulled it open, the hinges creaking with every inch pulling her nerves like taut violin strings being played with a broken bottle. The corridor was dark. A single strip light illuminated above that buzzed and flickered. Sheree moved barefoot, holding herself in her arms. Her legs bare. Cold settling into the joints. Her breath ragged as she moved, fingering the walls as she moved into that hungry black.

A door slammed somewhere, and the echo stabbed at her nerves. She let out a breath, but then she heard it. The sound of footsteps tapping the ground behind her. She held her breath. Darkness met her eyes. She stood frozen to the wall. A second passed. Then another.

A shape emerged through the darkness.

*Run.*

Sheree bolted down the corridor until she slammed into a wall. Rapid footsteps bounced along the walls.

"Oh, little giiiiiirlll…." The voice was menacing, laced with sinister cheer. Sheree fumbled at the wall. Was it a dead end?

"Fuck oh fuck oh fuck…." She yammered. Tears mixed with snot. Her fingers found the touch of a handle. She bolted through the gap and dared a look back.

A figure encased in shadow. The glint of a knife in its hand.

"Run, run as fast as you can…."

She slammed it shut and pressed her back against the wood. The footsteps drew closer.

"Oh, little girl, don't be like that… I have games I want to play." The voice muffled from behind the wood.

"What do you want?!" Sheree blurted, pressing all her weight against the door. The dull scraping of a knife point against the wood. Then silence. She took a breath. A beat of nothing.

Sheree screamed as the knife drove through the wood, its edge glinting off the dim light. Bursting into action, Sheree moved, turning, running through the darkness. She descended a flight of metal stairs that rattled as she moved, the bumps and patterns on the steps digging into her feet. The walls aligned with flickering lights. Some lit, some not, like a hockey player's smile. All windows were boarded up. Cracks of light bled into the dim black.

"Run, run, run!" His voice bounced off the walls, stabbing into Sheree's hope. She hit the ground and raced to the set of thick double doors at the edge of the foyer.

She gripped the bars and pushed, but they didn't budge. Thick chains coiled around them like a steel viper. The biggest padlock she had ever seen hanging from them. She banged on the doors, rattling them as hard as she could.

"Help!" She screamed as loudly as she could, feeling her vocal cords burn, fists erupting in hellfire as she pounded away. The door behind her flew open. The shadow stepped inside and closed the door behind them. Sheree ducked down, the sound of the chains swinging in the air.

Moving slowly, her mouth running dry, feet shredding from broken glass and sand on the cold floor. Sheree darted behind disused machinery. Some kind of old milking contraptions. Hay and straw mixed with the blood on her feet. The figure stalked down the stairs. She couldn't see its face. Thick hair falling from the crown of its head.

Sheree clambered inside a broken cabinet, pulling her shaking knees to her chest and carefully pulled the door closed. Breath rattled in her throat. Footsteps drawing closer. Sheree watched her assailant move slowly around the warehouse through the crack in the cabinet doors. He was covered in shadow, all but for the giant knife in his hand. He touched the chains of the door and rattled them, the clanging of metal raking along her bones. The figure began to whistle a song, long and drawn out.

*Alouette, gentille alouette, Alouette, gentille alouette.*

The figure moved away. The heavy footsteps disappeared. She held her hands to her mouth, trying to abate the scream that wanted to break through those tight lips so badly.

*God help me.*

That was all she thought before the door flew open and a large hand grabbed hold of her hair, and that scream finally came.

# Chapter Twelve
# Laura

Laura sat back at the station in the cafeteria. Her breath was rancid from the five cigarettes and three cups of extra strong coffee she had just thrown down her neck. Mary Dutton's mouth was moving, but Laura just stared at the fourth cup of black tar in her shaking hands.

*That photo. It's impossible,* she thought as the strip lighting above bore into her unblinking eyes. *That photo. The photo he had in his pocket when he died. They did never find his body…*

"Laura!" The name slammed into her ears like something alien. She looked up from the cup of black. Mary stared at her with pale eyes, her face twisted like she was chewing on a hornet. "Are you listening?"

"Yeah," she lied. She tried to remain focused, less fall back into her spiralling mind.

"Do you have any idea why your photo was there?" Laura shook her head. "Have you ever seen that photo before?"

*Yes.*

"No, ma'am." She lied, holding back her tears. Mary leant back in the creaking chair and folded her arms. "Do you have anything you want to tell me?"

"Am I a suspect?" She said. She didn't mean to, but the phrase ran from her mouth before she had a chance to catch it. Mary's eyes widened. She leant forward.

"No," she said. "But I think you're in danger." The door pushed open. It was Craig with two more cups of coffee. He spotted Mary, and his expression soured. Moving to Laura, he sat beside her and touched her shoulder. She was stiff as a rock, her face turning the same shade of white as the walls.

"Hey, Boss," he said tentatively. "Got you a refill."

"Thanks," Laura said deadpan, eyes dropping to the cold coffee. "So, what do we have?"

"Forensics came back with nothing," Craig said. "The victim had been alive when the incision was made. Heart missing. No next of kin. Low profile victim. No CCTV. *He's come back to hurt you again, Laura.*" Laura's eyes snapped to Craig.

"What did you say?" She bit.

"I said how are you getting home, Laura?" He said. "You look like you've seen a ghost."

Craig drove Laura home. He didn't need the sat nav, which he boasted was because of his memory which is how he managed to pass his detectives exam the first time around. Nothing to do with his mother running the whole Northern Complex Investigation Division. No, nothing like that. The same reason he was already up for an acting DS position in the Spring. Laura didn't pay heed. She watched the grey skyline pass them all the way home, hardly muttering a word.

Outside her house, she cracked the door and slipped out, pulling her keys out of her pocket. Craig called after her. "Boss!"

She turned. He was out of the car and moving towards her. He was a broad guy, with muscles straining against his shirt, and right then, he terrified her. He drew in closer, extending out his arms, ready to give her a hug. He was a giant, ready to consume her. Those big hands moved to her body. Laura pushed him hard to the chest and bolted for the door, keys scratching against the lock before she slipped inside, leaving him standing in the road.

# Chapter Thirteen
# Laura

That night, Laura took out the extra-large bottle of wine she had under her kitchen cabinet. Dark red Malbec. The way she liked it. She pulled the cork off and drank straight from the bottle. Three gulps later, she felt her anxiety and worries struggling to swim. Another few mouthfuls and they were drowning. She closed the curtains and locked the back and front doors and put some music on. Loud. Just the way she liked it. Metal, but harder. Guitars. Drums. Screaming. She wanted the music to fuck the thoughts out of her head. She turned it up even more until the house started to rattle. She danced in her underwear and work shirt, spinning around in false bliss. Her bloodstream swimming in ethanol, sipping from the bottle. Laura eyed Bagpipe tucking himself behind the couch, those yellow eyes poking through the dark crack.

Laura fell to her knees, nearly spilling the bottle onto her rug. She laughed and fell back, feeling the world spiral around her. The booze taking a sledgehammer to the walls of her mind.

*So what if he's back? So what! He died once before. I guess maybe this time he'll say goodbye! Maybe I can tell him what I really think of him? That I think his haircut is stupid, and the bruises he gave me have healed and now I have a great fucking body, fuck great and I can deadlift 80KG for reps.*

She turned onto her front, laughing, dancing in her own mind. Her feet nestled into the carpet. The world around her began to turn dark, so she shouted and slurred for Alexa to turn the lights on. She shouted once more for the lights to change, and she saw the lights turn from blue to purple, to red to green. She felt twenty-one again, dancing with an old boyfriend in Morocco – Darren? Daniel? Daz? A kind man but had serious mummy issues. *Ha!* She thought. *And I thought that was bad!* Life was simpler then – A new career and not a care in the world. And then she found the house of the dead that Alex Thompson had left for her, and she met Ron.

*Fuck you,* she thought and let that box of pain overflow.

Laura rolled onto her back and jammed the bottle in her mouth. The liquid bubbling and flowing down her gullet. She sank it with a grimace. Stumbling to her feet, she looked at herself in the living room mirror and smiled a red toothy smile at her swaying reflection.

Moving to the kitchen, she dug another bottle from the wine rack and pulled the cork open and sank a quarter of the bottle in one go. She eyed herself – The wine dribbling from her mouth like she had devoured a bag of plumbs, the liquid pattering on the floor like a bloody nose.

She fingered a wine glass but it tumbled, and she was too shit-faced to catch it in time, it exploding along the floor.

"Fuck you!" She screamed. "Fuck you!" She took another swallow of red and got on her knees, the glass digging into her legs. The pain seemed far away, and she watched the blood seep out of her. Another drink down the hatch, she could see his face once more in her mind's eye. Ron. Ron was back. He had come back for her. "Fuck you!" She screamed louder.

The music had reached new decibels. She moved to the front room, dragging her fucked up and bloodied body onto the cream carpet. Bagpipe was on his feet. She moved to him and he hissed loudly, back arched and fur ruffled. "Hey!" She barked. "Don't you dare speak to me like that!" She reached her hand out and the cat clawed her hand, shredding a layer of skin from her fingers. Bagpipe raced out of the room. "Come back!" She stammered; the pain lost in the numb.

She eyed her rug and clothing. She didn't know what was blood and what was wine. Nor did she care. He was back, and she would see her blood again, all over the walls and the carpets and her clothes and her makeup bag and her purse and on the hospital gowns and "Fuck you!" She howled, tears mixing with her saliva. She crumpled to the floor.

*The photo. How did he get the photo? How could he be back? He is dead. He died. There's no way. It's impossible.*

*But baby girl,* she heard his voice lick her ear. *You saw it remember? Or are you going crazy again? You know how you get when you're stressed. I thought you had stopped drinking? You know how loose you get when you drink baby doll. So loose…* She drove her hand to her face, pinching her cheeks, clenching her teeth together so hard she thought they would crack. Her face met the carpet.

"You should have just killed me…" She sobbed. "You don't have to live with what you did. I have to live with it every day. I can't… I can't…" She stood up, ready to take another drink from the bottle but she found it empty. Inspecting the ground with horror, she had spilt the contents all around her. She howled again, launching the empty betraying bottle against the television that blasted hard rock. It plunged into the screen and shattered on the ground, fragmenting on the floor and walls in an explosion of dirtied diamonds. The music carried on blasting, and rage gripped her. She clambered to her feet and grabbed the TV set with both hands like an enraged primate, rattling it, throwing it to the floor and screaming over and over and over.

"Fuck you! Fuck you!" She jammed her hands into her hair and began to pull. The searing pain numbed his voice.

*Kiss kiss baby. Kiss kiss.* A blood-curdling scream erupted from her throat as she felt hair begin to come away from her scalp. Her eyes squeezed tightly shut, as the agony finally broke free.

"Hey!" A voice came behind her. It was *him. He was here to finish what he started.* Laura grabbed the broken bottle and turned, mad with rage ready to kill that motherfucker once and for all.

Craig recoiled, moving, grabbing the broken bottle before she shredded his throat.

"Laura stop! Stop!" She thrashed frantically, screaming incoherently over and over. "Stop!" He screamed, grabbing her arms, tossing the bottle across the room where it joined the other littering of destruction. She pounded and scratched, kicked and bit into his jacket. She pulled and pushed, screaming over and over again, her tears breaking through in full force as Craig soothed her. She dropped to her knees slowly, collapsing to the floor. Craig moved with her, his back to the wall, her legs curled into her chest, hair sticking to her face as she pawed his coat. Laura pawed at him as pain washed away in tears and blood. He stroked her face, whispering into her ear, nestling his face into her hair. He held her and she sobbed into his jacket. Laura stopped fighting, and they sat a moment in that quiet space between breath and heartbeats.

"Come on," Craig said, hoisting her upstairs to her bedroom. A stumbling few moments later they reached her bed, like bringing home a drunken stranger after a night on the town. He pulled the covers back and laid her down. Her eyes were closed. Her breathing deep. "Sleep it off," he said, as he moved to the bedroom door. She grabbed out at his jacket.

"Stay…" Laura slurred. "Don't leave me…" He turned and crouched to her. Her eyes barely open. He didn't think she was conscious anymore, or if she was, she was barely clinging on.

"Sleep it off, boss," he said. "I'll be right back outside. I won't let anything happen to you." He touched her head and slipped away. Her fingers relaxed and she slipped away into nightmares. He turned her on her side and propped a pillow against her back then took a towel out of the suite and placed it by her bedside on the floor should she need to hurl in the night. Next, he found some painkillers and made two drinks – One water, for the pills and dry mouth, and the other a glass of fresh orange for the vitamin and sugar boost in the morning. His eyes fell onto her sleeping body.

*Took it hard today haven't you boss?* He leaned in close to her, her breath mixing with his. *But it's good to have you back.*

Downstairs, he cleaned up the broken glass took the busted TV set into the back garden and fed the cat. He sat a moment on the couch, looking through the window to the darkened street outside where his car sat empty. Dutton had told him to keep an eye on her.

"She needs to return to the Met. She can't handle it up here." Dutton had said to him. Craig felt anger run through his chest.

"She isn't going anywhere." He pulled open a bottle of beer from the fridge and sank it. He wasn't supposed to be drinking. He was working. But given the state Laura had gotten herself in tonight, he doubted she would say anything.

He finished the beer, locked the house up and posted the keys through the letter box. The night air was crisp and a thin layer of rain squelched under his feet as he moved to the car. Slipping inside, he felt his eyes grow heavy. He turned on the radio and opened up his Kindle on his mobile. He was reading a story of a man that goes insane following the death of his wife, locked into a spinning nightmare that revolves around the same time. Like Wuthering Heights but with fewer cravats. His mind fell back to the tent. The way the forensic expert eyes were undressing Laura by the riverside. He felt jealousy begin to rise in his chest. He pushed the thoughts away, deep down into his stomach where he let his stomach acid dissolve them like a parasite that crawled down your throat.

He had helped her tonight. And she would remember that in the morning. He knew she would. And she had better. He deserved to be happy.

# Chapter Fourteen
# Laura

"Hey baby," Ron said. "Look at this." His features were haloed by the bright sun as he stood at a backdrop of mountains and a clear blue sky. She moved higher up the steps, the water under them smooth. She didn't like boats, but Ron insisted on it, so she agreed. They were having an amazing time so far on their holiday, and she didn't want to rock those calm waves they were sailing along.

"What is it?" She took his hand. He was wearing a white shirt and his hair was combed to the side. *Gelled to the side*, she mentally corrected herself. Only balding guys comb their hair over. He was just a little *thin* on top. He wasn't going bald, which is why he used the gel. The expensive stuff too. Not VO5 or some other cheap matte. His beard was shaped and carved like a fine sculpting, so she could mention that first. He liked her to compliment him when she greeted him, but only something genuine. He knew when she was just saying it and not feeling it, so she had better feel it.

"A little further," he said, those teeth gleaming white against his tanned skin. The sun caressed her. Her dress flowing and white. He had picked it out especially to compliment her figure but keep her modesty from the wandering eyes of the locals in Cape Town.

Her eyes fell on the scenery and the breath was stolen away from her lungs: the sea was stretching and blue. Not a cloud in the sky, the sun sat high above them like a great orb of gold watching over them. The wind licked her skin like a loving breath. In the distance, mountains kissed the sky. Their boat rocked on the sea in the alcove of a small hidden beach with golden sand. Ron had picked it specifically and hired boats at a discount price. Laura had wanted to go shark diving like the rest of her friends, but Ron didn't like the idea of sharing holiday stories and wanking each other off at how much fun they had doing the same thing as everyone else. He wanted to make their *own* memories, and not just piggyback on the dreams of other people.

*"You need to be more ambitious,"* he had said on the morning of the trip, before throwing the tickets to the boat hire at her feet.

Ron squeezed Laura's hand. 'See,' he said smiling, wrapping his arms around her waist. He nestled his chin into her shoulder and neck as they looked at the serenity around them. Not a pinprick on the horizon, like staring at the end of the world. "Incredible, isn't it? Much better than being down there with the fish."

"Absolutely," she said quickly. She turned and kissed him, and they held each other's gaze a moment. His face was hard, but then his lips curled into a smile.

"Great," he said, letting her go. Laura noticed not a single soul was around and she felt her breath quicken. *Why had he picked a remote cove?* "Champagne?" He said. She turned and saw him standing with a bottle of *Armand de Brignac* dripping with ice from the silver bucket that sat on a small table. She smiled and nodded. His face lit up once more and he pulled the cork, blasting it far into the water.

He poured two fizzing glasses and handed one to her. She took it quickly, moving to taste the bubbles. His hand grabbed her wrist and a bolt of fear shot through her. Her eyes met his.

"Not yet," he said. "Eager beaver," he laughed. She giggled nervously.

"Sorry," she lowered the glass. "I forgot my manners." Ron cleared his throat.

"To a wonderful life," he said. "Your turn."

"To us," she said quickly. He nodded in approval, moving and pressing his lips to hers. He smelt of booze already. How long had he been up here drinking? The scent of the coconut sun cream lingered on her lips as he pulled away. He gestured to her glass. Ron sank the champagne quickly but Laura took a sip. He furrowed his brow.

"Something wrong?" He enquired, looking at her barely touched glass while filling up his own. She shook her head, the rocking of the boat under her feet growing steadily.

"No baby. Just, it's such a lovely bottle and such a wonderful day. I don't want to get too drunk and ruin it."

"Why would you ruin it?" He said sharply. "It's great champagne. It cost more than that dress you're wearing. The one I bought you. Why aren't you drinking it?" She felt like a rabbit in headlights. Laura felt a vice around her throat. She nodded quickly and knocked the glass back with a soured look on her face. Ron's face contorted. "Jesus," he said distastefully. "I said drink it not down it. Are you dying of thirst or something?" He snatched the glass from her hand and filled it up once more. "Try again." He handed her the drink. She stared at the golden bubbling liquid. Tentatively, she pressed the drink to her lips and took it in slowly. Not too fast, not too slow. Just right. "Amazing," he said with a smile. Laura felt the vice loosen.

They finished their glasses and Ron poured them another. Laura tried to keep her belch in her throat from rushing out. She was a lady. *His Lady.* And a lady doesn't belch expensive champagne on a nice boat on the South

Atlantic Ocean. "Jesus Laura," he said scoldingly. Those headlights rose in her face again. "Talk? Say something. You seem so agitated. Loosen up!"

"I'm just enjoying the drink," she said quietly. His face crumpled.

"I buy you a great dress, bring you out here in this wonderful place and all you can think about is getting hammered?" He slammed the bottle back into the ice bucket. "First you don't drink, then you ignore me? Fuck me I don't know why I bother."

"Sorry," she said, almost instinctively. "It's so nice of you. I'll relax. It's just so nice here." She vomited more excuses, more phrases, words that worked. Eventually, he moved in when she was near to tears and held her once more.

"It's okay," he said, the rage in his voice vanishing quickly as if it had never been there in the first place. He pinched her chin and pulled her face to his. "Stop being so worried. You can relax." His eyes locked into hers. "Kiss kiss…" They locked lips. "I know you wanted to go diving," he whispered. "You did this for me. I love you."

"I love you too."

"And that's why," he said, stepping away and reaching into his pocket. Laura's world crumbled around her. The wind no longer kissed her but instead dug into her like dull knives. The sun seemed to grow hotter, ready to bubble her skin and shred it from her bones, tossing it into the deep for the hungry monsters below to feast on. Ron pulled out the engagement ring and dropped to one knee and Laura's world caved around her. Mountains crashed into the abyss. The sky fractured and the world began to burn.

"I want to make you mine forever."

# XXX

I hope you found the parcel I left you. I know you like that picture and I wanted you to have it back. You thought it was lost forever, didn't you? I'll come for you soon, but not yet. I still have work to do. I need to make this new one perfect. I need to show you the work I am doing. Trying to be the man you deserve.

The fat man in the car was a pig. A big dirty fat pig that slavered over my new toy. A big stinky pig grunting and making piggy noises. He squealed when I put the knife in. Even through my mask, I could hear him. He bled a lot. But I'm getting better.

My dolls are growing. The world will know soon. They will know of the work I am doing.

And you will know how much I have missed you.

# Chapter Fifteen
# Sheree

Sheree awoke to the feeling of something nuzzling her mouth. She opened her eyes and spied a giant swollen rat sitting on her chest.

*Morning. How do you do? Any food around here? I'm STARVING.*

Sheree bolted upright and let out a sharp cry as she threw the rodent off her, the beast bouncing onto the floor and then scurrying out of sight. She breathed a moment, touching her face, and pulling her knees into her chest. She felt it then. Around her throat. Sour dread flooded her body like an injection from a viper bite. She fingered the steel clasp around her neck like a cold necklace. Turning her head, she saw a long rusted chain dangling from a fitting in the wall. Like a trapped animal, she grabbed the chains with her hand and heaved, straining her neck and back as the metal cut into the back of her neck. She screamed as loudly as she could, heaving and yanking, the chain rattling like an iron snake that wouldn't let go. Finally, her little strength left her like smoke from a bubbling puddle.

She collapsed onto the filthy sheetless mattress. Her clothes were missing. Only her mid-section was covered, and her bottom in nothing but a pair of piss-stained underwear. Sheree sobbed loudly, heaving staggered breaths.

The door pushed open, scraping along the floor. He walked in, and she began to scream even louder. His face. The skin was tanned leather that stretched around his head.

Hair wiry like black spiders' legs. His eyes baggy slits and his mouth stretched in a drooping scream.

He moved to her, his hands outreaching as she kicked and flailed, trying to keep the monster away from her, from touching her. His hands found her ankles, and she kicked and pulled herself back against the wall. He drew closer, the stench of the corpse mask pushing its way up her nostrils like solid disinfectant. Rotting teeth fastened into black gums. Bloodied straw pushed from behind the mask making the skin bulbous and grotesque.

"Get away from me!" Sheree howled, her voice horse and her chest burning. She socked him with a heel to his shoulder, then another to his chest. He reeled his hand back and gripped her mouth, those dead eyes staring back into hers. He lifted a finger.

*"Shhh,"* he hissed. Sheree felt her body turn to rock. He slowly peeled his hand away. She wanted to scream more but knew that she dared not.

"What do you want?" She whimpered quietly. "You want to fuck me? Fine, go ahead. I'll even pretend to enjoy it. Drugs? Money? I can get them for you. Just let me go. I'll go away and I won't tell anyone I promise! Just please… please let me go…" Her tears slid down her dirtied cheeks like parting a sea of grime. He peeled back, moving into the dark hallway, leaving the door open. The empty space taunted her to run again.

He came back with a bowl and a glass of water and placed them down on the ground by her feet. Brown lumps sitting in yellowed liquid. Clumps of what seemed to be vegetables bulged from the dish.

"Eat," he said vacantly. "Eat. Drink. Be pure." The words were like an alien speaking to her behind that leather. Sheree eyed the meal with trepidation. The hunger in her belly rumbled and her mouth salivated. But everything in her brain told her to not eat that food. She eyed the meal, and then dove into the bowl.

The soup was lukewarm and the liquid thick and sloppy. She ate by the handful, her appetite awakening, ravaging down the bowl of slop before she could even taste it. She felt it land in her barren stomach like a bomb of substance, and the water like a silky stream of cold. She coughed and spluttered, her cracked lips soaking up the moisture like the first rains in the desert.

"Thank you…" She said quietly. "Can I have another water?" The man reached down and took the glass from her, left again for a minute, and then returned with a refilled glass. He moved to the end of the room and grabbed the bucket filled with piss and shit and placed it by the mattress before leaving and closing the door. Sheree eyed the bucket, and a blanket of despair smothered her. He left without saying a word.

Then she felt it. A churning in her stomach, and it was heading south and fast. Using both her feet, she pulled the shit bucket under her and managed to evacuate herself before the bomb went off prematurely. She turned and heaved into the septic-filled bucket. Alternating between fluid exits. When she was empty, she collapsed by the container and the tears started again. Thick clumps of vomit covered her hands. The stench was unbearable, and Sheree fell backwards, eyeing the black ceiling.

She fingered the ground until she found the fresh glass of water. She swilled and spat lingering bile onto the floor.

*If he wanted to kill me, he would have done it already. He wants something else.* She thought.

She saw it then. The remnants sitting at the bottom of the glass.

"Laxatives," she whispered. "He put laxatives in the food to clear me out." His voice snaked into her mind as she felt her stomach again twisting into knots.

*Be pure.*

# Chapter Sixteen
# Laura

Laura peeled her eyes open and the daylight bore into her retinas like someone was stabbing hot pokers into her brain. She threw the covers over her head and wished that the marching band in her brain would take it easy on the bass drum. She sat up and she felt the steam train of last night's debauchery flying up her gullet and hurled red bile onto the floor. She pushed her hair back from her face, letting the string of vomit drip down onto the towel that had been laid out by her bedside. She queried the garment. She didn't remember putting it there, but then again, she didn't remember getting into bed.

Laura wiped her face on the bedsheets and made a mental note to change them when she had sorted her shit out. She clambered out of bed, stepping over the defiling puddle of regret. She regarded the glass of juice, water and painkillers. Either she had anticipated the hangover from hell when she stumbled up to bed last night, or she had gotten them in her sleep. Neither made much sense, so she put it down to *the unsolved mystery of the drunken* bitch and let the thought go.

"I'm never drinking red wine again," she sniffled, the smell of half-digested Malbec souring her nose. The next express train of vomit was hurtling down the tunnel. She made it to the bathroom just as the defiling liquid painted the porcelain. Laura Warburton heaved until she was sure she had nothing left, then for good measure, she stuck two fingers down her throat and scraped the last of her stomach lining out.

She sat back, panting heavily. The night before came through in shaky flashbacks. What had happened? She hadn't been in such a mess in a long time. She knew exactly why, and the thought made her feeble promise to stop drinking, want to head straight to the local off-license and buy another big bottle of *feel good*.

*Had he killed that man? Had he killed the others? Was this a trap to get her to follow him up here?*

Laura pulled herself to her feet, flushed the toilet and went into the bedroom. She sank the water and pills and then the orange juice too. The liquid was like velvet on her arid throat, and it landed like an explosion in her twitching stomach.

She set the shower to cold and dove in. In between yips and howls, she cleaned herself, washed her hair and sang holy murder when it came to doing her back. She scrubbed her teeth so hard her gums bled and finished up with a generous helping of mouthwash. Switching off the tap, she towelled, got dressed and dried her hair. She was beginning to feel better already.

She had seen that cold water helps hangovers on Reddit when she was down one of her many internet rabbit holes. It started with *How to make yourself better following a breakup*, then *How to make yourself better after a toxic relationship*. Then finally, *How to not kill yourself*.

A million coping mechanisms later and after practically getting a degree in abusive personality disorders, she found that above all else the cold water helped her mental health more than any bullshit counsellor ever could. They too helped, of course, but the cold showers were the thing that kept her from jumping in front of a bus.

Laura wrapped up the wine-soaked towel and stripped the bedding. She threw open her wardrobe. She furrowed her brow. There were more empty hangers than she could remember having.

She pawed through her clothing, then threw on a plain vest and a pair of shorts before heading downstairs. Bagpipe greeted her at the foot of the stairs and weaved through her legs. She was a black moggie-style cat whom she had rescued him from a drug den.

"Hey buddy," she said, reaching down and nestling her fingers between those pointed ears. He meowed playfully, before leaving Laura to carry on sorting her shit out. People had wondered why she had named him *Bagpipe*. Her answer was a simple one – *No matter what you call a cat, they won't come to you, so I called him Bagpipe.* That seemed to stop the questions from coming.

She checked her phone and had four missed calls from Jeremy and one from the superintendent. *Fuck.* She tried to call them back but it went straight through to voicemail. She checked the time and the pounding in her head came back. She was only a few days into her new job and she had pissed of the superintendent, alienated herself from her team, had clues of herself at the crime scene of a brutal murder, and was now late for work with a hangover from hell.

"Brilliant," she hissed, before collecting her stuff and rushing out the door into the cul-de-sac with her third cigarette in twenty minutes pinched between her teeth. Her long brown coat and handbag fought with her arms as she threw her wet hair in a bobble. Her heels clicked on the cold ground as she made it to her car fumbling with the keys. The air was cold, and Laura saw her car had a thick layer of ice over the windscreen. It was a bitch to scrape off at the best of times. Never mind when you needed to be at work thirty minutes ago.

"I don't want to breathalyse you," a voice shouted from somewhere. Laura looked up, scanning the quiet houses. She saw the black BMW idling, Craig's unshaven face poked out from the driver's side window.

"What the hell are you doing here?" She barked, moving towards him.

"Playing guardian angel," he said. "You were a mess last night."

"Watch your tongue Detective," Laura snapped, her pride cracking. "Why were you here? Your mother tell you to keep a watch on me?" Craig waved the comment off.

"She stopped telling me what to do years ago," Craig snarled. "She never gave a shit when I was younger, so she doesn't give a shit what I do now unless it's something to benefit herself." He ran his palm along his tired face. "I did it myself. After what you saw. I wanted to make sure you were okay." Laura let the silence hang in the air.

"I'm fine," she bit. "I didn't need you last night."

"From where I was standing," he said, "You needed me more than ever, and it's a good job I was here. Heard you screaming at the top of your lungs. You smashed your television. You frightened the hell out of your cat and could barely stand when I came in. If someone had called the police from the noise, then your career could be over. But I won't say anything. I even put you to bed and put a towel down for you and spent the rest of the night out here watching the place." Laura wanted the ground to swallow her whole. She *should* be thankful, but she didn't need a man in shining armour to rescue her from the big bad wolf.

"I didn't need your help," she said. "You should have gone home and knocked one out to porn hub like normal single guys do after work." Craig's brow furrowed.

"If I may be so bold ma'am, fuck you with that shit. What? I look after you the night after you find a picture of your face stuck into a dead guy's heart and I'm the bad one? You would have drank yourself stupid! Who is Ron anyway? You kept saying his name last night."

Blades tore through her body. What had she told him? What had he seen? Craig watched as Laura's face was ravaged with pain. He lifted his hand up. "It doesn't matter. I overstepped. Look, we need to get to work and you can't drive for a few hours. Get in, and I'll give you a ride." Laura contemplated this. She wasn't one for taking handouts or favours from men. It had never served her well in her life, but he did have a point. It would be too long to get a cab, not to mention the whispers of her turning up looking half-dressed in a taxi, and there was always the worry that she might slip up and let some details go to the public which she shouldn't…

*Hi, where are you goin?*

*The police station, please. By the way! I'm a new inspector in the Major Investigation Unit. Don't mean to alarm you but there's someone out there abducting women and butchering men, ripping out their hearts and filling them with straw. I know, crazy right! But that's not the worst part. I think it might be my ex-husband that died a year ago in South Africa. No! We never found his body. Isn't that strange? But the nightmares keep him alive in my mind. Not to mention the drinking problem I've started to lose control of.*

"Boss?" Craig said. Laura refocused.

"Okay," she said. "But just this once. Don't make a habit of it." Craig laughed. Laura cracked the passenger door open. She queried the bobble lying on the passenger seat with strands of brown hair clinging to the rubber. Craig pulled it away.

"My daughters – Millie. She leaves them lying around." He pushed it into his leather coat. Craig shifted the car into drive. "I thought you didn't have a car? You got the bus to work yesterday."

"I like to take public transport when I am somewhere new. Gives me more of a feel for the place." Craig pursed his lips.

"Makes sense." The humming of the engine filled the silence between them.

"Look," Laura said. "I'm sorry. Thanks for helping me last night." She looked out the window. The quiet houses drifting out of sight. Craig smiled.

"I think you're in danger boss. They left that photo there for a reason. I don't know why, or who, but they know you and that you're on the case. And if someone knows *that*, then they might know where you're living."

Laura sat back and closed her eyes. The world started to spin and nausea began to resurface once more. She thought she was here to catch a killer. But instead, turns out she was trying to catch a ghost. The question was… who would catch who first?

# Chapter Seventeen
# Laura

The station was a circus: officers running around like headless chickens, darting out of the back door and diving into their cars. Craig and Laura watched as they raced past. Laura grabbed the arm of a passing constable.

"What's going on?"

"It's bad Ma'am," he said, barely able to string the words together, the radio yammering in his ear. Laura let him go before he ran with his colleagues and sped off into the distance with horns and sirens blaring. Laura felt the world rushing around her. She steadied herself on the wall. Craig touched her shoulder, and she shoved him off like his hand was made of fire.

"I'm fine. Grab a car." She gasped, her fingers digging into the walls. Craig stood dumbfounded like a rabbit caught in headlights. Laura eyed him fiercely. "Now!" He moved and she grabbed his arm. "Do you have a taser?"

"I'm out of ticket."

"I'll reinstate it. Grab a taser and stab vest. Shits going down." Laura donned her stab vest from her locker. It was much looser since the last time she wore it but a diet consisting of wine, sleepless nights and anti-depressants, will make those pounds fall right off. They piled into an unmarked car. Craig pressed the centre console and the BMW lit up its sparkling blue lights. He took the handbrake off and was about to let the engine rip when a set of knuckles rapped against the window.

"Let me in!" It was Jeremy, his face looking redder than usual. Laura unlocked the car and he jumped into the back seat. "Here's the address," he said, punching it into his phone and docking it. It was on the other side of town.

"What's going on?" Laura barked. Jeremy looked at her like he had just heard a mouse sing the *Nessun Dorma*.

"Have you not listened to your voicemails? They've found another body." Craig looked at Google maps. It was an industrial unit on the other side of town. ETA seventeen minutes. He could make it in eight.

They burned through the streets like wildfire through a dry forest. Craig got to a busy junction and hammered the wheel, the concurring blare of the horn changing the tone of the sirens from a long stretching wail to a fast sporadic chatter. The lights were showing red and a sea of brake lights before them. He snatched a glance in his rear-view mirror and saw the other cops behind them. He must have gotten the lead on them, taking the back streets and driving like a lunatic with nothing to lose. He approached quickly, still doing a solid sixty towards a road of standing metal. Laura pressed her foot into the ground, trying to find a brake pedal that wasn't there, her hands clinging to the handle above the door. Heart hammering in her throat, radios going haywire.

"M.O.E NEEDED. DO WE HAVE A LOCK SNAP? IS THERE A DRONE? A DOG?"

Craig pressed the clutch and smashed his foot on the accelerator, the rev counter burying into the red before he banked onto the opposite side of the road, oncoming traffic swerving out of the way, before snapping from fourth to second, the engine screaming as they narrowly missed bonnets that blared and screamed at them, before slicing back into third. Momentum and adrenalin carried them back onto the right side of the road, slipping back into fourth, giving hellish power.

"Fucking hell!" Laura screamed, a huge smile on her face. Body tingling. Craig had a smile lingering in the corner of his mouth.

"I always wanted to drive fast," he laughed, cool as snow over a frozen wasteland. Not a break of sweat on his forehead, hands relaxed on the wheel. Jeremy looked as if he was about to give birth, sprawled across the back seats appearing rather dishevelled and gasping.

"Just get us there in one piece."

They turned down an estate that had so much graffiti painted on the walls it would make Banksy jealous. Children ran along roads filled with disused shopping trolleys and played with broken fence panels. A young girl, no older than four with her hair in pigtails and missing her two front teeth mouthed something at the cop car that would make Santa Clause expel her from the Christmas list forever.

People looked out of their windows holding cans of Stella and Special Brew cider. Some sat on couches in their front gardens. Others stood tinkering with cars.

"Turn right here," Jeremy said, pointing to a small off-road. An easily missable dirt track. Craig banked hard, the wheels bouncing off the asphalt, ripping up loose gravel and narrowly missing the brick wall that flanked the edges. In front of them, a woman with her hair pinned back standing in last night's pyjamas – Purple with polka dots – saw them hurtling towards her and grabbed her bottle of Lambrini and tucked into the wall. Laura heard her scream something obscene. *That's a complaint*, Laura thought.

"Who called this?" Laura barked to the Sargent.

"Anonymous," he said. "We're trying to trace back the call, but nothings come back so far. Maybe using a burner phone." Laura's brow furrowed. Was it the one responsible? Was it a member of the public that didn't want to get involved?

They turned up to a wire fence that guarded a tall, dilapidated building with windows either barred, smashed or boarded up. More graffiti stained the old brickwork. It looked like an old mill of some kind. Old storage units stood empty eroded by the rain, bleaching them in rust and bird shit.

Craig pulled up to the chain-link fence that was sealed together with thick and rusted chains. Laura pushed the door open, the stench of the clutch of the BMW burning her nostrils. More cars arrived behind them and officers carrying bags of tools followed. People from the estate were gathering at the entrance to the dirt track. A huge, rusted sign stood above the fence –

WELCOME TO WELCH MILL

"Get those people back!" Laura called to a group of officers. "Seal off the entrance with tape. Start a scene log." Officers dipped their heads and ran to the growing crowd of onlookers. Some began arguing, holding bottles of cider, their teeth missing and their heads shaved and gesturing to the officers. Some complained about the noise, and some shouted at the officers about the property they had never had returned when they were last nicked. One male – tall, bald and with skin a dull yellow, pressed forward and protested police couldn't impede his movement. An officer – Older in the tooth with flecks of grey on his beard - pushed him back with an open palm to the chest. Chaos erupted then, as the rabble surged forward. Another officer – A young female with blonde hair gripped a hold of the male and pulled him to the floor. Mobile phones were pulled out and shouting and chaos emerged. Other officers joined in the melee as handcuffs and Captor spray were drawn.

"What a start to the day," Laura hissed, shaking her head. The cops had it under control. They always did. A couple of guys in cuffs later and a few more onlookers holding their eyes after a nice spray of '*Do as you're told*,' and the chaos seemed to subside. A van was called, and the officers began to tape off the entrance.

"People will find a way of getting themselves nicked, regardless of the chances you give them." Sargent Jeremy said discontentedly. "You can't fix stupid, but you can lock it up." He flashed a smile to Laura who did not share his enthusiasm. Jeremy dipped his head, his silence falling dead in the air. He cleared his throat. He pointed to the chain linked fence. "How do we get through that?" Laura eyed the officers with heavy bags.

"You!" She called. A constable stepped forward – a tall red-haired man who looked like he enjoyed smashing things. "Get this open." His face lit up. He dropped the bag to the ground and pulled out a huge set of bolt cutters and placed their toothy jaws around the chains. He pressed them together, his face turning the same colour as his hair. The chains came loose in a loud *crack* and dropped to the floor like a dead metallic centipede. Laura pushed the gate open and moved onto the car park. "Transmit," she said to the officer with the big stick with the metal jaws who looked very satisfied with himself. He began chattering on the radio.

Craig, Jeremy and other officers followed. Craig drew his taser, his finger over the ark trigger, holding it down to the floor. No red dots yet, but they were ready should the Bogey Man come out to play.

They heard the barking of a dog behind them. Laura turned. It was the dog handler from the scene at the riverside. He dipped his hat, pulling on the lead of his land shark.

"See what you can find," she said. The officer did so, shouting commands to his dog as they moved around the permitter. "Nobody comes through here without my permission, and if you see anyone leaving, you grab hold of them and bring them directly to me." The officers at the gate nodded, feeling like glorified bouncers for the day. They didn't mind. It was an easy Tuesday morning at the office. Look for bad guys, grab the bad guys and hold onto the bad guys until the bad bitch with stars on her shoulder told them otherwise.

Laura moved with Craig to the front of the building. She peered through the large double doors, peeling away the wood covering the windows and peered through the filthy glass.

Disused machinery. Spider webs. Bulbs like translucent eggshells hanging from the ceiling.

"Is there a way inside?" She spoke.

"We're looking to see if there's a back entrance," Craig said, peering through the glass. "But so far, it's all locked up."

"That will take too long," she snapped, trying the door in vain, the sound of chains rattling on the other side. "The door is locked from the *inside*," she said, which made her even more confused. "If someone has seen something inside here, then there must be a rat run or something. Search the windows, crevices or hell bang a few bricks in if you need to. I am getting inside this building." Craig nodded and moved to the permitter of the building. Jeremy did the same.

Officers followed them, leaving Laura on her own for a moment. She eyed through the dusty windows again.

*Come on you son-of-a-bitch,* she thought. *Show yourself to me. Finish what you started.*

Laura played with the chains again hoping that somehow the lock will come undone. She peered through the dirtied glass once more, cupping her hands around her face. Was anything even here? *Who had called this in?* She wondered. Spiders prickled her skin. Maybe it *was* him? He was playing with her. Like a rat caught in a maze, each exit filled with traps and cats with hungry mouths.

Something moved. Holy shit, something moved. She swore it. "Hey!"

She could see him. He turned to her. Features drenched in shadow. Her stomach plummeted. Face to face with a ghost. The figure moved away from the window. She pulled out her radio.

"Suspect inside!" She hollered. "I need the building secured now! Nobody gets out, not even a dam rat!" Bodies began to race towards her, but Laura couldn't wait. She wasn't about to let this son of a bitch get away from her. Not when she had him cornered. Less for the case to be solved, but to prove to herself that the ghosts of her past, as impossible as they were, hadn't resurfaced from a watery grave.

Laura pulled more boards away. The rotten wood splintered and snapped under her fingers. She looked again through the window. The figure was cloaked in shadow, staring back at her.

*I see you…*

Laura picked up a brick and threw it as hard as she could against the glass. It smashed, falling like heavy rain on the floor inside the building. The figure was on its toes, disappearing down the dark corridors. He could find a rat run or a crawl space and evade her. Laura had no time to waste. She threw off her jacket and covered the shards of glass on the broken window and clambered through into the darkness. The glass nicked her ankle, but adrenalin powered her toned five-foot-eight build through the tiny hole.

"Boss!" Craig yelled after her, but she was already through and making headway through the corridors. Craig slammed against the door, yelling at officers to haul ass and crack the door open, losing sight of Laura as she vanished, his heart yammering in his chest. "Hurry up!" He yelled as the big and daft ogre of an officer hauled a large crowbar with more spikes on the end than Vlad the Impaler's front garden.

Laura slipped through old machinery and down the halls hot on her toes with her torch in her hand. She blasted through a closed door. She was in an office of some kind. Disused and dusted monitors sitting on old desks and the walls home to abandoned spiderwebs. The room was still. She stepped slowly, her feet crunching on broken glass. She looked down. She was bleeding. Her ankle bracelet was missing, and the stinging of her flesh made her wince. She racked her baton – 18 inches of hellish steel ready to break skulls, should a shadow charge at her with fists or a knife.

*Come on,* Laura urged. *Show yourself, Ron. Show me I'm not going crazy.*

She could feel eyes on her, as she moved slowly through that office space doused in dirty sunlight that bled through broken windows. Every corner had a shadow. And every shadow had teeth. She gripped the steel 8oz handle that little tighter. She snaked her hand to her radio.

"Lima Yankee Two Three to patrol."

"Ma'am, where are you? We're coming in after you!"

"I'm closing in on him," she whispered. Her mouth ran dry. "Hurry. He won't come without a fight."

Then, right on cue, arms flew from the shadows. Laura swung her baton through the air. It connected and she heard a hard growl escape a mouth, before seeing a body dressed in black sprint through a doorway, feet hammering on metal stairs.

Against all training, rational or God damn common sense, she raced after him. He turned; his face covered in shadow. She screamed something, she didn't know what, but she screamed back, diving over desks and old furniture as he moved through disused shelving, throwing them to the ground. She darted like a sprinter on the track before the clock ran out. Red mist taking over. She had to know. Needed to know if it was him. Ready to break him until he resembled nothing of the monster he was. Just like he had done to her for all those years. Carve him into pieces and leave her alone to put herself back together.

He darted around a machine block and Laura moved the other way to intercept, baton raised.

"Stop!" She screamed. The suspect faced her, face covered with a hood. A flash of daylight bounced off the blade in his hand. He charged at her, and Laura felt time stop. A crack split the air and the suspect frenzied like he was on fire, before falling to the floor. A loud crackling erupted. Two small harpoons dug into his leg and chest. A beam of light with two red dots danced around him like frenzied fireflies.

"Stay down!" A voice barked. Hands gripped Laura's shoulders. She shrieked, turning with the baton over her head.

"Hey!" Jeremy called, shielding his face from an incoming belt across the jaw with a steel hitting stick. Craig rushed in, his taser primed on the suspect, coil wires unravelled. The suspect tried to rise to his feet, still holding the blade in his hand.

"Stay down!" Craig screamed as he recycled the weapon for another five seconds of pain, his thumb buried on the ARC switch, the cracking splitting the air once more. More officers moved around them, some taking Laura into their arms and moving her away. Others transmitting. The dog handler moving in, the fury land shark going bat shit crazy. The suspect tried again to get to his feet. He was persistent, she gave him that. Craig let him have one more cycle, this time keeping the electricity going. "Move in! Get him cuffed!" Craig ordered. Cops dove onto the male, forcing those stiff arms into justice bracelets. Laura stepped forward.

"Ma'am," Jeremy said, reaching for her.

"I just need to see," she said almost in a trance. The cops hauled the male to his feet. He was the right size. The right build. Caucasian male. She moved her fingers to his hood. He was panting heavily. What if it was him? That would make her lose her mind. And if it wasn't, then would that be worse? Her trembling hand snaked towards his hood.

The dog was barking insanely. The Dog handler called him to heal. Laura felt something hot on her shoulder. The hood came off. Laura screamed.

It wasn't Ron. But she wasn't screaming at that. She continued to scream until other officers looked above them. Some joined her in her horror. Some threw up. Some stared as the blood drained from their face.

A woman hanging from the chains that swayed from the ceiling of the roof with her arms stretched out like a bloodied angel, her hands fingerless stubs. Her stomach was torn open like a fleshy mouth with a pale tongue made of intestines and organs laid out for all to see. Her eyes were gone, just two pits of soulless black. Her jaw hung loose in one terrible, never-ending scream.

# Chapter Eighteen
# Sheree

The sun fell mute and darkness descended. Sheree lay on that soiled mattress. Her skin felt like it was being peeled off with a blunt blade. Her body shaking. Bones rattling. Hallucinations of every terrible thing she had done, and every sordid act of debauchery committed against her came thick and fast. Her eyes ached. Vomit coming thick and plentiful. She didn't have the strength to move, so she slopped her guts onto herself. She wanted to sleep, but sleep wouldn't hold her.

Over forty-eight hours without heroin was the closest thing a person could come to death whilst still breathing. She had tried it before. Going cold turkey. She got the idea from the Danny Boyle movie *Trainspotting*.

It was a year ago, after she narrowly missed prison and was handed a suspended sentence instead for her part in a knife point robbery. *Joint Enterprise* is what they called it. She needed to work with probation workers and turn up to meetings. She nearly got caught swapping another girl's piss test with hers, and she decided to try the *rattle* herself.

She had barricaded herself in her room and had buckets for the piss, shit and vomit. She had canned food to eat and a vibrator to help when things got really tough. Paracetamol and ibuprofen to take the edge off and sleepers to knock her unconscious. A TV with a Netflix marathon for the boredom. Bottles of water for hydration and Lucozade for her sugars. Wipes for cleaning. Clothes for changing. She was ready. Ready for the *rattle*. Ready to go cold turkey and get this crap out of her system once and for all.

Six hours later, she was back on her knees earning money for another hit.

This time, however, she could do nothing but feel it. Every bit of it. No painkillers. No food. No comfort. No dignity. No conversation. Just her and her body turning inside out. She screamed. As loud as she could she screamed. Lying on her back staring at that mould-devoured ceiling she screamed and screamed and screamed until the dawn crept through the filthy skylight. Sodden through with sweat and all other delightful fluids that came freely.

From writhing on the mattress, her iron necklace cut into her, scouring her skin raw like she had tried to scrape a bad tattoo from her flesh with sandpaper.

Sheree woke from a dreamless sleep. She wasn't dead, and she would have sobbed if she could spare the liquid. It was night again. *He* hadn't been back in over a day. He was the only person that knew where she was. That could feed her. Could save her. Reliant on your taker. Reliant on the person that had taken everything from her to give her a little bit of it back.

How long had she been here? She couldn't remember. Was it one day or seven? How long could the human body go without water? Three days? In her state? Maybe two?

Had he left her? Was he tired of her and left her to rot? Had he been injured and couldn't come back for her? She felt dread in the pit of her stomach. Maybe one more day and she would be free from this place in one way or another. The sound of footsteps in the distance. Were they real? Were they there to save her? She tried to move, to make a noise, but she couldn't find the strength, slipping under that blanket of unconsciousness once more.

# Chapter Nineteen
# Laura

Laura's insides painted the asphalt, flecks of bile landing on her pants and shoes. A small hint of red wine lingered in the air. She took out some tissue from her pocket, wiped her mouth, and threw the tissue into the wind.

The CSI vans were here already. The fire service pulled up in their giant wagon. An ambulance. Police tape was stretched over the perimeter of the building. Detectives and senior officers with more crowns and stars on their shoulders than you could shake a stick at had been to check out the situation. And once they had seen it, left with scars that would stay in their minds no matter how deep they buried them. Laura was getting a nice collection now.

"I need you to keep this under wraps," Superintendent Mary Dutton had said, her face even more waxy than usual, tears breaking through those hard eyes. "We can't let this get out."

"Yes Ma'am," Laura had said, as they dragged the suspect out into the courtyard and threw him into a van. "What are we going to do about the news? The local press will be all over this, and then when that happens, the national press too. There will be hysteria."

"I'll handle that." Dutton eyed Laura and her paling complexion. "How are you?" The question knocked Laura off balance.

"Fine," she said, stretching out the word. "Shit happens." Dutton drew in.

"You don't need to be on this unit if you don't want to," she said. "You have gone through a lot. With your ex." Dull knives cut through Laura's heart. Dutton saw Laura's expression change. "Oh, I know about that. Most of the station does. People talk."

"I don't know what to say…" Laura's mind stopped working.

"All I'm saying is, if you want to take some time off the unit, then that's okay. I can transfer you to a nice cushy desk job at headquarters. We can see the rest of this out without you."

"I can handle it," Laura said, burning tears gathering on her eyelids. Dutton pursed her lips.

"Well, consider this your only chance to walk away with your head high. No one will judge you. I don't want you losing it or having a nervous breakdown."

"If this is some kind of loving mother '*I'm here for you*' crap," Laura eyed Dutton with ferocity. "Then with all due respect ma'am, I can handle my own shit thank you." Dutton gave a sour look.

"Don't say I didn't try to help you." Mary Dutton moved away from Laura and headed out of the courtyard. Laura pulled out a cigarette and smoked it without taking a breath in between.

*Was she right?* The niggling in Laura's mind came pressing. *What if I can't do this? Everyone has their limits. What if I have reached mine? How many other grisly packages will she find before this is over? Was this even their guy?*

Laura stood quietly with her back against a shipping container. A couple of pigeons nesting in its crevices. The next few hours passed like she was in a dream: she debriefed the troops. Gave the coroner what information she could. Filled in logs and transmitted radio messages. The world a faraway place to her now. She got to see the worst of humanity. The darkness that the public didn't get to witness.

She didn't live in the land of the living anymore. She lived in the land of chaos and death, but that was what you signed up for when joining the police. Fighting battles in a secret world so others can sleep safely in their beds at night.

The body, the *girl,* would go to the pathologist's lab and a full autopsy be completed to establish the cause of death, and for the identity of the girl to be established so that a proper debrief of the family – if she had any – could be completed.

Laura called the office. Catherine answered.

"Ma'am?"

"I need you to look into any missing person reports for the last fourteen days in the local area. Woman, aged between eighteen to thirty, dark hair, olive skin. Distinctive tattoos on her ankle saying 'Bruno,' and another on her right hip saying 'God is with you always.' Also, check the local hospitals for admissions of anyone matching those descriptions, and if you can't find anything, I want you to check with every hospital within fifty miles."

"I have the fraud file to complete," Catherine snapped back. Laura hung up the phone. She called Dennis.

"Ma'am." He sounded as sick as a dog. She gave him the same instructions.

"Yes ma'am," he said, the sound of a pen scribbling away on paper against wood. She hung up the phone. She paused a moment and called him back. "Ma'am?"

"Get better soon. Have some chicken soup and get some vitamin C down you. Try to get some sunlight. Oh, and have a cold shower. You'll thank me later." She hung up the phone again. She took another second and called him back. "Run the number for Local subscriber checks. Event and entity data. If they want you to jump through hoops give them my number. Go for cell site data for the past two weeks. Same for CCTV and ANPR checks. Check local intel and see who the last owners of the Welch Mill were." Laura moved to different cops that stood talking to members of the public. She sent them to complete house to house enquiries. If they could find out who the girl was, they could work backwards, track her movements and hopefully build a case.

"Haven't we got someone ma'am?" A cop said. She stiffened her lip.

"We have a suspect, but we still need to see if it is connected with the first murder down by the lake. It may be connected, and I hope to God it is, because if it isn't it means that there is still someone out there at large that has murdered someone."

"Gotcha," the officer said. He was older, and Laura felt a little condescending in giving him the basics of jobs to do. "What are you going to do now?" He asked. Laura took out another smoke, cracked the lighter and took a chug.

"I'm going to interview this fucker. See what he has to say for himself."

"He's nailed to the wall isn't he boss?" She shook her head. How naive. These days, being caught with your hand in the cookie jar didn't mean shit.

"Not exactly," she said. "He was at the scene of the crime. Doesn't mean he did it. I need to get him to talk, so I need to throw as much shit at him as possible in the hope that some of it sticks, and then the CPS can remand him rather than bail him and let a potential murderer go free." The cop nodded with a smile. He knew the score. He went off with another officer, a young redhead, and began knocking on some doors.

More cops parked up and took out scene logs and tape. She instructed cops to park up by the main entrance, then one to always remain at the front of the warehouse and the back, changing every shift, maybe for half an hour here and there to allow for a comfort break. A familiar face approached her.

"Ma'am." Laura smiled.

"You look different without the mask on your face," she said to Celine.

"Nice of you to say." She handed Laura a stack of photos and paperwork. "They aren't pretty, but I know you need them."

"You could have emailed me them?"

"But then I wouldn't have gotten to see you…" The two shared a stare. Laura felt a warmth, one that she had long forgotten, rising up in her stomach. A feeling that scared her. Made her think of the sea. A photo burning by a dismembered heart. A world of pain rushing in at once.

"Thanks," she coughed, tucking her hair behind her ear. "But email me next time. It's less resources." Laura moved away, leaving Celine to watch as she drifted into the distance. Without looking back, Laura got in the car and signalled for Craig to join her, before leaving the crime scene, not wanting to look back.

Back at the station, Laura placed the radio on the desk, took off her stab vest and moved straight into the Quiet Room where officers would go for some time to relax away from the chaos of the station. At least that was what it was meant to be for. Most of the time, it was a place to let the horror of being a police officer and process the things you have seen that you don't ever want to repeat before you had a complete breakdown.

Laura turned on the light. It was soft and gentle, buzzing like a milky eggshell. She placed her ass on the couch that was lined with chakra pillows and meditation cushions. She threw them off onto the blue carpet. Around her were counselling and holistic feel-good pamphlets. On the ground were boxes filled with incense and even a singing bowl that was still in the box. A thought diary lay in front of her and for a second, she felt like opening it up and pouring all her mind into those pages. But she just sat there in quiet solitude.

The face of the woman. Her features were unrecognisable. The only way she knew she was a female was because of what that bald son of a bitch had done to her body. Her breasts were missing, sliced off like she was a pig in a slaughterhouse. Her insides fell out of her torn belly and hung like slippery rotten fruit. She could still hear the sound of the blood *tip tip tapping* onto the ground below her. Fuck she needed a drink. Hell, she needed a full wine aisle. She was going to get so hammered tonight it was going to be the stuff of legend. She didn't give a shit right now. She didn't need Craig watching over her. She didn't need anyone. She had coped perfectly fine on her own since Ron, and she wouldn't ever put herself in a vulnerable position again. Look how that turned out.

*They think you pushed him,* a voice crawled in her mind, one that she thought she had drowned many times with copious amounts of Merlot. But it just got better and better at swimming. *They think you pushed him. He wasn't that bad was he? He wasn't as bad as you made out. He loved you.*

*Cognitive Dissonance,* the voice of her therapist rattled in her mind. *When you start to think you were the problem, and that it wasn't that bad.*

"He was abusive," she whispered. "And now he's torturing me again." But that was impossible.

*They never did find his body.* The voice whispered again. *He said he would never leave you alone. That you were 'mine all mine baby.'*

A knock at the door. Laura wiped her eyes and composed herself. She answered it. It was Mary.

"I believe these are yours?" She said, eyeing Laura with hard eyes. She took the bundle of papers from her and closed the door with a strained smile. She sat back down and eyed the brown envelope.

TOXICOLOGY REPORT.

Laura took a breath and opened them up. Inside the envelope, there was a PNC and a local database breakdown of the victim.

'Olivia Murray, age '26.' She was a known drug addict of crack and heroin and sold it from the back of Baxter Street downtown to fund her habit. Her PNC history was lengthy –

Theft and Kindred Offences x 28

Drug offences – x 7

Possession With Intent to Supply Class A Crack Cocaine – 36 months imprisonment.

Conspiracy to Supply Class A Heroin – 36 months imprisonment.

Drunk and disorderly x 12

Conspiracy to Supply Class A Heroin – 28 months imprisonment.

Olivia was a single mother with her child 'Ruby,' currently in the care system. She was in and out of prison and in and out of rehab clinics. She had large traces of both Methylcellulose and Opiates in her body. Laura let out a breath. At least she couldn't have felt what was happening to her. She hoped. Her eyes glanced over the injury report –

'*Laceration to Femoral artery…Hematoma to cranium…*
*Fracture to C8 – T8 vertebrae...Fracture to Orbital bone…Tongue removed…*'

The list went on and on. The victim had had in total eleven broken bones and several organs removed. Her eyes landed on one line that made her world cave in.

'VICTIM'S MOUTH AND STOMACH CAVITY WAS FILLED WITH A STRAW-LIKE SUBSTANCE.'

"Oh god," she whispered. It's the same killer. She flicked through the pages some more. Olivia had been reported missing many times in the past 12 months, often by her probation worker, meaning when she was found, usually at a local drug dealer's friend or hanging around on the dark streets of Wigtown, then she would be thrown back into prison for violating her licence. Her last missing person report was from three weeks ago when she had been graded as 'Low Risk,' due to her age and her frequency. Seven days in, she was graded medium, then four days ago graded high. Her missing person report was closed and passed to the CID unit to manage.

Laura felt a light bulb go off in her mind. The missing person reports in the office of the Major Investigation Unit. There were seven of them. All fitting the same profile. The reports slipped from her hands and cascaded around her feet. The pictures of Olivia's mauled and mutilated body staring up back up at her. "There's more."

# Chapter Twenty
# Sheree

Sheree floated into her mother's arms, her face a blur wrapped in a warmer, loving world. A world she had forgotten could exist. A world that she was no longer allowed to enter. She was disposable. Just a *thing* to be used and then tossed aside like an old winter jacket when summer came around.

Her eyelids peeled open. The footsteps sounded far away. Alien to her fogged mind. Her body was numb. It was dark. So very dark in this room. Her neck gnawed raw from the collar. She touched the bloodied flesh and the pain bolted through her like sticking her hand into a fire.

She winced and scrambled once again, the footsteps drawing closer. Her mind was primed. Animalistic. When the door opened, she would escape. She would run and scream and fight and kill if she needed to. But her mind forgot one vital detail of her plan: there was no escape. She was going to die here. It would be slow. It would be painful. Would she starve? Or would she die of thirst first? Shock from some kind of poison in her food? Or was he going to defile her body as all the others had and leave her unable to recover? Only time would tell, and as this realisation cracked open in her mind and festered like a sack of writhing maggots, she felt the cold set into her body once more.

The slide of a bolt. The jingling of keys. The door scraped open, and *he* walked through. His face covered with his insidious mask of stretched flesh and teeth. A sight she knew she would never forget, and if he held her down by her throat until the world slipped away from her right here and now, then it would be a mercy killing. There would be no nightmares that way.

"Eat," the man said, placing another bowl of watery slop by her feet. The blinking light crept through the dark. She knew she shouldn't. God knows that her stomach was carving itself in half, but that instinct kicked in again. She was hungrier than she could ever recall feeling.

Sheree lunged forward and grabbed the bowl with both hands and brought it to her mouth. She knocked down the slop without so much as chewing. It tasted like watery vegetable piss, but she forced it down her neck. If she was throwing up out of both ends later, then so be it. But she couldn't pass up any meal. She had heard marines on tv shows say that.

*"Never waste a meal opportunity. If your captors are feeding you, they don't want to kill you."*

Next, a glass of water came.

"Drink." Sheree went to take it, but her hand hesitated.

"What's in it?" She whispered through cracked lips.

"Drink," he repeated. Sheree took it from his dirtied hand and put it to her mouth. It tasted a little perfumy, but that could be from the old pipes in the building. She let that liquid slither down her neck and she revelled in the feeling in her stomach. The man took the glass and bowl and moved away.

"Wait," She called. He stopped. Sheree's heart hammered in her chest. She licked her lips, leaning towards him. "I need your help." The man regarded her. She presented the chain around her neck like a giant black millipede. "I have Reynard's, from the drugs. Bad circulation. I need to keep mobile." On cue, she stretched out her legs with a wince. Her skin was patch and white like a drumstick lolly pop. Her toes were blue and her veins painted a pattern of blotchy salami. "I might lose my legs…" She gestured to the chains again. "I won't run, not like last time. I'm sorry for that I promise. Please, just let me walk around." The man stood silently, hot breath pushing through the mask. He turned back towards the door.

"Wait!" She cried, stretching out her arm like a drowning woman reaching for a life raft. "Please!" She begged, the chain tightening around her throat, eyes bulging, lips swelling. "I'm begging you! I can't sit here any longer. I'll do whatever you want! You can fuck me up the ass if you want I don't care just let me loose!"

His shovel-sized hands consumed Sheree's face like he was picking an orange from the fruit aisle in the supermarket. His eyes stared through those drooping holes. He threw her onto the mattress. He stood over her like a giant amongst ants. Sheree wished he would stomp on her neck or jump on her ribcage. Anything was better than this. She longed for death, longed to be released from this living hell.

"Just kill me," she cried, fumbling the soiled mattress. "Just get it over with. I have nothing to live for anyway. I never have. You'll be doing me a favour." She fell inside herself then. She was going to throw up. Not because of the food. But because her being had rejected life. He turned and touched the handle.

Those hands found her again. No, not his hands. His foot. A big size 14 pressing down on her neck. She couldn't breathe. Her eyes snatched open and she grabbed at the leg. Annihilation standing over her with a blinking halo. She wanted to live. She didn't want to die. To start anew. To bathe in the sun. To live by the sea. To drink champagne for breakfast and eat lobster for lunch.

Sharp pain in her wrist. A familiar sensation. A sensation from another life. She cried out. She didn't want it. Didn't want the poison. Her body had rejected it. Rejected the pain. Her bones had stopped rattling. The nightmares and hallucinations from withdrawing off gear had receded. He watched the plunger descend into her veins.

Sheree screamed as loud as she could. The sound of her shrieks bounced off the world like an orchestral ensemble of a living nightmare. The toxin jumped on the highway of her veins as her old friend consumed her. Chemical joy hooked into her, pulling the flesh apart and seeping right into the cracks, like the love from her mother she could never have again. Heroin. It was the next best thing.

Sheree stopped fighting. The pressure released from her throat as she fell on a wave of euphoria, floating high above her body, looking down on herself. She lay there, a wasteful body in a wasted life. Her eyes rolled to the back of her head. Mouth laying open. The man grabbed her legs and pulled her to the top of the mattress. Sheree tried to call out as he began to undress her. Shouting from her sunken place to let her free, to not touch her. But her screams came out in low gargles as she lay there like a lump of flesh.

She stirred awake. Her skin felt like daggers against her bones. Her teeth ached, her eyes burned. She wasn't naked. She didn't feel devilled or violated in her insides. Instead, she was dressed in loose clothing. Her legs were covered in loose joggers, her skinny appendages sticking out from the bottoms like draping a car engine in dough. A heavy jumper coated her arms and chest that itched her skin. She sat up. Her back popped and clicked as she moved. Surprise struck her. She touched her neck and no metal kissed her fingertips.

She turned. The chain dangled on the wall like a dead metallic snake. Slowly, Sheree stumbled off the mattress like a child learning how to walk, using the wall to keep steady. The blood rushed to her toes and muscles and they lit up like they were filled with tiny needles.

She stretched, a long series of clicks running along her feet. The lactic acid struck then like a dog bite in her calves, crumpling her to the floor, biting her jumper so as not to call out. After what seemed like forever, the spasming began to pass, and she continued to move around her tiny cell.

A steam train of bile bubbled in her stomach, before blasting up her gullet. Sheree raced like a mother with morning sickness and painted the foul bucket with what little she had to give. She lay on the ground wiping her mouth on her clothing. She spat the remainder of half-digested vegetables into the bucket, peeling her hair from her face.

The door went again. Sheree scrambled to the edge of the room. Was he coming with more drugs? Did he mean for her to wake up unchained? He stood there and regarded her behind the mask. She noticed a small sports bag in his hand.

"What's in that?" She said meekly. He opened it up and threw the items onto the mattress. Three bottles of Evian mineral water, a bunch of apples and a toothbrush. She eyed him with trepidation, waiting for something to happen.

"Naloxone Hydrochloride," he said.

"What?" She said, unsure of what language he was speaking.

"It reverses opioids. You were upset. You would have run or hurt yourself. I fixed you."

"Oh…" She said. "So, the heroin?"

"All gone. That's why you threw up. Metabolises in the body, but some still has to come out." Sheree let the relief set in. She didn't have to go through another rattle. She eyed the dangling chains.

"Why did you unchain me?"

"You have been less trouble than the others."

*The others?*

"Thank you..." Sheree said, trying to keep a lid on her terror. She could charge him or hell even play dead. He would have to take her to the hospital if she hurt herself. He wanted to care for her, why else would he have brought the food and water? If he wanted to keep her in one place, he would have kept her locked up. What was he playing at?

*Be pure.* The rattle of his voice in her mind again.

"What do you mean, *better than the others?*" She said, then immediately wished she could swallow the words before they hit his ears. She sat suspended in terror. Had she angered him? Was he smiling? She couldn't tell behind that mask. So much communication comes from someone's facial expressions. Even micro-expressions. When you remove those, then it makes them much harder to read.

It was terrifying.

He took out something else from the bag. A towel. He gestured to her.

"You need to shower."

# Chapter Twenty-One
# Laura

Laura charged into the Major Investigation Unit and pulled the papers from the pinboards like she was escaping a burning building. Her eyes ravaged them.

"What's going on?" Catherine said, looking up from her crossword puzzle. Laura didn't answer. She stared at the bundle of papers and scribbled notes down. Dates. Times. Locations. Times previously missing. Anything she could put together.

"You okay ma'am?" Jeremy said concerned, moving over to the bundle of papers.

"When did we last look at these missing person files?" She barked. The pair eyed each other curiously.

"They were closed down," Jeremy said. "It's force policy. Over twenty-eight days and they get closed and we go off intel. Normally these people just show up or get locked up. We have a review every fourteen days from there. Discussing at panels of any new information –" Laura cut him off.

"Don't tell me about the procedures, I asked you a straight question." She stabbed her finger into the bundle. "When did these last get looked at?" Jeremy gulped.

"The last one, before Olivia… Was a lady named Katherine Hargreaves. She went missing three months ago. Before her, Jennifer Delany, six months. April Withers, nine months."

"So, we just let these people fend for themselves without making so much as a single effort in what, *nine months* to find them?" Laura's nostrils flared. "How the hell can you be an investigation unit if you don't investigate?" She was furious, her teeth tight, her fist clenched into a rock-hard ball just begging to be buried in someone's face. She looked around the office. "Where's Craig?"

"Said he needed a minute after the warehouse," Jeremy said.

"Get him on the phone," she barked to Catherine. She rolled her eyes and Laura met that roll with a wall of annihilation. Catherine rebuked then nodded quickly and picked up the phone.

"What's going on ma'am?" Jeremy said weakly.

"The murder today. The murder at the riverbank. The missing women. They're all connected. Both victims were filled with straw, like some kind of ritual killing." She touched the pictures of the missing girls. "We have a serial murderer on our hands."

"But we got him?" Jeremy gasped from his flabby mouth. "The Super said she didn't think they were connected."

Red rag to a bull.

"I am your mother fucking supervisor, not her!" Laura barked with a ferocity that rocked the shit out of Jeremy. "Did we get a trace on the tip-off?"

"We're working on that," he said quickly.

"Work faster." Laura thrust the paperwork into his chest. "Email these to Dennis."

"He's sick!"

"I don't give a shit. I want associates, cell site data, CCTV footage, offending backgrounds, last known address, and last time they took a shit. Witnesses. Bus cameras. Anything and everything." She eyed Jeremy who looked at the paperwork like a baby that wouldn't stop screaming. "I want you to send units out to every warehouse, landfill, and God damn hole in the ground in a twenty-mile radius. We're no longer looking for missing people. We're looking for bodies."

"You can't authorise that?" The Sargent barked. Laura grabbed a cup of cold coffee on a table and hurled it against the wall.

"Do it!" She seethed, her chest rising quickly. Jeremy scurried to the scanner with the papers, picking up the phone to call Dennis. Catherine gestured to the phone in her hand.

"It's just going to voicemail," Catherine said, but Laura was already out the door with her coat. She had a murder to solve and someone in custody, and the clock was ticking down with every second.

# Chapter Twenty-Two
# Sheree

Sheree was led down the long corridor. She could make a run for it. Hide under a table somewhere. Maybe she would get lucky and find something heavy to break him with when he wasn't looking. Smash a window and climb through. But if she failed, that chain would find its way around her neck again, and this time there would be no second chances at redemption.

*Fool me once, shame on you. Fool me twice…*

They stopped at a door, and he pulled out a rung of keys. The lock was heavy, and the door yearned for oil as he pulled it open, the bottom scraping along the floor like an old foghorn of a forgotten ship.

The floor was tiled and filthy and thick mounds of sludge gathered where the wall met the ground. The walls were green and filthy: handprints, smudges of grime and shit ingrained in the cracks and creases of the chipped plaster. Sheree followed him under the flickering light. She passed closed doors that read 'STAFF ONLY' and 'PRIVATE' on the top in marred dusted plates. What was this place?

They moved down a set of rickety steel stairs which were bubbled and ribbed with metallic patterns that stung Sheree's bare feet. She was so weak, needing to hold onto the freezing cold handrail as she moved. At the bottom, they moved along a straw-littered floor, passing pens and old machinery. The smell was rancid. A mixture of shit and slop of some kind.

Hooks that were stained with old blood hung from the low ceiling. Gates open that led to pens with hay bales stacked high. Old pig troughs. Milking bays that had turned solid with rotting milk and bubbling cheese. The flies were the worst part. They buzzed around Sheree's face and she had to use what little strength she had to swat them away when they landed on her cold skin. Little did she know, they would be eating her flesh soon.

Sheree eyed a large frosted window above a chained door. The only place that she hadn't seen covered in bars. She made a note of it. But it needed to be the right moment. Nothing stupid. She needed to be compliant, but devious. Cunning, yet invisible. A good little girl to get what she wanted.

She moved into a large room that greeted her with a wall of putrid-smelling antiseptic and bleach that burned her eyes and nostrils. She was led into a large wet room with tiles and lights fitted into the ceiling. Shower heads were fastened against the walls. Against the mould and the stained tiles, the shower heads were sparkling and clean, with two copper pipes feeding into them through the wall.

"Strip." The word cut through her, her skin prickling. Sheree turned, holding herself. She felt tears welling in her eyes, body beginning to fold in on itself. He was going to rape her. He could have done it when she was tied up and chained to the wall, but he wanted to wait. Let her think he was being kind. Some sick game. He was going to hurt her. *Really* hurt her. If she didn't make a run for it now, she wouldn't get another chance.

"No," she said, fighting the fear in her throat. "I won't do it." His eyes fixed on hers.

"I'm not going to hurt you," he said calmly through the rotting mask. "Get undressed. Be clean."

*Be pure.* The sound of his voice ran through her mind once more. Sheree thought about everything she could and shouldn't do. He had the keys to the exit. She was weak. She was trapped in a maze, and he knew all the turns. She eyed the shower heads. When faced with her own annihilation, what choice did she have?

Fighting all urges otherwise, she began to take off her jumper.

"Not here!" He barked. He pointed. Sheree followed his hand. A small cubby was built into the washroom. She hadn't even noticed it. "Get undressed and wash." He placed the items from the sports bag onto the ground. "Soap, feminine products and things to scrub yourself with." He began to close the door. "Knock when you're done," he said, and then with the sound of a deadbolt sliding into place, she was alone.

Her heartbeat thumped in her ears. The light bounced off the white tiled walls. There was a towel hanging up in the cubby on a peg that had been screwed into the wall. She undressed and paced her clothes folded on a shelf that was dusty and filled with cobwebs. She pulled out the shampoo and the bar of soap and stepped out into the cold air of the wet room.

The water came slowly – spurting out in splashes then slow trickles, until becoming a long steady stream. The sound of a boiler fired into life somewhere in the distance. Sheree put her head under the water, and she nearly cried at the feeling. So long spent so cold, she had forgotten what warmth felt like. She pulled the toothbrush out of the packet and dabbed a generous helping of toothpaste on the head and scrubbed the thick muck from her mouth. The lingering taste of the watery soup and bile disappeared into minty freshness. She swirled and spat it onto the floor, and it disappeared down a gurgling plug hole that was fixed to the floor.

Lathering her thin body in soap, Sheree scrubbed her skin raw. She felt dirty, like the filth was engrained in her flesh. She turned the heat up to as hot as she could tolerate. She wanted to strip this place from her skin, strip all the pain, the anger and the degradation from her flesh. But it went deeper than that. Clean her soul, purge her old life of drugs and debauchery from herself. She winced when the water hit her neck from where the collar had been chewing on her. But she didn't care. She didn't want this time to end.

A short time later, the water shut off abruptly. Sheree stood under the final trickles of the shower head and washed the last few suds off her skin. She towelled off and got dressed again. She had never felt so clean, and dare she say, she felt a slither of happiness run through her. She knew she would have to go back to her room. She wasn't free. She wasn't his equal, but a small part of her wished to thank him for such kindness. She could no longer smell her own body emanating rot and filth. But instead, her nostrils were filled with the scent of lavender and berries. A scent of a better time. A glimpse at better things to come. But that asked another question -

Why?

Why was he keeping her? Why was he letting her wash? Why not just throw a packet of wet wipes into her cell and make her clean herself that way? Why give her a tour of the building and expose possible escape routes? Was this all a test?

*You're better than the others…* If she wanted to survive, she must show him she is worth keeping alive. He wants her to be good. Be clean. Be *pure*. She would have to fake it 'till she made it. That was good, because she had been pretending to be something she's not her entire life.

Strong.

She pulled herself from her thoughts and noticed something clinging to the plug hole. It was hard to spot and made sense why he hadn't seen it. But Sheree had a keen eye for detail. Another thing that she had brought with her from her childhood. She learned it from checking how much vodka her father had drunk that night. It would be the difference between him smashing the house up or smashing her mother up. Fighting every instinct to stay put, she scurried to the plug hole.

She crouched down, moving her wet hair from her face and pushing it behind her ears. Sheree studied it. It was small and round. Yellowed like the nub of a hoof. She looked over her shoulder at the door again. She knew she didn't have time.

Sheree eyed the shower head. She hadn't noticed earlier, but there appeared to be something *behind* the fitting like something was there before but had been removed. A brown line that had been roughly painted over and sealed away. Then it clicked.

*This must be where the animals were washed and cleaned before they were slaughtered.*

That thought sent a bolt of unbearable horror through her mind.

*Be Pure. Make yourself clean.*

"Oh god," she whispered, her old friend terror running through her veins once more like the poison she had ejected from them. She would rather have the poison right now. A huge, big brown bag of it melted on a spoon and delivered right into her brain. Call it intuition or simple curiosity, she

127

reached down into the drain, sludge and shit clinging to her fingers.

Footsteps in the distance. Fear ravaged her.

*Get your hand out!* Her brain screamed. But she couldn't. She *had* to see what that little yellow stub belonged to. She doubted she would get another chance. She needed to know. Her life depended on it.

A door scraped along the floor. The sound of nonchalant whistling broke the silence.

*Alouette, gentille alouette, Alouette, gentille alouette…*

She could feel it kissing her fingertips. It was lodged in, coming loose.

*Just a little more…*

The deadbolt began to loosen. The door opened. A flash of cool air burst into the room. He eyed the empty space, his breath pushing through the mask of a dead girl.

"Just getting dressed!" Sheree called from the cubby. No answer met her ears, only a shuffling of weight. Sheree hung the towel back on the rack. She eyed the screws that were pinned into the wood. One of them was loose. Like a child stealing one last cookie before her parents returned, she yanked the screw from the wall. She had to be quick.

He stood in front of her. She fumbled, dropping the screw on the floor, quickly crouching and throwing the towel over it. He had caught her. She had betrayed him and he was going to notice. She needed to be good. *Stupid, stupid girl!*

"Ready?" He said standing over her. The tightness in Sheree's chest loosened slightly. She pretended to dry the floor, palming the screw.

"All done," she said, trying to mask her bubbling fear. The man eyed her intently. Sheree cracked a nervous smile. He turned and moved away. She nestled the item in her hair.

Something she had done from her days of being stopped and searched. You'd be amazed what she had hidden in there.

She was led back to her cell. He locked her inside and she sat on the soiled mattress, inwardly smiling. She had gotten away with it. A small victory on her part. He wasn't invincible. He could be fooled, and if he could be fooled then he could be beaten. She had a chance after all.

She took the screw from out of her hair and stuffed it under the mattress. Then, she remembered the yellow stub and pulled it from her hair too. She eyed it intently, then dread consumed her, trying to hold back the scream in her throat.

It was a human tooth.

# Chapter Twenty-Three
# Laura

Laura pulled out her phone and dialled Craig. It went straight to voicemail.

*Where the hell was he?*

He was her lead detective. Even if he was dying in a car accident somewhere, he hadn't asked her permission.

"For fuck sake…" She spat, scanning the car park. She pulled out a pair of keys from her coat and a car chirped to life. It was an older model Peugeot 306. Laura slipped in and punched in the sat nav for the custody suite. She looked at the ETA. With her driving, it would take her a third of that time.

She fired the engine to life and it rumbled under her like a steel horse. Laura sped out of the car park, the wheels springing and bouncing on the road as she hurtled away. She hit the 'EMERGENCY/999' button on the centre console and the hidden blue lights came to life. Her hand pressed into the steering wheel and the sirens began to blare.

She approached a set of traffic lights, the siren hammering quickly as cars slowed and flashed her across. How kind of them. She was going anyway.

She made it to the custody suite with the engine crying for reprieve. It had been a while since she had been able to drive like a bat out of hell. It often helped her to clear her mind. The adrenalin. The danger. The rush of it. She felt better than she had in months.

The building was square and old looking, with chipped walls that gave way to brickwork like peeling the flesh off a corpse. Black windows reflected the overcast sky, and tall green gates with barbed wire encased the grounds. Laura followed the sign that said, 'STAFF ENTRANCE.' She imagined she qualified as such.

When she first made Sargent Laura cut her teeth in the custody suites for a couple of years. It was more relaxed than the madness of response, but it had its drawbacks. Better work-life balance was the first, with more sociable shifts. It was a good job, but my gosh those around you were energy vampires. When she was working nights, her colleagues either sucked the life out of each other and went on about their pensions or the fact they only had '34 more paydays' before retirement. What a way to wish your life away.

Laura used the time to study and was often found in the refs room at 3 am with her head in a book. She left the role before she lost her mind and managed to get a job in the Major Investigation Unit as a seconded DS, before becoming a DI.

She wanted a drink. A drink so badly. Did she even have a plan of action? She was so out of her depth. So out of touch with the investigation. And now she was about to walk into the real case of her new posting without so much as a sniff of what she was going to ask him. It all felt so rushed. She should have a full team with her for an interview like this. Two officers doing the interview, and one in the next room watching and analysing on the camera. But it was just her going up against a monster who she so desperately wanted to be the bad guy they had been looking for. But she doubted it. Monsters don't reveal themselves so easily.

The place was a circus, with sergeants sitting behind the desks and booking in prisoners – One, a woman so thin Laura was surprised they had clothes able to fit her, with her hair matted and skin yellowing and filthy was screaming at the custody sergeant.

"I need my methadone!" Seemed like it was the most important thing in the world. Not her health, her children that she had been neglecting for the past three days while she went and scored, or the fact that she was facing a custodial. No. Just her methadone. Just her drugs. It hurt Laura to see people in such circumstances. She joined the police to help people, and she still tried in whatever way she could to lift the veil of darkness away from people's lives. But some people, no matter how much light shined on them, wanted to live in the dark forever.

Another prisoner was brought through into the suite. A tall man so built he had to be double handcuffed. He was screaming so loudly and incoherently that the custody sergeant – an older woman with deep wrinkles and her hair tied back so tightly it appeared to be the only thing keeping her face attached to her skull – ordered the officers – five of them – to take the male straight to his cell.

Laura stepped onto the custody platform where phones were ringing out and computer screens with cell CCTV cameras sat behind Perspex glass. She regarded the screens, like watching animals in a zoo, then turned away and slipped into the back room.

"Who's in charge of Mark Shaw?" Laura said to the room of detention officers. One turned – an older man who looked like he should have retired years ago.

"Cell 28. Solicitors already in consultation." He said, not turning to look at Laura. Confusion slapped her.

"Solicitor?" She said. "Who is in there with them?"

"A detective," the detention officer said, tucking into a bag of Cheetos with Netflix playing on his phone whilst inputting commands into the computer. "Young guy. He's not been here long." Sensing Laura's questions that were bubbling in her mind, the officer turned and pointed to a small door that stood behind her by the side of a raft of lockers where arrested persons have their belongings stored until they are released or sent to prison. "Go out that door, turn right and you'll see the consultation rooms to your left. I think they're in the third or fourth one. Been in there for a few minutes or so." Laura nodded a thank you, but the detention officer was already turned back towards his computer and was crunching more of that cheesy goodness and washing it down with black coffee.

In the corridor, Laura sighted three more officers waiting to have their prisoners booked in. Some were quiet. Others not so much, screaming to be released and that they will sue/fight/kill themselves if they weren't. Basically – Insert 'empty childish threat' here. Laura remembered a phrase she heard once –

*If you want to know someone's real personality, then tell them 'no.'* It had always proved as a useful tool in recent years. Ever since meeting Ron, she had learned the importance of maintaining boundaries.

Laura stood outside the consultation room.

"The trick with Gin is you have to get it when it's on offer and you MUST drink it with lemonade and not tonic water," the solicitor was yammering on.

"I'm a whisky man myself," another voice came. Laura eyed them through the tiny window in the door. It was Craig. Where the hell had he been? She wrapped her knuckles against the door. The talking stopped. The creak of a chair, then the handle depressed.

"Ma'am," Craig said with a smile. "I thought I would come here straight from the scene and get the ball rolling." Laura's nostrils flared.

"Did I instruct you to do that?" She said, smiling through gritted teeth. A flare of worry slipped along Craig's eyes.

"Well, no but…"

"What have you told her?"

"Nothing," he said. "I was going to see what you wanted us to do." Laura eyed the solicitor, who was typing away on an iPad.

"Just follow my lead." She pushed the door open. "Detective Inspector Warburton," Laura said. The solicitor smiled and went to speak but Laura cut her off. "Me and detective Sinick need to have a chat about the case and the interview. We won't be long." If the solicitor wanted to protest, Laura didn't give her a chance to fill her lungs with the air to do so. She left the consultation room with Craig following slowly behind like a badly behaved dog. They moved through the custody suite and past the lady that was still yelling about her methadone and was now sitting on the floor refusing to get up.

"I want my fucking script!" She screamed, wailing like an infant throwing a tantrum. The Sargent tried to reason with her. Laura and Craig slipped past.

"Excuse me," Laura said, moving through the wall of bodies.

"Cunt," the prisoner barked. Laura stopped dead and smiled. She tucked her hair into a bobble. She turned and faced the woman.

"I beg your pardon?" She said.

"I said fuck off!" In a flash, Laura grabbed the wretch by her arm and yanked her to her feet. From there, she looped an arm under the woman's bicep and cupped her shoulder, forcing her head to the floor, gripping the back of her neck.

"What cell?" She said calmly through the prisoner's screeches and wails.

"Fourteen," he said, completely slack jawed. Laura did a quick scan of the halls and dragged the woman kicking and screaming into the cell before slamming it shut with a thundering crash. She moved back to the charging desk when she saw a hand snake out from the open hatch of the cell, the woman's rabid face pushing through the gap.

"I'm going to get you fucked for that you bitch! Just you wait!" Laura nodded to Craig.

"Go close her hatch for me. I don't think we're getting on." Craig smiled and moved to the cell hatch.

"Move your arm," Craig said, his hands pressing on the hatch door to close it, her fingers gripping hold of the hole like she was being thrown into a furnace. Upon seeing Craig, her eyes widened and a smile curled along her lips.

"I remember you…" She hissed, eyeing him up and down. Laura's ears pricked up and she moved to the cell. Craig's face turned a wash with horror. The woman's sneer grew larger. She eyed Laura her gaze ravaged Craig. "Want me to suck you like a lollypop again?"

Laura snatched the hatch and moved away.

"What was that about?" She snapped to Craig as he moved away. He shook his head.

"Never seen her before in my life."

# Chapter Twenty-Four
# Laura

Laura followed Craig through the custody suite as they moved to one of the back offices. Her stomach was churning. Something wasn't right. She could taste it in the air. She gripped his arm.

"Spill right now," she blasted. Craig looked to the floor. "You know that woman." Craig's face looked like he was chewing on a wasp.

"Don't worry about it." He said and tried to move away. Laura pulled him harder.

"How do you know her?"

"I said forget about it, ma'am."

"Fuck that ma'am shit," she bit. "If we are going to go in there and go to war with a possible murderer, then I need to know if you're hiding something. He is some kind of street rat, so if you know him or any of his clientele, then you need to tell me right now because I need to be fully prepared for anything that will come out of his mouth." Craig looked up to the ceiling, trying to find the answers. "Look," Laura said more coolly. "Whatever it is, you need to tell me, or I can't have you in there with me." Craig squirmed in his skin. He let out a long exhale.

"It was about a year ago," he said. "My ex-wife and I were separating." Laura didn't like where this was going. "I hadn't slept in the same bed for months. I went out of town and found a girl on a street corner. She gave me a blowjob. I felt terrible for it."

"You used a prostitute?" She said, the words like vomit in her mouth. "You went and gave someone money to touch your dick and then went home to your wife?"

"Our marriage was over," he bit, eyes filled with fire. "We hardly spoke. It was like living with a ghost. Do you know what it feels like to love someone so much, and they don't even want to touch you? Do you know what it's like to see who a person really is and not the thing they pretended to be?"

Laura felt a stab in her heart. She knew all too well what that felt like.

"It was like living with a ghost," he continued. "Seeing the death of a person right in front of your eyes even though they're still living." She could hear the rawness in his voice. He looked away, eyeing the walls like he wanted to run through them.

"There's more, isn't there?" Craig pursed his lips, then nodded.

"My badge fell out of my pocket, and she saw my name and where I work. So fucking stupid. She took my wallet and ran out into the night. She knew I wasn't going to say anything. After that, I packed my stuff and left and moved back in with my mother. One night, I got drunk and broke down. Tried tying a noose around my neck when my mum came home and talked me out of it. I told her everything." Craig spoke vacantly like he was speaking about someone else. Like he was recalling the terrible scene in a movie or a book he had consumed. Complete dissociation. Laura stayed silent.

"So, then my mum being my mum and not wanting this to get out, I went with her to find the woman. I pointed her out and we paid her some money to keep her mouth shut. I don't know what happened to her after that. I never saw her again until today." Laura felt her skin crawl.

"Does anyone else know?" Craig shook his head.

"No." Laura put her hand to her lips, trying to hold back all that she wanted to say. They were about to walk into an interview with a suspected murderer and her lead detective had used one of his girls. He would know. God knows word travels fast on the street, certainly something like that. He had been compromised, but she needed him. He was the only detective on her team that wasn't completely inept. But then again, did she need him? Did she really? His integrity was in question, but his reasons behind it were somewhat valid albeit flawed. And then the superintendent knew all about it. Could she challenge her superior for trying to protect her son? If Laura kicked him off the case then questions would be asked. Who would believe the woman in the cells anyway?

The web just gets thicker and thicker. What kind of police force was this? It reeked of corruption at the highest level, with bodies piling up, a crumbling investigation unit and a wall of silence that was impenetrable.

"Okay," Laura said after a moment. "We do this today together, but if at any point he recognises you in the interview..."

"He won't."

"But if he does," she said firmly. "Then you make your excuses and leave, and I'll deal with the rest. Okay?"

"Okay." Craig cracked a smile, but Laura's face stayed hard.

"Good," she said. "Now let's go prepare."

# Chapter Twenty-Five
# Laura

The Solicitor put her phone down as Laura and Craig walked through the door. She smiled, but Laura kept her face stern and pulled out the chair before slamming the thick evidence file on the desk. Craig stood back, writing in his daybook.

"Emma Fishwick," the solicitor said, extending a hand. Laura took it firmly.

"Detective Inspector Laura Warburton, head of the Major Investigation Unit." Emma took the hand back. Laura could feel the sweat from her palm lingering on hers. This was her first rodeo, and what a case to be undertaking.

Laura opened the file and stole a look at Emma's face. She was overweight, blonde and wore way too much make-up. Maybe it was the way she sat or the cheap perfume she was wearing. Either way, Laura didn't like her. A lot of cops try to placate the solicitor before an interview to get them on side. That wasn't Laura's tactic. They were there to give the best chance to their client, and in Laura's experience, their clients normally deserved to be locked in a cage for the rest of their lives.

"Your client," Laura said, her voice cutting through the tense air. "Mr. Shaw." The solicitor began typing on her tablet.

"Correct. What's he in for? Your colleague alluded to it being serious. Drugs again?"

Laura passed Emma a sheet of paper that was embedded in the mound of forensic reports and photographs. She slid it along the desk. Emma eyed the paper and her brow furrowed. She studied the document, then placed it on the table and took off her thick-rimmed glasses.

"What is this?"

"That is your disclosure," Laura said. "I know my colleague is a little more forthcoming with the details, but I will be leading this interview."

"I need a full disclosure, under the Human Rights Act," Emma began, rattling off the usual rhetoric.

"I work under the Police and Criminal Evidence Act, not under the Human Rights Act." Laura sat back in her chair. "I will tell you this though," she said, tapping the file of evidence. "I hope you have a strong stomach for what he has been up to. It's not pretty." Emma picked up the document again, trying to hide a hard swallow.

"Arrested on suspicion of kidnap, torture and murder," she whispered, then began to rhyme off his rap sheet. She put the paper down. "What evidence do you have against my client?" Emma said. Laura didn't bite. Her face stayed solid like hard rock. She gestured to the paper.

"That is your disclosure. Your client can tell you the rest." Laura stood up and took hold of the file. "I'll go get him for you, shall I?"

# Chapter Twenty-Six
# Laura

The clock on the back wall ticked loudly. Emma typed on her iPad and Laura sorted out her evidence and questions into order. Craig sat with a notebook open, scribbling down some notes. The tapping, ticking and scribbling. It was enough to drive someone to murder.

"Have you been interviewed before Mr. Shaw?" Mark nodded. "Do you prefer Mr. Shaw or Mark?" He was dressed in the customary grey jumper and sweatpants to match. His feet were bare. His knuckles were tattooed with four dots. The infamous sign for 'All Coppers are Bastards.' They were going to get on just fine. She could feel it already. He was a bald man with mismatched eyes – One blue, the other green. One was swollen badly, painted with purple and blue and leaking brownish red fluid.

"Fuck you." He said, folding his arms and sitting back in his chair. Laura smiled to herself.

"Suit yourself, Mr. Shaw."

"You can call me Daddy," he said. Laura pursed her lips.

"Let's begin, shall we?" She said, a tight smile across her lips. Laura pressed the big red button on the digital recorder. The black screen illuminated with the reference number that she quickly wrote down before it disappeared. The screen changed from 'START' to REC' and they were on their way.

Laura introduced the interview, herself and the location. Craig and Emma introduced themselves also. Laura eyed Mark.

"Also present for the interview is?"

"No Comment."

"Mark Shaw," Craig piped up. "Born 26th of November 1972." Laura cautioned him and asked if he understood, to which he remained silent. She explained it anyway, and she could see his agitation growing. His lips grew tighter and his arms folded that little further.

"So," Laura said, pausing in her notes. "You were arrested today on the suspicion of the murder of Olivia Murray. Can you tell me what happened?"

Mark looked at his solicitor, then sat back.

"No comment."

"Okay." Laura opened the first document. A list of questions. "Where were you last night?"

"No comment."

Laura asked Mark about his whereabouts over the last 48 hours. Who he was with, where he went and what he was wearing. He either remained silent or faintly uttered 'no comment.' Craig asked questions about if he had gotten on any public transport or if he had used any kind of ATM. Again, he remained tight-lipped.

Laura opened the folder further. She pushed the photos of Oliva Murray's mutilated body in front of Mark, tapping on her face.

"We believe before you murdered Olivia, you strangled her."

"You don't know if my client murdered anyone officer," the solicitor piped up. Laura almost forgot she was here. "You can't ask him that."

"I will ask your client anything I see fit," Laura snapped, her eyes burning into Emma's. "So again, I repeat what I was saying." Emma returned her gaze to her computer. "Did you strangle her?"

"No comment," he said, looking away from the picture and staring at the blank walls that encased them. Laura pulled out another photo. One with Olivia laid out on a metal slab. Her eyes vacant like two frosted windows. Her stomach and chest cut open, breasts falling down onto the table, and her insides brown and decomposing like rotting meat. You could almost hear the maggots that had begun to nest inside her corpse.

"Olivia Murray was strangled and drugged. We found toxins in her body. We also know that she was cut open very roughly. We imagine she may have been conscious whilst the incisions were made, but she couldn't move whilst it was being done." Mark continued to look away. Laura could see the colour draining from his face. Her mouth went dry. "How did you do it?" Laura said. "How did you cut her open?"

Mark remained silent. Laura let out a breath and pulled out another photo. One of the straw that was clumped in blood and bile on a scale.

"This was pulled out of Olivia's stomach, mouth and anus. Straw and hay, of the weight of 4.22 kilos. Why after you killed her did you place this inside her body?"

"I didn't kill anyone," Mark whispered. His solicitor raised her head and fired a look of death at him. Seeing a crack in the armour, Laura went in.

"Then why were you at the crime scene Mark? Why were you in the Warehouse? Why did you run from me? Look," she said, softening her voice. "If we have got the wrong person, you have to tell us. You have to tell us what happened." Mark searched his head. He licked his lips and leaned forward onto his elbows, eyeing the photos. His face reddening. The solicitor continued to tap away on her tablet.

"I didn't kill anyone."

"I advise you to go no comment," the solicitor jumped in. Mark eyed her.

"Fuck off," he spat, and turned back to Laura. "I didn't kill anyone. I know who the girl is. She worked for me. She went off with someone a few weeks back. Haven't seen her since. Thought she was in a den somewhere."

"Who did she go off with?" Mark shrugged.

"I don't know," he said, like he was talking about where he misplaced a chocolate bar. "She was a good earner but she was trouble."

"Trouble?" Laura said. Mark nodded.

"With clients. Always bringing shit to my door. Tried robbing a couple of them. I just figured she pissed off the wrong person, or she ended up in a den somewhere. People do this sort of shit all the time. I figured she would turn up eventually."

"Why were you at the scene of the murder?"

"I take some scrag every now and then. I don't dig it, I toot it. Put it on some tin foil and burn it. Chase the dragon. That's why my lips are burned." He took a sip of water. "I went there to take my gear in peace. If you check in the upstairs offices, you'll find my sleeping bag. I have been in some trouble with some people."

"Who?" Laura asked. Mark burst out laughing.

"Nice try. But I'm not a grass. If I tell you, then you better lock me away for good because they'll peel my skin from my bones and feed it to me. But just some bad people. That's all I'll say. Anyway, I can't go home because they might turn up there, so I've been sleeping rough wherever I can. I saw the warehouse and crawled in through a window. I was there for a couple of days out of my face before you lot turned up."

Laura wrote it all down.

"So, you know the victim?"

"I just said that," Mark said.

"Were you lovers?"

"We fucked once or twice. She gave me a few blowies for some gear when she had nothing. Never kissed her on the lips though. Like I said, she's a good worker." He let out a rasping laugh. "But no. We never were *together* if you get me."

"I get you," Laura said. Laura pointed to his swollen eye. "Your friends do that to you?"

"No comment." He said. Laura sat quietly and stared at him. Craig eyed her, but seeing her completely silent and still, he mirrored. Both eyed Mark. Emma ran out of things to type. All eyes on Mark. The ticking of the clock in the background. Seconds dragging over glass. The hum of the overhead light. The sound of Mark's rattling chest filling the air. "I said no comment." He repeated. Laura stayed sitting there eyeing him. She pulled out the photos again, pointing to them. Still, she said nothing. Mark folded his arms once more and shrugged his shoulders. He averted his gaze to the table. She counted to twenty, letting that silence suffocate him. When Laura hit nine, he looked up again. At twelve, he let in a deep breath. By seventeen, he began to chirp once more.

"I was mugged," he said.

"By who?"

"I don't know."

"I said by who?"

"I said I don't fucking know. That's the truth." He was leaning forward. Laura could make out the tarnished gold on his back teeth. "I was with my girl Sheree. We were out working. I stay hidden in the back. Protection."

"Did you have a weapon?"

"Fuck off." Mark spat. "I have things for protection, and that's all I'm saying. It was a few days ago. I was stood having a smoke. Sheree got into a car and complained about the client. Some big fat fucker. Always stank of shit but he always paid extra. Sheree got in his car and they disappeared. The next thing I know, I get a strike from the side. Didn't see or hear it coming. I woke up the next morning with my jacket missing and my eye the size of a golf ball."

"Why would someone take your jacket?"

"The hell if I know. It was real leather too. Nice and fresh. I went asking around but no one knew who could have done it."

"Why didn't you go to the police?" Craig said. Laura felt like slapping him for asking such a dumb question.

"Because you're all rats and pigs," Mark spat. He leant forward and pressed his finger into the table, the tip turning white, his face flooding with red. "Like I would want to come to you lot for help. You've got the wrong person," he said, sitting back once more. "You've got the wrong person. I didn't kill anyone. What happened to Olivia is fucking awful and sick. I rob, I steal, I push girls and I push drugs. I'm not a monster. I'm a businessman. I did not kill anyone." He enunciated the last sentence with a slam on the table.

Laura made a mental note of the panic button behind her.

"What fucking evidence have you got on me anyway?" He spat. "I've been sound with you lot. I came quietly at the warehouse. I have been sweet with you all and you haven't told me a single thing as to why you have locked me up other than I was there. I've told you why I was there, and there is proof I was sleeping rough. I didn't hear anyone or see anyone."

Laura held her palm up to Mark.

"Okay," she said. "I'm nearly done with my questions, and then we'll get you out of here okay?"

"Bout fucking time," he spat. "I'm going mad in these clothes and this building. Makes me sick. Claustrophobic as fuck."

"Okay," Laura said. "Just a couple more questions." She looked at her notes. "You mentioned Sheree. Who is she?"

"She's my newest girl. From down south. She's a feisty one to be fair. But she does what she's told."

"Last name?"

"I don't know," Mark said. "I don't ask."

"Age?" Mark pondered this.

"Young. Not as old as you. She's hotter too. To be fair to you though, if you weren't a pig I'd bend you over."

"And have you seen her since?" Laura said, ignoring the bait. "Since she got in the car with the male?" Mark shook his head. "What car did she get into? Can you describe it to me? What about the male?"

"What does this have to do with my client?" Laura ignored the comment.

"Anything you can give us would help massively." Mark thought about it.

"From what I can remember," he said. "It was a silver Ford Mondeo, I think. Few years old. 63 plate."

"And the male?"

"Fat fuck. Around fifty or something." Laura felt something snap in her mind. She wrote down the description, putting the dots together. *The body at the lake.* She felt a spike of adrenalin. She was getting somewhere.

"Strange one," she said, eyeing her notes. "Where did Sheree usually take her clients?"

"Why?"

"Humour me." Mark took another drink.

"Normally the car park by the reservoir. Nice and quiet there." He looked at Laura. "Why?" He stretched the word out accusingly. "Is Sheree okay?" Mark said.

"We will try to contact her and we'll let you know." Laura had no intention of letting him know if she was okay. The CPS wouldn't remand him for the murder. He was right. They had nothing concrete on him. But she had a trick up her sleeve to keep him right where she wanted him. Behind bars for 23 hours a day.

"We will look into your alibi and your defence. But I need your movements for the last few days to verify your story."

"You asked that earlier," Emma piped up.

"It's to prove him innocent," Craig interjected. Emma smiled. Laura knew what was coming. She had mistaken her as being inexperienced. That was a fault on her part. She had played dumb and played it well. But she was about to be handed her ass on a plate.

"No," Emma said. "At this time, the only evidence of any crime you have on my client is that he was at the scene and has given you lines of enquiry regarding this." Emma eyed the pictures of Olivia. "Tell me officer, has my client's DNA been found on the victim at all?" Eyes fell back to Laura. The tables had turned, and that clock seemed so much fucking louder now.

"Not at this time."

"Has any kind of murder weapon been found?"

"Not at this time."

"And lastly, you said my client strangled the victim before mutilating her. Have you found any of her blood on his clothing? Any strands of straw, hay or pollen? Or do his fingerprints and palm size match that of the deceased?" Laura licked her lips, feeling her world fall apart.

*This is why I like to be prepared,* she thought.

"Not at this time." Emma smiled. Laura wanted to bash the smug bitches face in with that damn iPad. "Well then, I should expect he will be given bail and not remand?" Mark smiled. He knew he would walk.

"I'll be out of here in time for the football tonight," he said smiling widely.

"Not quite." Laura said, holding up her hand. Mark's smile wavered. Laura flashed her eyes to the solicitor.

*Watch this.*

"Mark Shaw I am further arresting you on suspicion of assaulting a police officer, of which being myself, possession of a class A controlled substance which we found in your hoodie, possession of a bladed article and also a failure to appear warrant that was generated following your last arrest for drug possession."

"You're taking the fucking piss!" He screamed.

"You didn't disclose this!" Emma raged.

"I'm disclosing it now," Laura said. She eyed him intensely. "You might have to watch that football match another day. You're going back to prison Mr. Shaw, but I thank you for your cooperation during this interview."

"You fucking cunt!" He screamed, leaping to his feet and diving over the table to her, murder in his eyes. Laura slammed her hand on the panic button. The loud rattling of the emergency alarm blared and cops, detention officers and hell, even a custody Sargent piled into the room and dragged Mark kicking, screaming and cursing back to his cell.

# Chapter Twenty-Seven
# Sheree

Sheree nestled her face into the sleeves of the jumper. She had been pacing non-stop since he left. The tooth. An actual human tooth.

*Oh my god. What was he going to do to me? What had he done to the others? How many other parts of human beings were scattered around this place?*

The jumper no longer yielded warmth. Instead, it was itchy, rough and burned into her skin. She could almost smell the last person it belonged to. How many others had worn this jumper? The stains on the mattress. Is that where he had done it? Killed them and gutted them while they slept? Had he tied them up and forced that shit mix of soup and water only to drag them down to the shower room and pull her teeth out whilst she lay there unable to move, moaning as water cascaded on her and the touch of plyers wrapped around her teeth?

Sheree tried to think clearly, but she couldn't. The only thing in her mind was a screaming voice telling her that she had to try and get out of here and fast. She had tried once before and she had failed, but she would try again. She *had* to try again. She knew the layout of the building. Plenty of places to hide. So many dark places she could crawl into. She had a weapon, a loose nail. She could wait until he came to her again, then she would strike and make a run for it. She could grab those keys he had on him and run right out the front door. There must be a road or a house somewhere close, or he had a car?

Sheree's legs began to turn blue, the cold dampness of the ground absorbing into her feet. She needed to get off the cold floor, but she couldn't bring herself to go near that mattress. The stains now had history. A tragic origin that would seep into her bones and infect her if she lay on it too long. She believed in that stuff. In *energy*. That when something horrific happened, it latched onto the environment around it. And this room, these walls, the clothing on her back were laced with pain.

Sheree stood under the skylight and tried to climb up to it but it was too high. She leapt, willing her tired body to move. She had been cleaned, both inside and out by *him*. She was nearing purity, and she didn't want to know what happened next.

Popping the tooth back in her pocket, the touch of it almost making her skin peel away from her bones, she moved and grabbed the mattress. It was heavy. So. God. Damn. Heavy. It came away from the wall inch by inch. Sheree heaved. Her energy bleeding from her.

Finally, she made it to the wall. Folding the mattress in half – the old springs creaking and breaking under her weight, the underside of the mattress twice as filthy as the top side – she climbed on top and stood on her tiptoes. Sheree took hold of the lip of the skylight and pulled her body up so she could peer over the precipice.

Through the grime and mould, she saw what looked to be a disused junkyard: old JCBs, tractors with their windows smashed, and even what looked to be a barn of some kind with its windows broken, old wood hanging from its frame. Around the grounds, she saw what seemed to be thick forestry. A tall metal gate with spikes and rusted barbed wire hung on top and a large fence with a thick chain looped around the centre and a mean-ass-looking padlock. Beyond that, a gravel path filled with potholes and grass.

Her arms began to give and she steadied herself to the ground.

Her spirit was dampened. Even if she managed to get out of the building, there was no way she could get out of the compound. She only had one option. She would need to fight to survive. Running and hiding wasn't an option. No matter how hard she tried, he would find her. She was so weak. How long could she go without food and water before she fainted and he dragged her back to that wall with chains wrapped around her neck? Claustrophobia began to constrict her mind, and she felt a tight pain like the swelling of a balloon filled with thick oil expanding in her chest. Her throat felt like it was stuffed with cotton wool, and tears began to fall from her stinging eyes. She couldn't breathe. She was suffocating.

*Oh god,* her mind raced. *What's happening? Has he poisoned me? Is this it?* She clutched her chest, tumbling off the mattress into the wall. Mould marred her jumper and her hands. He would know she had moved it. He would see the marks on the walls, the mattress not quite where it was. Her fingertips on the skylight lip. She was going to be discovered.

*Breathe!* Her mind raced. *Breathe! Breathe!*

Sheree felt the walls closing in around her, her chest unable to expand like someone was lying on her with all their weight and was carrying a 50KG dumbbell on her for good measure.

*Break yourself. Get to a hospital or a morgue. Because it's the only way you're getting out of here.*

Her hands grabbed her hair, nails digging against her scalp. She back-butted the wall, then began to hammer fist the floor and her head. She had to end it herself before he did. He would be slow. He would pull her teeth from her skull. He would do horrific things to her body, ravage her whilst she lay there paralysed unable to move. She slammed her head as hard as she could against the wall once more. Her chest still unable to find that breath. Sheree's head exploded in white hot pain as heat doused her face and neck. Might have begun to crack her skull. Good, she needed to go harder. Take herself out of this world for good.

One more slam and Sheree felt the world spinning. She could do one more. Had to do one more. Take herself out of this place. Out of this world forever. She reared her head back, annihilation staring her in the face. Sheree gripped the wall and pulled her head back. Knees digging into the ground. She felt weary, slipping, falling. She fell forwards, the world around her spinning. Her hands pushed into the wall. Something came loose. She eyed it. Something from the wall came off and fell onto the ground. A small square the size of a fingernail. She went to touch it, her hand trembling, trying to grab a still object in a room of funhouse mirrors, her vision swaying and morphing.

The world tumbled around her and she felt the slap of the ground against her face. Things began to turn dark. The last thing she saw was the dirtied outline where the mattress had been moved from, and then the sound of footsteps growing closer.

# Chapter Twenty-Eight
# Laura

The taste of her cigarette lingered in her mouth as she leaned against the wall. She pulled out the pack and sparked up a second one, closing her eyes. She had sent a request over the radio to have officers on the scene search the rest of the warehouse. She knew they would find Mark's belongings. His sleeping bag. His drug paraphernalia. She had interviewed murderers before. He wasn't one of them. They wouldn't find anything on the victim's body linking the two together. Even if they did, he had an alibi that they had hooked up a few times. That just shows they were together, not that he had mutilated her. Although sometimes, human beings often irreparably damage each other with words alone. A sharp tongue is like a sharp knife. It cuts without drawing blood. People can strip away every part of them until they are just a shell of their former selves. It was experiencing a death that was more than skin deep. Something she knew all too well.

He would be in jail by the morning and she considered that a small win. But she knew the murders were connected, and now she had another girl, 'Sheree' to find before it was too late. The more she knew, the more questions sprouted in her mind like poisonous flowers. The way of execution, the *coup de grâce*. It was so unique. Gut the body and fill them with straw. On both bodies. It made no sense. Why would someone do that? It was almost like the killer was making dolls out of them. Preserving them. Some kind of psychological or even more accurate, completely insane way of trying to preserve someone in time.

She had seen it before. A case she had worked on five years ago when she was just a detective and didn't have the respect she had now. She let out a laugh that was laced with loathing.

*Respect. I have nothing of the sort.*

She was into a string of murders that had been happening around the slums of the city. She got a call to an old farmhouse. The owner of the building, a writer that had moved to the states to pursue his fortune in publishing had been left the estate in his uncle's will. It was falling apart and the land hadn't been tended to in years.

He attended and found the building to be locked with an ungodly smell emanating from the insides so strong that Laura had to burn her clothes afterwards. Laura attended with Ron. They didn't know each other well then, but they would do soon enough.

They broke down the door with some help from the local cops, and the sight she saw that day would haunt her for the rest of her life. More bodies than she could count, all lined up and left to rot in the hot sun that beat down through the broken wooden roof in various stages of decomposition. The sound of the flies and the writhing of the maggots still festered in Laura's mind on dark nights. Bodies so rotten they had to call the underwater rescue team in to scoop their liquified flesh off the ground.

The killer, Alex Thompson, aged forty-two, had had a bad childhood. He owned a cattle farm. When police raided it, they found his wife dishevelled and his child locked in a backroom. They were taken far away. The papers never got to hear about them. Thompson was disturbed. The mind of a child. No sense of right and wrong. A good barrister got him a lifetime in a psych facility. Ron had been great on that case and coordinated it well, earning him a promotion, and foolishly earning Laura's heart.

They were hailed as the detectives who solved one of the most grisly murders in UK history, and Thompson rose to infamy rivalled by Jack the Ripper and Harold Shipman. Thompson was prolific. He murdered fast, dumped the bodies, and went for another round. He was sloppy, almost begging to get caught, which his defence used as evidence to show an unstable mind.

But this killer. He was calculated. At least two bodies under his belt and no doubt many more to come. He was good at what he did. Praying on the scourges of society, the ones that people wouldn't miss or wouldn't bother to look for. The one responsible was aware of data footprints, CCTV, and even forensics. Which again made her think the impossible. That the ghost in her past had come back to make her life hell.

It made perfect, yet impossible sense.

Hopefully, they got some kind of break. Dennis was going to find some kind of pattern in the disappearances. CSI would find a fingerprint or a rogue hair. Hell, maybe even their good old buddy Mark might remember something. But then again, now she had thrown him in prison, Laura felt that she had pissed on her own chips with that one.

"Sheree," she mouthed. "Who are you?" She pulled out her phone and called Dennis.

"Boss," he said. He sounded like shit.

"Can you find me a 'Sheree' linked on Mark Shaw's known associates?" She heard the sound of Dennis grunting. The sound of creaking and then cupboards opening.

"Go ahead," he said.

"Sheree. We don't know much more about her, other than she's around her early twenties and from the South of the county."

"That's not much to go off ma'am," he said. He coughed down the phone. Laura pulled the receiver away. She didn't need anything else adding to her already growing headache.

"That's all I have for you," she said. "Check the associates. Do some digging. Call me if you find anything."

"Will do. Bye." Laura went to hang up the phone but then brought it back to her ear.

"How are you feeling?" She said. There was a slight pause. She checked to see if the call was still connected. It was.

"I've been better," Dennis said, a faint laugh rattling from his lips. "I don't know what it is. I've been to the doctors, but they just said to keep hydrated and rest. Which is tough when you have a serial killer on the loose." Laura laughed, but then her mind stopped. Dennis continued to talk. "All this paperwork, all these checks. I'm starting to build a little picture of the girl's movements. Trying to pin it down." Laura went to speak, but something sparked in her mind.

"Dennis –" She cut in. "Who told you we're thinking a serial killer?" Laura heard a dry swallow.

"I just assumed."

"Don't lie to me," she bit, trying to remain somewhat calm. He spoke meekly.

"It's on the news." Laura's stomach plummeted.

"What did you say?"

"I thought you knew? It's been on the news all morning. They're saying there is a serial killer on the loose. That we have someone in custody." Laura hung up the phone. So much for keeping a lid on things. Laura opened up her web browser, her fingers trembling.

She went onto the BBC website. She didn't have to look long. It was on the front page. A picture of Olivia, the deceased girl from the warehouse, and the male that was found dead on the car park, Charles Steward. Their faces side by side, bright-eyed and teeth shining. Below, the caption –

*LOCAL CITIZENS FOUND DEAD AND MUTILATED. POLICE INVESTIGATION ONGOING.*

*The town of Wigtown was shaken to the core as police discovered two grisly scenes of mutilated bodies in the last forty-eight hours. Olivia Murray (26) – Left picture and Charles Steward (54) Right photo – were identified as the deceased as they were found by officers following routine patrols and investigating missing person reports.*

*Superintendent Mary DUTTON of the Wigtown Constabulary has released a statement following the grim discovery -*

*"OUR HEARTS GO OUT TO THE TRAGIC LOSS OF THE FAMILIES OF THE TWO CITIZENS OF WIGTOWN. IT IS WITH GRAVE SORROW THAT THIS HAS OCCURRED, AND A FORMAL INVESTIGATION IS UNDERWAY. POLICE REQUEST FOR ANYONE WITH ANY INFORMATION TO COME FORWARD."*

*Information was brought to the attention of BBC News from an anonymous informant that the police were treating the deaths as suspicious. We are yet to see what further developments occur in this ongoing tragic case. Police have urged the public to proceed with caution and to travel with friends and not after dark. A local newscaster has…*

Laura shut the browser down. Her smoke had completely burned out and her face reflected back to her in the black mirror of the phone screen. Who had said something? Who had broken the confidentiality? Who was a wolf in sheep's clothing? Was it one of her team? They were the only ones that knew about the possible connections. The autopsy reports. The missing girls... And why the hell was the superintendent giving a public statement on Laura's investigation?

Laura looked up past the tall, barbed wire fences and up to the sky, trying to quell her racing mind. But then she saw something else which made her skin crawl.

At the front of the custody suite in the visitor's car park. She saw men and women with cameras and wearing suits diving out of vans which had every news station from every channel. Some sighted her and tried to call out to her, but Laura moved to her car and slipped inside. Someone else could pick Craig up. She needed to get out of here right now.

She fired up the engine and drove to the gates. They creaked open, and the mob descended on her thrusting microphones to her window, descending on her like a pack of hungry dogs for a piece of meat. Laura blasted on the horn of the car and revved the engine. She tried to keep her cool, but she was ready to blow like a pressure cooker on full heat with the lid sealed on too tightly.

Laura put her foot down, speeding through the crowd and narrowly missed a cameraman who managed to avoid kissing the bonnet of her car. In the rear-view mirror, the reporters turned to the camera, some fixing their hair, some fixing their suits, but Laura had so much to fix she didn't know where to start.

# Chapter Twenty-Nine
# Laura

The precinct was no better. Reporters and news cameras flooded her when she arrived at the barriers of the station. She unwound her window to tap her pass on the car park barriers, and her face was flooded by microphones and booms and cameras. She used every inch of resolve she had to not dive out of the car and not stick those cameras up the reporter's asses. She had had cases like this in the Metropolitan police. The news just loved a good 'cop controversy' story. She had been used to it then, but they weren't as frenzied. The news stations down south were well fed with content. Up here, In Wigtown, they were starving.

The barriers opened lazily, and Laura drove under them as quickly as she could, nearly hitting the roof of the vehicle. She parked out of sight, near the back of the car park. She cracked the door and stepped outside. The cawing and screeching of the vultures pierced the air. Two officers stood by the gates and were being mobbed relentlessly, reporters moving right into their faces and snapping photos. The cops stood there stoically.

A Sargent – Tall, bald with a large nose – moved past her in the car park. Laura took his arm.

"How long have those officers been there?" She said, pointing to the two mobbed bobbies. The Sargent eyed them.

"About two hours," he said. Laura grimaced.

"Get them relieved immediately, and then have a turn around of two officers every thirty minutes, and tell them to have their body cameras on at all times. Bring out some barriers. It's not safe for them to be close to the cops." The Sargent appeared confused by the order, but immediately turned around and went back indoors. A moment later, two fresh officers came out with barriers and placed them in front of the station, only to be moved when police vehicles were to enter the compound. The newscasters weren't thrilled of course. They could smell blood and wanted a taste of it, but the officers looked relieved. Laura felt a small swelling of pride in her heart.

"Now let's see who has been talking," she said, slipping through the back entrance.


Officers raced around like headless chickens. Senior officers with more badges and stripes on their shoulders than the US Flag filtered around looking less than happy. The CID desks were stacked with notes and paper. Officers that would normally have Netflix shows on their phones were now running riot on their keyboards, pulling up data spreadsheets and trying to find the missing piece to the puzzle. Laura slipped into the MIU office. Catherine was reading a magazine.

"My office. Now," she barked, casting her eye on the abandoned ship around her. Catherine stood up quickly and slipped into the back room. She called Craig, but it went to voicemail. Dennis too. Someone had talked. Jeremy didn't like being told what to do. Catherine was as useful as a condom machine at the Vatican. Dennis, she didn't really know. He seemed good at what he did. Same as Craig, but he was the son of the Superintendent, so there was that to consider. Then there was the Superintendent herself. But why would she let the press know what was going on before they needed to? It made no sense. Why let water in your ship when it was staying afloat? Only one way to find out.

Laura marched upstairs to Mary Dutton's office. Senior officers stopped in the corridor wanting to pick her brains but Laura blanked them and continued on her way passing every bullshit PR poster that spouted mental health awareness days when cops on the ground were so stressed they were ironically taking mental health days off work.

Mary Dutton was sitting at the computer nursing a cup of camomile tea. *Stressed are you ma'am? You don't have a god damn idea what stressed means.*

"My office, now," Laura barked. Mary eyed her like she had walked into her house on Christmas morning and had taken a shit on the turkey.

"I beg your pardon?" She spat, nearly choking on her tea.

"I said, my office now. I don't care if you're my superior, we need to talk now."

"You better rethink your tone, Inspector Warburton," Mary said, her eyes like fire. Laura felt her resolve beginning to crack, but she couldn't back down now. This wasn't a case of rank, this was two wolves snarling at each other to see who backs down first.

"Fine," she said, stepping into the office. "We'll talk here."

"I'm busy."

"The hell you are!" Laura screamed, slamming the door. "You had no goddam right to deliver that statement to the press! This is my investigation! My team, my authority. You should have consulted me, you should have given me some kind of inclination that someone had leaked something to the press about all of this. We don't even know for certain if the murders are connected. We don't know anything other than there are two murders with a similar MO."

"Two murders within a short time frame of which both the victims have been disembowelled and had their mouths and stomachs filled with straw." Mary was relaxed speaking carefully, still with her tea in her hand, like a witch that was justifying why the children had to eat the gingerbread before she ate them.

"But the press doesn't need to know that!" Laura frenzied, pacing around the room and pressing her nails into her head. "You have just made this whole investigation a hell of a lot worse. Now, our suspect has infamy. It will become a game to them! They are going to up the ante, they are going to start toying with the press and giving them information that will derail the investigation!"

"You don't know that."

"I've worked on cases like this before."

"I am aware."

"Then listen to me when I say I *know* how these people work. They crave attention. Live for it. Zodiac? BTK? The Ripper? They all wrote letters to the press and the police taunting them." Laura stopped and caught her breath. "Why did you say something? Why did you give a statement?" Mary put her drink down.

"The press knew and they wanted answers, and I don't need to consult you. I am in charge of your team. You may think you have this under control, but you are hardly holding your drinking together, never mind the investigation."

"What did you say?" Laura felt like a truck slammed into her.

"You should calm down on the red wine." Laura felt fury growing in her stomach. *Craig. She sent you to spy on me. Not to help me.*

"How fucking dare you," Laura seethed. "What I do off duty is nothing to do with you."

"It is when it impacts *my* unit," she said. Dutton pulled a file from her cabinet and thumbed through it. "Laura Elise Warburton. Age thirty-five. Widowed. Detective Inspector of the Major Investigation Team in the Metropolitan police. Struggles with anxiety, depression and post-traumatic stress disorder following the death of her husband, Ronald McElderry. Highly volatile in therapy and is believed to not be taking her medication correctly." She slammed the file shut. "Struggles with substance misuse, namely alcohol." The silence on the death of the last syllable was deafening. Laura fought back the tears.

"How did you get that file?" She quivered. "That is confidential." Dutton shrugged.

"I know a few people that owed me favours," she said. "When you arrived on my team."

"My team…" Laura interjected.

"Anyway," Dutton continued without missing a beat. "Following the development of the case at the riverside, I asked my son to keep an eye on you. He protested of course, but he knows better than to disobey my request. He reported back that you were abusive, destructive and frankly, a complete mess." Laura began to sink into the earth. "I have a duty of care to my team and my investigation. I gave you the opportunity to resign to a less stressful post, but you refused." Laura could feel the world crumbling around her. She wanted to both run as fast as she could but equally smash this office to pieces.

*Calm down Laura. Calm down. Breathe. Remember what the therapist said. Count to ten. It's the PTSD. You need to forget about Ron.*

"Who the fuck do you think you are?" Mary leaned forward, her fingers interlacing together.

"Keep going Inspector Warburton and I will have you suspended." The threat did little to quell Laura's rising anger.

"Threatening me for standing up for my investigation? Digging up my history? You're going to suspend me during the biggest case of the constabulary's history?"

"Try me." Both women stared at each other. Electricity filled the air. Laura eyed a tiny smirk cracking Mary's lip. A smirk she would happily wipe clean off. Laura moved to the desk and jabbed her finger at Dutton.

"Go fuck yourself." Mary cocked her head and smiled.

"And there you go," she said with a sinister stare. "As of now, you are off the case." The words hit Laura like a silver bullet to a vampire. *What have I done?*

"What did you say?" She whispered, lips quivering.

"I'm resigning you off for twelve months with stress. Give you chance to get your life in order. I will let someone else take over the case. Jeremy, maybe."

"You can't do this."

"I'm afraid I just have," Dutton said. "You are getting far too invested in this case and you haven't dealt with your own demons. Cases like this need someone sharp and not filled with wine and trauma. The break will do you good!" She said the last word with a heightened inflexion like she was doing Laura a favour. "You clearly can't handle the pressure. Such rage Laura. Such untreated and unbridled rage and resentment when control is taken from you. You should really speak to someone about that."

"You set me up to fail," Laura said, a ball of pain swelling in her throat. "The unit was in disrepair when I arrived. The caseload was huge and nobody was looking in the right places. None of the team respected me."

"I don't blame them," Dutton said. "You are notorious Laura. Your story preceded your arrival. A quick Google and we can all see why." Dutton leaned forward. "Did your ex-husband *really* die in a boat accident? Or did you help a little?" Laura grabbed the cup of tea and threw it against the wall. It smashed into shards of porcelain like white jagged bone. The lukewarm liquid splashed along the grey walls, resembling an ink blot in a psych ward. Laura saw death. Nothing but death staring back at her. She left the office. Dutton's eyes cut into her, joining the knives that were already lodged in her back.

# XXX

Did you like what I made? I made it for you. I thought she was an angel. Her skin was pure. The colour of caramel.

She was a bad one. She was *filthy*. So sad. So much filth poured out of her body. She didn't take care of herself, and I thought I could make her beautiful, keep her to myself for my collection, but I couldn't. She was a dirty dolly. She didn't like the straw. It made her gag and feel bad. I had to force it down until she stopped screaming. But when she was full, her eyes were pasty white and filled with tears. It made me sad, and I couldn't have her in my collection. Never. Never, never. I wouldn't do that.

You almost caught me though. You did. I was there when you saw my blood angel. I was there watching you. Could you feel me near you? Could you feel my breath on your neck? I hope you liked the photo I gave you.

Just like my father and his house of horrors.

There's much more to come.

# Chapter Thirty
# Sheree

Sheree peeled her eyes open. Her body felt numb and she felt the chill of the darkness entomb her with its icy blanket. She managed to press the ground and sit up. She felt the blood flowing back into her limbs, and they erupted with millions of tiny needles stabbing under her skin like buzzing bees.

Her fingers met the swelling over her right eye. It exploded in fiery heat and she winced. Taking in a breath, she brought her fingers back to it. Tentatively, she felt it and the crusted blood layered around her face. She had done some damage. A headbutting match with a wall that was heavily one-sided.

Night had fallen, and the dark welcomed her into its abyssal glare. Scurrying met her ears as she looked around the dark. The door was closed. If *he* had discovered her on the ground, then he hadn't tried to help and he hadn't chained her up again like a dog. He would have found the tooth and the nail. She wouldn't have woken up. He would have slit her throat there and then. She was sure of it.

The mattress was still half under her leg, untouched. Her jumper stuck to her skin and she peeled it away, crusted with blood. How long had she been out? It was daylight before, and now she could see the bright moon bleeding through the skylight, a diamond bright against a cloudless black canvas. The air in her lungs felt alien, like it shouldn't be there. She could feel herself spinning on the whirlpool of despair again, but she pulled herself away from it. Her lungs expanded, soothing the chaos in her heart. A sanguine warmth built in her chest.

*Be pure*. His voice snaked into her mind once more. *Be pure*. The food that made her shit and vomit. The drugs to calm her down when she was frenzying, but then drugs to stop them taking hold of her and to flush them out of her system completely. Letting her rattle. Feeding her broth. Letting her wash and clean. She had never been treated this way before. In a way, it was almost kind.

She was better than the others. She had been hasty. He would have killed her by now, she was sure of it. He didn't want to hurt her. He let her roam free. Gave her a shower and food. She could be good to him, and in return, he would not harm her. She was off the drugs. Something she hadn't been able to do herself. He did care for her, and she needed to show him that she did for him too.

Maybe this was okay. The system didn't give a shit about her. Her foster family hadn't cared. Teachers? School? Past boyfriends? Nothing. She was a product of pain, and pain is all she had known.

But *him*. He didn't want her body. He didn't want to exploit her or hurt her. He wanted to keep her safe. To make her *pure*. To be the princess he knew she could be.

*The square off the wall*. Sheree lazily dragged her fingers around the ground trying to find it. Maybe it was something useful? Maybe it was a way out? Information from someone about her assailant. She crawled onto her knees and moved around the blackness.

After an endless moment, Sheree found it. The paper. It was a crumpled bit of paper. She opened it, careful not to rip it. It was tiny, maybe the size of her thumb. She squinted, but her eye was getting worse, and soon she knew that the bulbous egg on her forehead would consume her vision completely.

*In the world of the blind, the one-eyed man is king.* She didn't know why that saying came into her mind, but it was certainly apt. Something Mark had said to her before.

*Mark.* She hadn't thought of that son of a bitch since she had ended up in this hell hole. She hoped he was dead somewhere with a needle in his arm. He wasn't a good man, and even though a part of her had sort of loved him, it was purely because he could get her the drugs. The drugs he had gotten her into in the first place. A sour taste found its way into her mouth. She found what little saliva she could and spat it onto the floor. *Fuck you.* He was a predator. Praying on the vulnerabilities of those around him that are desperate to *feel* something, or more likely, feel *nothing*. She felt something all right. A stab in the arm, or a slap across the face, or being grabbed by the hair, choked, spat on or raped in a car, back alley, hotel room or out in a field somewhere by whoever passed him the money.

So why would he bat a damn eyelid if she never came back to him? Why would he go to the police and tell them that she has been taken? He was only interested in himself. It should be him in this cell, not her. She had something to live for. A chance at salvation. He was the devil in a flesh sack.

Maybe that was what she needed to do. Suicide was a permanent solution to a temporary problem, and this was only temporary. If she killed herself, she would never be able to live the way *he* wanted her to live. He was trying to help her. She needed to stop trying to fight it and just let it be. He had never harmed her, he had fed her, clothed her. Washed her and kept her safe from herself. She was on a one-way ticket to death when she was out on the streets, either from Mark, drugs or someone else. Now, she is safe, and she will one day be free. If only she can be *pure*. *Pure* for *him*. *Pure* for herself.

She clambered to her feet, stumbling against the wall, every part of her legs, hips and back popping. Maybe he had seen her on the ground, lying there. He didn't help or punish her because he believed in her. Believed that she can be better. That was it. She needed to do well. Be better for him and for herself. He was a good person. Whomever he was. He was good.

Sheree moved to the skylight and opened the note, squinting through one eye to try and see the writing. The light shone through the thin paper, and her bloodied, weeping face marred her vision, but she could just about make out the single word scribbled in dirt and grime on the note.

*NOT*

Sheree eyed the word. What did it mean? The serene feeling of surrendering came crashing down around her like glass suspended above a canyon. Why had she put so much faith in such a small note? The person that wrote it might have been crazy, or maybe they didn't do whatever *he* wanted so he didn't give them the nourishment and food that he had given her. She could think clearly. If she was to leave a note, it would be something more useful. A way to escape, a way to call for help. The location of a telephone. Anything was better than a single word with no meaning. Sheree scrunched the note up and tossed it onto the floor. She hauled the mattress back to where it belonged, careful not to make too much noise.

She fell onto her back, and the springs dug into her as though she was lying on dull knives. The night's featureless black began to blend with her good eyes vision as she stared at the ceiling, wondering once more if she could float away to happier places.

# Chapter Thirty-One
# Laura

Laura stopped off at the local off license on her way home and bought two large bottles of red wine and another packet of smokes. She paid on her credit card and stormed away from the counter without uttering a word.

In her car, she drove in silence, the hum of the engine quietly nursing her scattered mind. She couldn't make sense of anything. Not right now. Her thoughts were a ball of barbed wire that sliced deep when you tried to unravel it.

A car blared behind her. She saw she was sitting at a green light, angry motorists flashing and making obscene gestures. She drove off unapologetically, moving through the busy streets before turning down the quieter roads that led her home.

Laura arrived at her house, stepped out of the car placed the rattling keys in the lock. She cracked the door and stepped inside, shutting the outside world out. Bagpipe moved to her, purring and slipping between her legs. She didn't acknowledge him. Instead, she went straight to the kitchen and de-corked the bottle of 2020 Merlot and drank straight from the top. She chugged like she was back in high school again, sinking a quarter of the bottle before the urge to breathe made her take in air. A satisfied gasp left her red-painted mouth. She pulled out a stool and sat for a moment and stared at the bottle.

*You really shouldn't be drinking you know,* the voice said in her head. *It doesn't agree with you. You shouldn't drink when you're feeling sad.* It was the voice of her old therapist. She was young, around age twenty-one with zero to no life experience other than a university degree. She asked Laura if she could use her sessions to study for her PhD in psychiatry. Laura told her to go fuck herself.

The sessions did little or nothing to help. She found more comfort and sense from complete strangers on YouTube. Laura eyed Bagpipe jumping on the kitchen counter.

*Why so sad mum?* Laura reached her hand out and nestled her fingers into the creature's fur. Without a word, Laura pulled out some cat food and fed her little fury friend that was meowing incessantly at the smell. She emptied his litter box and refilled his water. Laura went upstairs, taking the bottle with her. She cried under the shower, turning it as hot as she could bear it, before slipping into a vest and some small shorts.

Her mind nattered for her attention. Details of the day, the case, from that bitch superintendent. To rationalise, analyse and hypothesise. Laura tilted the butt of the bottle to the heavens until the thoughts stopped.

The TV stand stood empty, shards of glass still on the floor. She pulled out the pan and brush and swept them away, before sitting on the couch.

The house was quiet, and the thoughts were getting louder. Laura tried to read, but the words wouldn't sink in. She tried some music, hell even tried to go to sleep. That wasn't going to happen. She sat there silently sipping the wine while her mind continued knocking on her skull begging for attention.

A thought wisped into her mind like a cloud blocking the hot sun. Less a thought, but a face. A smell. A touch in her memory. She took out her phone and found her number.

The phone rang twice before she heard her voice. Warmth, desperate and longing, flooded her body like the embers of a fire on a cold night.

"Hey," Laura said.

"Hey to you too." The voice replied, sounding playful.

"I'm at home with a bottle of wine, and I don't think I can finish it on my own." A pause in the air. "Sorry," Laura said after a moment. "I shouldn't have called you." Laura hung up the phone and placed it on the arm of the couch. The phone rang. "Hello?" She said, the wine mixing with her breath.

"Text me your address," Celine said. "I'll be right over."

# Chapter Thirty-Two
# Laura

When the doorbell went an hour later, Laura threw it open and found Celine standing there dressed in a long beige coat and heels. Her lips were a dull rouge, and her black hair was curled and fell over her dark skin. Eyes painted in a peacock blue, and Laura fell right into those compelling spheres. A small black bag hung by her waist. Laura saw a flash of black lace poking from under her coat.

"Can I come in?" Celine said with a devilishly immaculate smile. Laura wrapped her hands around her cheeks and pulled her inside. She pushed the door shut with her heel, their breath mixing, lips finding each other. Hands devouring each other like fire on kerosene wood. Laura took Celine's hand and pulled her upstairs to the bedroom.

Laura tore Celine's clothing off with the ferocity of a starving animal given its first meal. The coat was thrown on the floor in a careless crumple. Laura smothered Celine's corset with her lips, tasting her skin, her perfume mixing with her tongue as she slid along the top of her plump breasts. She had her belly button pierced which Laura's fingers caressed as she moved her hand further south, tracing her toned stomach and fingering the top of her underwear.

She was wet and she mixed with Laura's fingers as she found her lips. She was shaven, which Laura loved. With her free hand, Laura unclipped the corset – pitch black with magenta cups – and pulled it down, slipping her erect nipple into her mouth. Celine's breath heavy, moaning in Laura's ear as she kissed her neck. Celine dug her nails into Laura's scalp as she fell backwards onto the bed.

Laura's slender fingers gently worked their way up to the spot that made her breath sharp and longing. She felt Celine's breath catch as she teased and toyed with it.

Her skin was delicious like the best ice cream in town and Laura had a hell of a sweet tooth. Celine moaned louder, then brought her face to Laura's. They stared a moment into each other's souls. The rest of the world feeling a million miles away.

Candles filled the room with the scent of jasmine and sage. Red wine on the side counter with two glasses. Celine saw this and smiled devilishly.

"I thought we would just be having wine?" She giggled. Laura smiled, and brought her lips to hers firmly, tongues mixing together. Celine began to tighten around Laura's fingers. Laura locked eyes and kissed lower, tracing her lips down that smooth stomach until her tongue touched that sweet honey pot. Her breath quickened, growing deeper, faster, until Celine's back arched, fingers clutching at the bedsheets. Her nipples tingling, body setting alight until that building of heavenly bliss came to fruition, ravaging her skin, dumping pulsing waves of euphoria into her veins that stampeded along her bloodstream. Celine called out, writhing on the bed. When the tide of endorphins receded, she giggled, running her nails along her skin. She looked south to see Laura smiling, biting down on her bottom lip. Celine let out a small laugh.

"You've done this before…"

"I don't kiss and tell," Laura winked. Celine jumped to her feet and pushed Laura onto the bed and mounted between her legs, falling onto her, tongue tracing the inside of her thighs, tearing away the tiny shorts. Celine caressed her, finding her with her mouth, exploring places Laura had long since forgotten.

A gasp of air as Celine found that magic spot with her tongue. Laura eyed the top of her head between her thighs. She was good. Oh god, she was *really* good.

Celine worked, tongue licking and lapping just the way she knew women liked, slipping her fingers inside and out, exploring her, finding what she liked. Listening to her body. A sharp intake, a groan, a grip at the back of her head. Laura was on the edge. Moving closer to that place of heaven. The thoughts of the case came back, the face of the dead girl. She tried to push them away, mouthed to her mind to keep the monsters out, just for a few moments. Just for a little longer.

"Are you okay?" The voice broke through Laura's mind. She snapped her eyes open. Tears were running down her cheek. Celine was sitting up, her figure out for the world to see. She was so beautiful. It was as though God wanted to create the perfect woman and deliver her to Laura himself.

"Sorry," she said, sitting up and pulling her top back over her exposed breasts. She moved her hand through her hair, eyeing the bedding. "Tough day."

"You want to talk about it?" Celine said, her voice soft, so gentle and caring. Wanting to understand. Wanting to know what was going on inside Laura's mind. Laura shook her head.

"No." She reached into her bedside drawer and took out a smoke. "You should go."

"But I just got here?" Celine protested, voice deflated. "I don't want to leave."

"You have to," Laura said, sniffling, wiping away the tears from her eyes. "I'm no fun anyway," Laura resounded, her body turning numb. It was always better when she was numb. She was strong when she couldn't feel. She would deal with her emotions later. Something she got good at doing.

"I think you're fun," Celine said, stroking Laura's leg. She pulled it back like Celine's hand was a rattlesnake. "What's gotten into you?" Questioned Celine, brow furrowed. "I don't get it. You invite me over and what?"

"I don't want to talk about it." Laura snapped, reaching for the wine. "I want you to go and leave me alone. This was a mistake. I shouldn't have called you." Laura stood and moved into the bathroom and closed the door. She put the shower on.

Celine sat a moment on the end of the bed in a stupor. After a few minutes, she got dressed and stood by the bathroom door. She hesitated, then knocked on.

"I'm going," she called into the bathroom. She listened. No response other than the rush of the shower. She went to knock again, hesitating. She pulled her hand back. "You know, you really need to fix your head. This is fucked up. It's not okay." Again, nothing met her voice but white noise. "Just…," Celine said, rolling her mind. "Get better. Call me, okay?" She stood, waiting for a reply, before slipping out of the house. Laura continued to sit behind the door cradling her knees, staring at the empty shower.

*You need to get a grip of yourself,* the voice in her head rattled. *You're losing control.* The voice turned darker. The voice became his.

*You could always talk to me, couldn't you baby. And now look at you without me. You're pathetic. Can't even fuck someone else without thinking of me.* Laura forced herself to stand. She turned the shower to ice cold and walked in fully clothed. The thoughts blasted away as her body came to life. She stayed under that cascading cold until she began to shiver. The bathroom floor was soaking because she hadn't closed the door.

She shut the tap off and stepped out. She towelled. She heard it then, cutting through the quiet. The bedroom door opened, and footsteps clicked against the bedroom floor. Had Celine forgotten something? But as she listened, she realised they weren't Celine's footsteps. They were too heavy. Too booming. Laura's breath stopped, and the numbness in her flesh was replaced by something else.

*Fear.*

The sound of moving. The sound of weight on the bed and the duvet sliding along it. Wine glasses clinking. Laura's hair dripped water onto her feet.

*Tap tap tap…*

She put her hand to her mouth.

*It was him. He had come back for her.* Laura let out a silent scream. She moved to the bathroom door and as silently as she could, she turned the lock until it slid into place. Pressing her ear against the wood of the door, she heard his breathing. It was heavy and deep. Weight shifted, then more footsteps. A drawer opening, the rattling of jewellery. Then the click of the door closing and muffled steps down the stairs, and the front door opening.

Silence ate Laura alive.

She waited, terrified to move. After what felt like forever, Laura unlocked the door and crept out.

The room was filled with ghosts. The bed had been neatly made. The candles had been extinguished. The wine moved to the dressing table where her vanity mirror was pushed towards the ceiling. She stood at the door, her feet nailed to the ground, blood draining from her legs. A dry swallow.

"Hello…" She croaked. Only the void answered.

Laura took a step, waiting for a hand to snatch her ankle from under the bed. Her body was made of rock, hands nestled into her chest. She looked for her phone. She couldn't find it. Isolation slammed into her mind, and the walls grew teeth. She tried not to breathe, walking slowly along the carpet, fighting with the screaming voice in her mind with each step.

*Run, just run. Someone is in the house. Run you stupid bitch. Get out of here!*

Laura slipped her head around the bedroom door, analysing the landing beyond. Moving slowly, down the stairs, eyes searching the rooms as she passed. Gingerly, opening her front door to reveal nothing but a quiet and empty street. She slammed the door, locking it tight.

The kitchen was empty, only the sight of a half-empty bottle of red wine. The living room was vacant, as were the conservatory, and the back garden. She tested the back door. To her horror, it came open. She swore she locked it. She always locked it. She never used the back door. Bagpipe was a house cat. Celine had come through the front and left through the front. Why was the back door open?

She searched for the key. Panic began to constrict around her throat. She couldn't find it. *Someone* had it. Someone had been inside her home and had a key. How many times had they been in? When she was at work? Running errands? Had they stood over her watching her in her sleep?

The feeling of black putrid bile swirled around Laura's stomach. She needed to call this in. She took a step and stopped.

*I can't call this in. Not with the press and with work all over this case. Inspector Warburton begins to lose her shit because she can't find a back door key and forgot she had been outside.*

*How much are you drinking these days, Laura?* Her therapist whispered in her mind.

She was stressed, a little drunk and sleep deprived. She needed to call Celine and ask her to come back. She needed to call Craig and tear his head off, tell the team that she was off the case for a while. She had a million things to do, but first she needed to ditch that bottle of wine.

At the top of the stairs, the air felt cold. A breeze wafted through the house. Her bedroom door was closed. She froze. Why was it closed? She had left it open. She knew she had left it open.

Laura placed her hand on the door and pushed it open. All reservation, all rational and all reason crumbled into dust, sprouted black legs and scurried away.

Her bedroom window was wide open. Laura felt tears burst from her eyes and her throat began to close up. She darted to the bedside drawer where she had kept her phone. It wasn't there. She pulled out the contents and threw them to the floor. Where was it? Where was her phone?

"Alexa!" She shouted, fighting through the ball in her throat. "Call my phone." Silence. Then, the sound of something buzzing on wood.

It was coming from the dressing table. Slowly, Laura moved to the dresser. She saw the light of the phone illuminating under her mirror. She picked it up and cancelled the call. She saw it then, dangling from the bottom of the mirror. A small silver heart on a thin silver chain. Her ankle bracelet. The one she had lost when crawling through the door chasing Mark through the warehouse.

Laura threw It across the room like a deadly insect. She pulled the mirror down. She began to scream.

Written on the glass in dried blood.

*I'm Home Baby. Kiss kiss.*

# Chapter Thirty-Three
# Laura

Laura stared at the writing, paralysed by fear. The feeling of eyes on her. He was back. He had come back for her. How could he know where she lived? It wasn't hard. If he still had contacts in the Met, it was just a quick PNC check.

And found her he had. Laura felt a tightness in her chest like someone was twisting her heart, screwing into place. Her mind yammering a million things at once, screaming at her to run, to hide, to call the police. Could she trust them? Could she trust anyone? How did she know someone wasn't working with Ron? Who would believe her? Nobody believed her when she came clean about the abuse last time. Nobody believed her when she said Ron's death in South Africa was an accident either. So, who would believe her now, that he had come back into her life?

She was alone fighting a ghost. A ghost that had come to reclaim her.

Laura finally willed herself to move. She rushed, grabbed her phone and threw a jacket on from her wardrobe. Standing at the top of the stairs, she was afraid to breathe. What if he was still in the house? What if he was watching her right now? Hand on a blade, ready to carve her open and watch her spill out onto the floor.

*You ruined my life*, he would say, as his hands would wrap around her throat. *Now, I'm going to end yours.*

She raced down the stairs, through the house and into the kitchen. The backdoor was still closed. Bagpipe was sleeping on top of his scratch post in the living room, his tail swaying gently like a fury metronome. She grabbed him and bundled him into her car and he fought every step with teeth and claws.

She was still going to leave for the night. That was an absolute given. There was no way she could sleep here until the locks were changed and she got some kind of security camera installed. Maybe even a guard dog, or hell, a damn moat and portcullis would do just fine.

Laura ran back into the house with keys pressed between her fingers like crooked knives. She just needed a few things, and if he was in there…

No monsters came from the shadows and Laura grabbed a small night bag. Her nerves so tight she thought they would snap at any moment.

*Maybe you have lost it completely Laura? Maybe this is all in your head. That's what he used to tell you wasn't it? "You're going crazy baby. That never happened. I didn't say that. You need to speak to someone about the way you've been acting recently."*

Laura left the house, stabbed the key into the ignition and drove away without looking back.

# Chapter Thirty-Four
# Sheree

Sheree awoke to the sound of the door yearning open. He stood there, his face again covered by the mask. She bolted up, a sharp pain striking through her back.

He stood there silently, his breath heaving heavy wheezes that vibrated through the mask's dead lips like the sound of a blue bottle's wings. He surveyed the room slowly. Sheree matched his eyes. He stepped his big boots into the room, stalking around the room like he had found a secret chamber in an old hall. His fat fingertips traced the walls, marking them with bulbous prints. Sheree eyed him cautiously, her stomach beginning to bubble with fear. Had he seen something? Did he know she had been looking? Was he looking to see if she had been good? She had been. She would tell him. She would reason with him. He wasn't going to hurt her. He couldn't. She was special. She was pure. She was doing as he wished. Being a good girl like he wanted. He had rescued her from her old life, and when she was better, only when she was better; would he let her leave.

He stood by the window and touched the windowsill, wiping grime onto his fingers before dusting them onto the floor and smearing the remaining residue onto the walls.

"Food," he said. Sheree feigned a tight smile.

"I'm starving," she lied.

He eyed her sternly. What was he thinking? What was he planning? The dark things those hands of his could do. She saw it then by his feet. Her breath halted like someone pulled the emergency cord on a speeding train.

At his feet. Where the note had been hidden. The piece of wood that had broken off was crooked. He would notice. He would notice the note she had put back for safekeeping. In her sleep-deprived haze, she had performed an error. He would see that she had been bad. She had been looking for things she shouldn't have been looking for.

Sheree stood and stretched her skeletal body out, drawing attention away from her transgression.

"I would love something to eat please," she croaked, her throat tickling. "But first, I would like to use the bathroom." She eyed the bucket in the corner. He cocked his head and gestured to the bucket in a *go right ahead* movement. Sheree felt her body flush with heat. She smiled, pulling her arms under her shoulders.

"Alone, please," she said timidly. "I don't want you to watch." The leathery mask eyed her with its vacant eyes. "I want to be a lady for you. The best I can be. Ladies use the bathroom alone." A moment passed, and he left the room with a long exhale.

Sheree moved quickly to the piece of wood in the wall and took out the note. She needed to be quiet and quick. He would be listening through the door. She used an old trick she had learned when trying to smuggle drugs into custody. She took the note and wrapped it in a tight ball, squatted, then nestled it inside herself. She corrected the crooked wood, before sitting back on the mattress.

Like the blare of an alarm, the aching creaks under her signalled him to come back inside. She sat with her legs over the end of the mattress and ran her fingers through her hair. Something she had always done when things got a little tense.

*Nothing to see here officer. I'll be moving along now.*

The heat of his glare began to bubble her skin like a magnifying glass held onto a lone ant under the hot sun. She hadn't used the bucket. Would he check? *No,* she thought. *I am good. He won't hurt me. He is kind. I do as he asks, and he keeps me safe.*

"Can I eat now please?" She said quickly, breaking the silence. Again, he studied her like a mysterious painting before stepping out of the room, leaving the door to the dark corridor open.

She could make a run for it right now. Run like the devil was behind her. But where would she go? She couldn't find a way out. She needed to stay put. He would let her go when he was done with her. He just wanted her to be good. Well behaved. To be pure. Sheree's stomach began to churn. She was beginning to get hungry after all. The bounty of her captor's generosity would be received well. She would eat whatever he gave her. He was helping her. He was a good man and she was pure and clean and good. Yet the burning in her legs to sprint for sanctuary stayed in her muscles like a dull ache. Staring at that open door like an invitation to hell itself, took all of her will not to give into. She had spent a lifetime giving herself up to desires. This time she needed to practise restraint.

He came back in with a plate and a glass of water and paced it by her feet. She would be good, and he was going to be so proud of her for just how good she was being to him.

She smiled at him as he retreated to the open door. He stopped and watched her.

"Eat," he said through the mummified mask. The eye sockets had dropped since she last saw it, like a face of melted wax. Sheree smiled thankfully, then leaned over to see what delights he had prepared for her to consume. At the sight of the plate, her stomach began to twist. She felt like she was going to throw up. A lump swelled in her throat, and her eyes began to burn. Was this a joke? Some kind of test for her?

Her eyes met his. His hard stare bore into her like a dulled drill tip burrowing into her skull.

"I'm not hungry," she croaked.

"Eat," he repeated. She couldn't. She couldn't force that down her throat, washing it down with a glass that was littered with dirtied finger smudges like fat leeches. Sheree's stomach began to do burpees. She was going to vomit. Vomit right onto his fresh black shoes that didn't have a spec of dirt on them.

He wasn't kind. He was cruel. The way he stood over her like training a dog. Clarity pushed through her psyche. He was a monster, and no amount of being good and pure would change that.

"No," she said. As soon as the syllable died in the air, she saw his shoulders tighten.

"Eat!" He screamed; his voice ragged. He grabbed her by the back of her hair and yanked her head back. She let out a harsh scream which was then silenced by him forcing a fistful of hay into her mouth. It was dry, like chewing on mummified sandy worms. She felt it sticking to her throat, running between her teeth. Sheree tried to fight him off, catching his neck with her nails. He was so strong, the strength of an Ox and his fingers wrapped tighter around her hair, so hard so that she thought her scalp would peel away. Her neck was again forced back, and more of the straw was stuffed into her mouth. She felt it clumping at the back of her throat. She gagged and garbled. Unable to breathe and he kept on shovelling it in, forcing it deeper down. She tried to bite but her mouth was too full.

He threw her onto the mattress with her head buried in the shit and piss-stained fabric. Her stomach felt like it exploded, as a train of bile forced its way through the clot and seeped onto the makeshift bed. Hot, wet and sticky clumps running between her fingertips.

She pushed her fingers into her throat and managed to clear the blockage, the air finally finding her lungs. She began to sob, her face turning red like a squozen plum, panting and coughing heavily.

Finally, she righted herself. He was still standing there, adjusting the leathery mask. He was going to skin her. Disembowel her in her sleep and peel her flesh from her skull and wear her. He was going to show her face trapped in its one final eternal scream to the next person he had in here, and thus the cycle would go on and on. He hulked his body over her, his figure blotting out the filthy walls.

"Eat!" He barked, his rasping breath pushing through those tight lips with teeth protruding out of a dead mouth like old stones surface from a drained and stagnant pool.

Sheree needed to fight more, but her resolve was gone. She had nothing left in her. No strength. No will to go on.

"Just kill me now," she sobbed, putting her head in her hands. "Why are you doing this to me? Just let me go. I won't say anything. I'll move so far away even the crows won't find me. Please…" She fell to the floor then, holding herself.

"I want you to be pure," his menacing voice rasped. "To be part of my family. My collection. I need you to be a good girl, and not a dirty one. Or you will end up like the others – broken. I don't like broken dolls," his voice turned softer. His knees creaked as he crouched to her. "Do this, show me you want to be good." He spoke like a parent to a crying toddler, telling them that the other kids in their class were just jealous because they weren't special like them. Was she special? Was she going to be special to him?

Sheree sat up, pulling herself onto the mattress. She had no choice. She picked up the plate and took a straw between her fingertips. She popped it into her mouth like dried-out worms and began to chew, fighting back her sobbing that hiccupped in her throat. She nestled it between her teeth and swallowed, where it stuck in the back of her throat like a dead snake. He stood watching her as she put another piece in her mouth, his eyes never leaving her as she finished her plate in dead silence.

# Chapter Thirty-Five
# Laura

Laura drove to the edge of Wigtown and checked into a Travel Lodge. Normally she would want to stay in something with at least a bath, but that was the least of her worries right now. Settling down onto the bed, she tried to digest what had happened.

She pulled out her phone and arranged for a locksmith to change her locks. That was the first point of call. She was practical. Robust. Adversity had taught her that. Then, she lingered over her phone number and hit call. Three rings later, each stabbing at her nerves, a sleepy voice whispered through the receiver.

"Hello?" Celine said.

"Hey," Laura said, rubbing her eyes.

"Can I help you?" She did not sound happy. It was just before midnight, and Laura wouldn't have appreciated the same call at this time in the evening when she had just been blown off either.

"Sorry about today," she said. She tried not to sound robotic. She was calling as a matter of decency, but something inside her also wanted to make the phone call. She could invite her over? Maybe pick up where they left off? The thought of sex to Laura right now was the last thing she wanted, but she didn't want to be alone either.

"Don't mention it," Celine said, her voice laced with pain. "It was a little fucked up I won't lie."

"I know. Sorry, I have a lot on my plate right now." A pause hung in the conversation and dead air filled the silence.

"I heard that you aren't working on the Straw Man murders anymore."

"Who said that?"

"Everyone. It's the talk of the office."

"Do you want to come over?" Laura said quickly. Celine hesitated.

"So you can blow me off again?" Celine laughed. "I don't know who you think you are, but you aren't stringing me along. In fact, I think it's rude as hell for you to just call me up –" Laura began to sob. She didn't want to, but it came anyway like the bursting of a dam. Celine stopped talking.

"I don't know what to do…" Laura croaked, her head falling into her hands, hair devouring her face.

"Laura," Celine said, her voice sounding a little less harsh. "Are you okay?" Laura shook her head.

"I think my ex-boyfriend is trying to kill me." Laura wanted to take the words back and erase them from her lips and Celine's memory. The shuffling of fabric down the receiver.

"Where are you? Are you at home?"

"No," she sobbed, wiping her eyes. "I'll text you. I'm at a Travel Lodge. I can't go back there." Laura heard the sound of a car door closing and keys rattling. "I just. I just don't want to be alone."

"I'll be right there."

# Chapter Thirty-Six
# Laura

The bedside phone buzzed to life, jolting her out of her stupor, her mind drowning in a black sea filled with sharks.

She lifted the receiver.

"Visitor for you," the receptionist said, before killing the call. Laura took the stairs to the reception. Celine was wearing her trench coat, a white blouse and a pencil skirt. Heels the colour of melted caramel. A black leather bag hung over her shoulder, her keys in her hand. Maybe some kind of subliminal message to Laura that she intended to go home tonight when they had done whatever she was here for. What was she even here for? She hardly knew the woman. She was attractive, yes, and the taste of her body still lingered on her lips and the smell of her perfume hung in her nostrils.

"Can I get you ladies anything?" The receptionist asked from behind the glass. Laura and Celine continued to stare at each other like two lions ready to devour the same kill.

"No thank you," Laura said quietly. "Come on."

They walked through the foyer and down the hallway until they got to the lift. The doors closed. Just them two. Neither spoke a word. The surrounding thick silence the most deafening thing she had ever heard.

Why was she here? Laura thought to herself. She didn't want love. She didn't want human interaction, and yet here she was, standing in silence in this metal box as it hummed it's way to the third floor, with a woman to which she had only said a handful of words. But she couldn't stop thinking about her. She was like an insect that had burrowed its eggs inside her mind. From the moment she had laid her eyes on this woman, something inside her had fired to life an old furnace. There was something about Celine that drove her crazy, and yet repulsed her at the same time.

Which is why it could never work between them.

The elevator pinged and she stepped out quickly. She pulled the key card out of her pocket and opened the door. Celine slipped on through and Laura got a hint of that coconut perfume she had been wearing earlier. Had she worn it on purpose? She didn't want to be some kind of booty call and yet here she was looking as hot as ever and smelling equally delicious. Laura realised again why she didn't date. It was so complicated. Laura followed her into the room and closed the door.

"So," Celine said. "The case." Laura eyed her. She couldn't control it any longer. She took off her shirt and let her breasts hang out for Celine to feast on.

"Fuck the case." She embraced Celine and they fell onto the bed.

The sex was hot and incredible. Laura was a gentle yet generous lover. She was fast and soft in all the right places, taking her time, even teasing a little. When Celine wanted her to go slow, she would tickle and touch, caress and feel. But when she wanted to get there and get there good, Laura would hold back, making her beg for it. Forcing her to whisper those naughty words she wanted to hear, and when she was satisfied Laura would give Celine what she wanted, and that sweet song that ran out of her ecstasy gripped lungs would dance around her ears like a river through a desert.

They explored each other. A woman knew what a woman wanted. Celine was experienced, clearly. The way she moved, the noises that escaped her. Everything about her was electric, and Laura felt the worries of the world evaporate around her like snow on a hot pan. Celine was a drug to her. That's why she craved her. She was addicted to the numbing she felt around her. She was all she could think about, all she wanted her world to become.

"Where the hell did that come from?" Celine said, her heart beating under that sweat-laced chest, her hair long and black, spread out over the white sheets, eyeing the ceiling and gasping for air, eyes wide and body flushing red.

Laura appeared from between her thighs, a long sweet smile along her face. She climbed up to her lips and laid one on her. Celine could tell how sweet she tasted. Laura lay next to her, running her fingers up and down Celine's toned stomach.

"I'm sorry about before," she said, nestling her head into Celine's neck. She turned and locked eyes, Celine's eyes a jade green. Something Laura had never seen before. She kissed her and those jade eyes fell into Laura's blue ones once more. She smiled, her flawless white pearls dazzling Laura's vision.

"What?"

"There's something about you," Celine said stroking Laura's hair. "I never go with people from work, but you…" Laura fought away the growing panic in her chest.

"I'm damaged," she said sternly. "As cops, we try to fix things." Laura got up, Celine furrowed her brow as the comment rooted in her mind. Laura walked bent over, giving Celine a full view of the goods, almost teasing her like she was a poisoned fruit. Laura took out a hairbrush from her night bag and ran it through her hair. Celine eyed her figure in awe.

"You hit the gym?" She said, her eyes devouring Laura's toned back and legs. Laura didn't answer. Instead, she covered herself up with the dressing gown that hung from the bathroom door, wrapping it tightly around her. She took out a cigarette and opened the window. Thankfully it didn't have suicide locks on, and she could unhook it to let some air in.

"You aren't supposed to smoke in hotel rooms," Celine said.

"Call the police," Laura smiled. "See what they do." Both let out a laugh, but it died in the air quickly. Celine appeared next to her and took a smoke from the pack and lit it. Laura flitted her eye to the cigarette.

"Hey," Celine said, "After what you just did, I need one of these." Both leaned out and watched the world of Wigtown go by.

"Crazy isn't it," Laura said, sounding like she was speaking to the wind rather than anyone in particular. "All those people. All those cars. All those lives. Just going about their business. Debt. Kids. Bills. Jobs and problems. They can have it all taken from them in just a couple of seconds. A bad phone call. A car accident. Violence. Then it's all over. What seemed so important one day means nothing the next." She took a long drag of her smoke, letting the blue ribbons disappear into the darkening sky. "How many of them do you think ever really live before they're too old and broken to do so?" A silence fell between them. Celine eyed Laura's smoke with curiosity, then took it from her fingers and took a drag. She exhaled and nodded, coughing.

"Yeah," she said, wafting the air. "Exactly what I thought. Weed." Laura pushed her playfully.

"Behave," she laughed.

"Getting all philosophical on me," Celine joked. "I'll have to leave right away next time we fuck before you turn all Fredrich Nietzsche on me." Laura dismissed the comment, flicking the smoke outside.

Both showered and lay on the bed. Celine cracked open the bottle of wine she had in her bag, in between her spare underwear and hairdryer.

"What?" She said, catching Laura's eyes on the bag. "A girl has to be prepared just in case." Laura pushed her hand into the bag and pulled out a vibrator that was as long as her forearm and ribbed down the sides.

"Prepared?" Celine leaned forward and pulled it out of her hands, throwing the instrument back into the handbag.

"You never know."

Laura took the bottle and they both took turns drinking in the quiet. The passion had faded from their skin. They sat there like two strangers once more, the elephant in the room making itself known.

"So, I'll just say it," Laura said. "You'll think I'm crazy. But I think whoever is committing these murders has something to do with me. Someone from my past."

"What the hell makes you say that?" Celine said, choking on her wine.

"The photo of me and my ex at the crime scene on the heart? All the women are a similar age to me. They all have a look of me, and I found my ankle necklace at my home. The one I lost after we found the girl in the warehouse."

"Shit," Celine said, moving in. "I didn't know about that."

"That's not the half of it." Laura told Celine about the blood on the mirror and the back door being open." Both of their blood ran cold. Celine closed the bedroom window.

"I don't know what to say…"

"Tell me I'm not crazy."

"I mean…" Celine said with trepidation. "It sounds weird, but not impossible. What makes you think it's your ex?"

"Because…" Laura said. "On that boat trip in South Africa, he told me, as he went overboard, that he will never leave me. That no matter what, he will find me, and he will ruin my life forever. That he would always find me and I wouldn't be able to stop him."

Laura stared out at the cheap flowery wallpaper that wrapped around the walls over a wooden tiled-looking border that met the blue and purple chequered carpets.

Ron was on one knee holding the ring that had a rock on it so big the reflection of the sun was blinded her. The sound of the waves hitting the boat died away. The seagulls that soared above vanished from her hearing. Instead, just her heartbeat remained thumping in her head.

*Run. Run away from him. Run fast and never look back.*

Ron's flawless smile was slipping at the edges. Laura eyed him, her mouth dry. The champagne in her hand turning warm.

"Well?" He said. "Will you marry me?" Time seemed to freeze.

"Ron… I…." She croaked. His face changed. He got up from his knees and closed the ring box, putting it back into his pocket. He turned to face the sea and mountains.

"I knew it," he hissed to himself, his hands pushed so far into his grey trousers Laura thought he was searching for a gun he forgot he stashed in there. He turned, his fists clenched, head cocked, eyeing Laura with the crow's feet that linger in the corner of his left eye. Laura wanted the sea to swallow her alive. "I knew that me doing all this would be a waste of money." She could hear his voice bubbling. He was angry, yes, she could always tell when the pot was starting to boil over. And my god, there was no way to turn the heat down. You just had to let the water evaporate completely.

"To think I wanted to do something special for you. For you! Of all fucking people. I wanted to bring you here, blow a shit tonne of money. The boat. Private beach. Champagne? Even the damn dress you're wearing costs more than a month's salary." He shook his head, eyeing the mountains.

"Ron," Laura croaked, putting her hand to her mouth. "I just thinked…"

"Thinked? You just thinked?" He snarled, leaning in. "You just fucking *thinked?* That's not even a word you dumb bitch. How the hell did you ever become a detective? I got you where you are today. Because of *my work. My skills.*" He was an inch from her face. "You think you're better than me? Think you can find someone better than me is that it?" Laura shook her head quickly, tears rolling down her cheeks and falling onto the bed of the boat. She didn't want to be here anymore. Didn't want to be on the sea. Wanted to be somewhere she could run away and keep running until her feet blistered and wore down, and then run a little more until they wore away completely.

"I'm sorry," she whispered. Ron reeled his hand back and slapped Laura across the face. She collided with the ground, her mouth filling with salt water that had begun to spit over the edge. The sea was growing rougher. The boat began to shake, and the rolling clouds grew darker.

"Sorry? You don't know the meaning of the word! Won't marry me after everything I've done for you. What, you fucking someone else? Is that it?" He stood over her, red-faced, spit slapping against her stinging cheek. "You slut!" He screamed over her. Laura could taste copper in her mouth. He hadn't hit her before. Maybe a shove or a nudge. He was sharp with his tongue, always happy to push her spirit down, but now he had become something new to her. He was more than a monster now. He was what she always feared he would one day show her. That thing that was beyond words. "Get up!" He gripped her by the hair and dragged her to her knees, her scream was carried away by the wind. "What if I just throw you over the brow of the ship huh?" Laura let out another scream of anguish. Her eyes looked for someone to help. Someone to come and rescue her. Someone to see what he was really like. Nobody ever saw this side. They only saw the happy and the smiles and the fancy suits and the promotion photos around the office. Nobody but her saw this, and nobody was around to see it now. "Fuck it!" He pulled the ring out of his pocket and threw it overboard. "Look what you made me do!" He snarled. "You can pay for that. I'll make you pay." He grabbed her and dragged her to the brow of the ship. She was forced over the edge her hair and head dangling over the railings. The sea was black and angry. Thick swaths of foam bashed against the sides. The abyss stared at her. The wind howled in her face, hair ravaging the both of them.

Ron's eyes were wild. Filled with unchained hatred.

"I'll never let you go. Ever," he hissed. "No matter what the hell happens Laura. You will be with me forever, on my life. If you ever try to leave me, I will find you and I will cut your throat and drink the blood whilst you choke on it." He threw Laura onto the deck. Her dress soaked in sea water. The heavens cracked open, and a fierce downpour of swollen rain cascaded down on them. His shirt was soaked, and she could see his body sticking to it like it had turned into melted plastic, the fabric dancing in the sea air. "Maybe that's what I have to do," he said, the rain dripping off his head, his lips spitting the water back to her. "I love you so much." He moved to the railings. "What if I just jump off?

End this whole thing? You'd like that, wouldn't you? You want to live without me. I'll do you the favour and do it for you." He clambered to the rungs of the railings and turned his face down to her. "Tell me you love me Laura," he hissed. "Tell me you love me, or I will jump." Laura went to speak, to beg him to get down.

She didn't see the wave hit the ship, just the feeling of being weightless, sliding out of control and the world turning upside down before that icy blanket of death bled away from her.

The wind cut through her. She coughed and spluttered, back pressing against the railings. Lightning carved along the black sky like a blade made of fire. Thunder bellowed over the dark mountains that jutted like teeth from a deadly giant. She wiped the sea from her eyes. Through the blur, she saw she was alone. She tried to stand, but her heels slipped. Fish and crustaceans gasped for air around her hands.

Through the railings, Laura saw only the endless hungry sea. Ron was nowhere to be found. She called out to him, over and over until the lifeboat rescued her.

She never saw him again.

# Chapter Thirty-Seven
# Sheree

Sheree lay with her stomach in knots. She tried making herself sick when he left, jamming her fingers down her throat and wiggling them until she felt her body convulse. But she couldn't. Something was stopping her. If she threw up, she would have nowhere to hide it, and he would know she had been bad. He would know that she had been dirty and was rejecting him. She could throw it up in her bucket but she was sure he would check, and bloodied straw covered in bile wasn't exactly subtle. So she had to let her body try to break down the bundle of straw and hay, feeling it churn in her stomach as she washed it down with foul-tasting water.

She didn't know how long she had been here. Time seemed endless. The night became day and then the sun relinquished again. How long had she been here for? No way of tracking the days. Nothing to keep a note of the passage of time. She had the nail. She could scratch something into the wall, but then he could see it and he would know that she had something.

Her mind began to spin as she lay there huddling herself on the sodden mattress, feeling like she had done all those times when a client had chewed her up and spat her out. She was a piece of meat to be abused. She was a song sheet of pain, and the world played her perfectly. Her skin felt like it was filled with lice that raced along her bones. Her head beat loudly like a war drum.

What had her life been? Just a series of fuck ups among other fuck ups. She was paying for it now. This creature that kept her locked away. This was her life now. This is how she had been born and lived, and she had chosen this way of life. She had been offered help from services – prisons, probation, rehab. Twelve-step programmes. Recommended books, meditation, and hypnotherapy. Social services, domestic violence workers, friends and hell, even the cops that threw her in handcuffs that spent hours talking to her whilst waiting in the desolate custody cells. All of them had helped her turn to a different path, and she always told them she would. Even meant it sometimes. But that meant facing her demons, and the drugs kept the monsters on the right side of the closet.

And this, laying on a mattress filled with stringy bile and dried piss, was her prize for wasting her life. If she got out of here, she would do all the right things. She would change her life. Again, she wondered if this was an immersive rehab experience. Show someone that their life isn't forever, and make them believe that this is the end then let them go free with their newfound freedom and lease on life. Kind of like the *Saw* movies. Where those less favourable members of society were made to fight for the life they had been so quick to throw away.

How she wished to have another chance. Just one more chance at redemption. She would go back to school. Get out of the block of flats she was living in where the neighbours sold crack and the local police were on first name terms with the tenants. She would make something of herself. She would get clean for good.

Sheree heard the door go, the sound of old keys turning in a stiff lock. Like a beaten dog, she retreated to the wall, pressing herself against it firmly, wanting to pass through it in a whisp of smoke and disappear out of the window.

The door opened, it scraping against the ground. He stood there. She began to scream. Not because of the knife in his hand, or the dripping syringe in the other. No. She screamed because when he looked at her, his eyes were void vats of emptiness. That he saw no hope in her future. No children. No education. No sunlight to touch her skin once more. He regarded her as nothing more than a piece of meat to be thrown onto the butcher's slab.

# XXX

You're getting closer, my sweetest Laura. I know that you have found my notes and my photographs. I'm infecting you as you did to me all that time ago. From the moment I saw you, you have grown like cancer in my mind.

I know that you are thinking of me, and me growing closer to you. I will have another body for you soon, oh so very soon.

The smell of your hair, the warmth of your bed. You can change the locks. Barricade yourself away. But I will find you. I have forever. How long can your nerves hold out?

We can be happy together. When you see the work I have been doing. We both want the same thing – to make this world a better place. We will be so happy together. You'll see. Away from all the bad, from all the pain. You're hurting and I can feel it. The way you move. The way you speak in your sleep.

You found the bald man with the drug problem right? In the warehouse where I left my last doll? I put him there for you. To follow my trail of breadcrumbs, to then hear about the girl. There is more to come yet though my love. The pieces are falling together. The breadcrumbs leading you to my home and you will see all I have done.

For you. This is all for you.

Like drowning in an ocean, only to resurface alone.

You will know how it feels to be abandoned. Locked in a shell with nothing but the shadows to keep you company.

I will see you soon.
*Kiss kiss.*

# Chapter Thirty-Eight
## Sheree

Hands gripped Sheree's throat as he pinned her to the mattress. She screamed a hoarse roar, thrashing like she was being mauled by a rabid dog. He grunted, teething, spittle pushing through those dead leather lips. His hands were rough, digging into her windpipe. Her hand pushed into his face, finding the soft parts, pushing her fingers into the drooping eye holes. Her fingernails scraped along the gelatinous ball of his iris. He pulled away, screaming and held his eye.

Sheree powered to her feet, bolting to the door. Sausage like fingers grabbed a hold of her hair, yanking it back like she was on the front row of some out-of-control roller coaster, her back clicking and cracking. She met the ground, and the putrid smell of shit and piss pushed up her nostrils.

A fist slammed into her jaw and rocked her. Her mouth filled with the taste of copper and her teeth loosened like mislaid concrete blocks.

The glint of the daylight bounced off the syringe as he clumsily pulled it out of his pocket. He flicked the cap off, the tip of the needle dripping with clear noxious liquid.

He hammer fisted it towards her chest, like driving a stake through a writhing vampire. Adrenaline red lined, and Sheree kicked him in the stomach. The wind expelled out of him, crumpling him like tossing plastic on a fire. But not for long.

He descended again with murder in his bloodshot eyes. He was back on top of her and brought the syringe down again. Sheree darted her shoulder out of the way, the needle tip scraping along the concrete. She coiled around his arm and sunk her teeth into his flesh a starving viper on a lost rodent.

Like tucking into a slab of raw meat still pumping, the flesh shredded between her jagged teeth. He screamed a long howl of pain. He released the syringe and scrambled for his knife. The serrated edge of death missed her by an eyelash, burying and tearing into the mattress as Sheree released her vice-like bite, pieces of flesh flapping over the wound like shredded beef.

A solid shin to the groin and he went down again. She dove on him again like a frenzied animal, biting deep into his neck. A flood of hot blood filled her mouth as a muffled scream perforated her ears. His bloodied hand came back, grabbing her hair, twisting her scalp like tearing out a rotten tooth with a wrench. She released her jaws in a burning bellow of agony, fingers scrambling under the mattress. She wrapped the rusted nail from the shower room in her palm and drove it onto his neck. The man's hand snapped to her, fingers slippery and clumsy with blood, the instrument jutting out like a slim Frankenstein bolt.

Sheree slipped from under him and grabbed the syringe, jamming it into his shoulder and depressing the plunger. She fell backwards onto the ground, panting heavily. He turned, pulling the needle out from his arm. That dead face fell to hers. He staggered to his feet, his hand clutching the bloodied wound. He took a step before collapsing to his knees like a drunk fumbling their way home. He swiped at her slowly with the knife, until he crumpled to the ground, the knife clattering from his fingers.

Sheree grabbed the knife and wrapped it in her fingers and unhooked the rung of keys from his belt line.

Sheree darted to the exit but slipped on the pooling blood, her knee smashing into the floor lighting up in white hot agony. She climbed to her feet like escaping a burning building and raced out of the room and locked her captor in with a heavy slam and click. Her heart hammered in her chest. Breath ragged. Eyes darting along the dark hallway with the single blinking light.

Sheree didn't have time to waste. She hobbled down the corridor and moved through the old offices filled with silent monitors and chairs that had been eaten away by moss and rot.

Down the rickety steel staircase, she saw the light to the outside world that was chained away behind a heavy lock. Moving as quickly as she could, her feet bare and shredding under the harsh metal, she made it to the door. She heard banging coming from behind her. Someone smashing their body against a metal door.

*He would have a spare key*, she thought through her blind panic. *I have to get out now!*

Sheree fumbled with the keys and the lock. Hands slipping with sweat and blood. She dropped the keys.

"Shit!" She called out. Nerves electrified. She was so close. So close to freedom.

She heard footsteps on the stairs. Her neck snapped backwards.

A figure draped in shadow. He was coming for her. He had gotten free. Her breath stopped dead in her chest.

The key slipped into the lock and turned. The heavy clasp came free and Sheree pulled the thick chains onto the ground like uncoiling a metal snake around a child.

Bursting through the open doors, the touch of wind on her skin made her almost break into tears. Ignoring the pain in her knee, she let those legs fly. She ran faster than she ever had, her feet shredding on the gravel. Her mind locked and loaded for the compound gates in the distance.

She didn't have long. She was getting closer.

*Fifty metres.*

*Twenty-Five.*

*Ten.*

She slammed into the gates that rattled around her. Her mouth dry as she fumbled the keys on the large lock that held the gates shut. She tried another. No. Another…

Footsteps rushed quickly behind her.

She turned. He raced to her. Face covered with a balaclava. Not a drop of blood on him.

*Climb!* Her mind screamed. She wrapped her fingers inside the fencing. The wiring sliced through her fingers and toes like she was clambering over dull razor blades. She eyed the barbed wire above her, it rusted and brown with specks of feathers and leaves clinging between the rungs. It smiled at her, hungry for the flesh she was about to part with.

*Come play Sheree. Fight for your life.*

Sheree's mind scrambled. Trapped between the devil and the deep blue sea. She grabbed hold of the barbed wire and its rusted teeth tore into her arm, bleeding her thin junky skin onto the metal fence. Her blood bubbled and spurted. Breath blasted from her trembling lips in sharp screams. Body on the verge of shutting down.

She forced her arm through and then moved her face towards those teeth.

A hand wrapped around her ankle and pulled her backwards, the wiring tearing along her bicep and forearm. She screamed fiercely, as her vocal cords sounding ready to tear.

He pulled on her leg like trying to dislodge a stump from the ground. Her blood raining down on him. The wired fence buried into her fingers as she clung on with all she could. The fence bowed and rattled around them. The blood found her ankle and his hand slipped from her, snapping her back against the metal. She climbed again, the barbed wire hungry for more.

Sheree's world began to spin. The blood loss. The adrenaline. The lack of food.

An eruption of pain in her leg. She turned and saw the syringe embedded in her calf with the plunger depressed.

"No!" She managed in a harsh whisper. A leeching of all she had. Her fingers gave way and she slipped from the fence, crashing to the earth. The world began to slip away, as his shape eclipsed the daylight.

# Chapter Thirty-Nine
# Laura

Laura writhed in silent despair as her words sank into the room around her. She hadn't ever spoken about what happened to anyone. Not really. Even her therapist didn't hear everything. The parts that mattered. Yes, she was sleeping okay. Yes, the medication was working. No, she hadn't been having suicidal thoughts. The usual rhetoric you had to tell a therapist who only gives a shit about you so long as you were paying them. And when that well dried up, they threw you to one side and let you feed yourself any comfort you could find.

Work knew, obviously. But that made things much worse. Ron was a well-respected detective. No one knew that he was a monster, and nobody would have believed Laura if she had told them. He was good at wearing the mask, and some people didn't want to see behind the scenes because the performance is too good for them.

"I'm so sorry," Celine said, touching Laura's back. Laura welcomed the touch, yet it felt alien to her. She was lost far away in her own mind staring at the walls. The crashing black sea. The faint hint of salt in the air that lingered in her nostrils.

"I stayed on that boat for almost four hours," Laura said. "Clinging onto the side of the railing while the sea pelted me. I got pushed out to sea. It was a miracle they found me. I think that was because the boat was only rented for an hour. They didn't come because of the storm. They came to save their asset." She felt the tears burning to break through.

"They found me curled up on the deck, shivering and wet through. I don't remember much of it, only that cascading black that bounced and threw me around like a huge hungry mouth that wanted to swallow me alive."

"When I got back to England, the local newspaper came to see me in the hospital and they did a story on me. *'Detective couple in tragic boat accident.'* I can remember reading the headline which made me feel sick. Flowers began appearing at my home and the hospital. *'Sorry for your loss'* and *'thinking of you in this hard time.'* No one knew what he was really like. No one could ever know. To speak ill of the dead, even though they were a monster through and through, is not something that would have gone down lightly."

"So that's why you transferred?" Celine said carefully, stepping over the subject like she was walking on eggshells stuffed with razor blades. Laura hardly heard the question.

"I got back to the station and there were flowers waiting for me from everyone I could think of. Then, I got back to work. But people were different with me. What started as something lovely and well-intentioned, their stares grew longer. Whispers around the office that I was somehow responsible. That I had caused him to go overboard. That I had left him to die in the ocean. That I was written into his will, that I was only with him because of his status and the bereavement money."

"That's ridiculous," Celine said, tracing her nails along Laura's back. "How could people think that?" Again, Laura appeared lost in her own monologue.

"The cheque came through. Apparently, Ron had changed the details on his life insurance in preparation for us getting married. So, I got the pay-out. It was enough for me to pay off my house and my car and stay in the MET police and see out the rest of my career with much less stress.

Maybe take a different route in the cops. Settle into something a little more relaxing. Reduce my hours, hell even take a few more holidays a year.

"But I couldn't do that. The stares, the whispers. Known as the fiancée of the beloved dead detective. The detective who brought down the infamous *Alex Thompson*.

*The Warburton Black Widow*, as I had heard someone whisper once. That was the last straw for me. I threw a coffee mug at the guy who said it. Some probationer. Not even a fleck of hair on his balls talking shit about me. I got suspended. Started drinking. So, my choice was to either stay where I was and live in the shadow of my misery, or transfer to somewhere new and make a fresh start. Then I heard through the grapevine of killings that were happening up here and that the media hadn't gotten hold of it yet. It seemed like life was giving me a break. An opportunity to make a new name for myself. To catch my own *Alex Thompson*. I put in the transfer request and DUTTON accepted it within a day.

"Why?" Celine said, enthralled by the tale. "Why did Dutton want you here?" Laura shrugged.

"Because she knew I was good. She knew that I was the woman for the job."

"Seems strange to me," Celine said. "The amount of requests they must have had for this case, and yet Dutton has been a hard ass with you since you got here."

"Maybe I got lucky." Celine shook her head.

"Luck doesn't work that way," she said. "Someone wanted you on this case. You need to be careful." Laura brushed the comment off. Arrogance flared in her mind.

"It doesn't matter now," she said sharply. "I'm off the case. My reputation is in ruins."

Laura broke down, the pain flooding through her fingers. Her face swelling red and her throat clamping shut. Celine pulled Laura's hands from her face. She eyed Laura's vats of pain that leaked all the anguish and trauma onto the bedsheets.

"Listen to me," she said firmly. "You're beautiful. You're not going crazy. If those fuckers in your old precinct want to think that you were to blame somehow for your abusive dickhead boyfriend's death, then let them. Like you should give a shit anyway. You are amazing and you're beautiful. From the moment I laid my eyes on you I knew that I wanted to get to know you. You are not going crazy. I believe you." Those three words broke through Laura's agony like a cannonball in a hall of mirrors.

"Sorry," Laura said, wiping her eyes. "God I'm such an ugly crier."

"You're a whiny little bitch," Celine giggled. Laura pushed her away and stood up, swaying her naked form to the bathroom.

She showered and came back in a dressing gown. Celine was helping herself to her cigarettes.

"Your phone hasn't stopped ringing," she said. "Dennis?" Laura felt confusion rattle her.

"He knows I'm off the case?" She took a smoke from Celine and sparked it up. The phone lit up again. She answered.

"Boss!" He said quickly, sounding out of breath.

"I'm off the case Dennis," she said, "you should call the Sargent. He's the one in charge -"

"Ma'am, be quiet and listen," he barked. Laura's train of thought stopped like the slamming of a door. He spoke quickly, rapidly like he was using his last breath. Laura's heart picked up.

"Go on."

"Where are you?"

"Busy."

"Well, you better get *unbusy*," he barked down the phone. Laura's body went rigid. "We know where he is. And he's got another victim."

# Chapter Forty
# Laura

"I have to go," Laura said, throwing her clothes on. Celine eyed her with worry in her eyes.

"Now? Who was on the phone?"

"Dennis. My data guy." Laura threw her coat on and grabbed her keys. "We think we've found *him*." Laura put her shoes on. "The units are en route."

"I'll come with you," Celine said, jumping to her feet.

"No!" Laura commanded. "I must do this on my own. My career is already in the shit. I'm not dragging you down with me."

"Fuck my career," Celine said. "I'm coming."

"No," Laura snapped. "You stay here. Go home. Whatever. But you aren't coming with me. You can't be seen with me or your ass is gone too. You have your life to think about. Me? This is personal now." She moved for the door. Celine grabbed her arm.

"What if it is *Ron*?" Celine said, worry lacing her voice. Laura halted, fingering the door handle. She turned slowly to meet Celine's terrified eyes.

"Then I know I'm not crazy. But at the same time," her voice barely audible. "Then my worst fear will have been realised."

Laura slipped out of the door and dialled Craig's number. Straight to voicemail.

She dialled Dennis back.

"Dennis."

"Ma'am," he said breathlessly.

"Text me the address. I'm on my way."

"Will do," he said.

"How did it come in?" She said, deciding to take the stairs rather than the elevator.

"From a witness. Saw a bloodied woman being dragged from a fence into a warehouse."

"Dead?" Laura said, moving into the reception.

"Unconfirmed," he said.

"Then we could still save her," she said resoundingly. "Text me the address now. I'll meet you there. And Dennis," she barked, moving along the car park. She heard his breath down the phone. "Don't do anything stupid." She killed the call

She tried Craig again. Straight to voicemail. She left a message. *"Call me immediately."* She fired the engine to life. It was probably nothing. Maybe they were just busy or the radio reception was shit. Or maybe it wasn't so clear-cut, and they were in trouble.

*Kiss kiss.*

Her phone pinged. An address from Dennis showed up. It was a warehouse of some kind. A disused abattoir on the outskirts of Wigtown. Laura hit the EMERGENCY button on the switchboard mounted to the dash and the flickers of blue and white came to life. She activated the horn, sending the sirens wailing and she drove like the devil himself was chasing her.

# XXX

Are you excited about the big finale? This is your moment. I can't wait to see you. Every minute I have spent without you has been like a knife grating along my soul. If I had one. I am convinced now that I don't.

But aren't good and evil just speculation? Completely subjective depending on the motivation or the information available? How can something like *good and evil* exist when it is completely dependent on context?

If I kill someone that is a murderer, a rapist or a child molester, does that make me a bad person? What if the local milkman, George, seventy-four years old and an upstanding pillar of the community all his life, was delivering milk to a local nursery laced with cyanide? If he was murdered, then is that a good thing or a bad thing? Is that good or evil? The line is so blurred…

You will find that I am not a cruel devil like you have been made to think. I have done what I have done for you. These people. These dirty, dirty fiends are scourges of society. What is more humane – cutting their life short, or for the rest of the country to work all their hours in their perfect little lives to pay for them to be locked in cages until their dying day? Does that sound like *justice* to you?

I am in pain. But through my pain, I am making a new world. A new life for me and you.

The bracelet. The photo. The phone calls. Mark. It all leads to me. The time for the conclusion is here. The big reveal. The climax of our tale together.

So, tell me, Laura. What are good and evil?

I will show you very soon.

Lots of love.

*Kiss Kiss.*

# Chapter Forty-One
# Sheree

A flicker of light pushed through her blurred vision coming from a small orb of white that flickered above her head. Her brain felt foggy like she was staring through someone else's eyes, unable to string a thought together. Her brain was a long drone of nothing: no thoughts, feelings, emotion. Just a white room of emptiness. She lifted her head. Her mouth was bone dry like she had been eating sand.

She could hear something. The sound of metal scratching together. She saw a figure in front of her draped in shadow. Their hands moved. The scraping coming from them.

Her feet nestled on the ground. It was soft. Sheree craned her neck to get a better look. Blinking hard, trying to clear the blur from her vision. Daggers carving up her back to the base of her skull. The light reflected in bright halos back at her, like the floor was coated in some kind of membrane.

"That's for the spillages," the figure spoke casually like he was simply telling someone what day of the week it was. The floor was covered in plastic sheeting, the same kind a painter might drape over your furniture, or that your grandmother would wrap around her couch to keep the leather fresh. A thought as clear as crystal pushed through the brain fog.

*You're going to die.*

Her arms were bound in bandages soaked in blood. She tried to move but her limbs wouldn't budge. Thick duct tape bound her to the chair that yearned aged groans under her weight. Under her forearms was a strip of metal attached to the arm of the chair. Under her ass, the chair was hollow with a bucket underneath. The only support was a small shelf that supported her lower back.

*To piss and shit in my dear,* a voice scraped along her mind. *We're in for a long ride.*

The figure continued to move items around on a small trolley, like the kind you would find at a dentist's surgery. Next to him, he had large white plastic buckets and jugs each with names she had never heard of – Sodium Hydroxide. Butyl Cellusolve. Ortho Phenylphenol. Formaldehyde. Each with huge orange labels supporting a picture of skull and crossbones. Her breath stuck in her throat.

Her arms and legs pulled against the restraints with what little strength she could muster until the duct tape began to chew her skin raw.

"Keep doing that and you'll wear yourself out," he said. Sheree pulled as hard as she could until she relented, letting out a defeated exhale. Tears breaking through her puffy eyelids. He turned towards the light. "And I want you full of energy for when our guest of honour arrives," The Straw Man said as he eyed the butcher's knife.

# Chapter Forty-Two
# Laura

Laura drove like hell hounds were nipping at her heels. She tried Craig again.

*Voicemail.*

"Craig, answer the fucking phone!" She put the call down and called her office. Catherine answered.

"Major investigations."

"Catherine, it's Laura."

"Oh," she said. "I'm not supposed to speak to you, ma'am. I have to go."

"Don't hang up!" Laura barked. Catherine hesitated.

"If Dutton finds out, I'll get sacked."

"If she does, I'll tell her I threatened to fire you." Laura banked hard on the other side of the road onto oncoming traffic that anchored on their brakes. Horns blasting through the air. The revs of the Audi redlining.

"Are you driving?!" Catherine yelped.

"Is the Sargent there?"

"No," she said. "I haven't seen him all day. What's going on?"

"Is Craig there?"

"No. Again, not seen him…"

"Have units been dispatched?"

"What units?" Catherine queried. "What's going on?" Laura's voice stammered.

"The call?" Catherine let out a frustrated sigh.

"Boss, I don't know what you're talking about?" Laura slammed her palm on the wheel.

"Just get units to the address I'm going to send you." Laura killed the call and opened up the messenger. Cars blurred past her as the speedo crept higher. She typed out the address, flicking her eye up at the road, cutting drivers off, slicing through traffic. She hit send. She called Dennis. He answered in one ring.

"Why haven't the units been dispatched?"

"What?" Dennis croaked. "Craig and the Sargent have already left."

"No one knows they're going!" She barked. "They're walking into a death trap!"

"Fuck!" Dennis shrieked. "It makes sense. Dutton's name is all over the log," he said quickly. His voice tinny, like he was on hands-free. "Something is wrong," he continued quickly. "I saw the call come on the list and then it was gone. Restricted, like she didn't want us to see it."

"That doesn't make any sense?" She yelled, hurtling through a red light. Tyres screeching in her ears.

"I had to break into the server to get the details. There's one more thing Ma'am," he yammered. Laura's heart plummeted. What other delights was he about to divulge? "We got another call after the witness. It was from *him*. He asked for *you* specifically." The blood drained from Laura's face. The revs disappeared into a distant echo. Headlights blurred like a torch through frosted glass.

*It is him. He is playing with me. Like he said he would.*

"Boss, you there?"

"I'm here." She said meekly. "Make the call. Get us back up." She tossed the phone onto the passenger seat.

She didn't see the lights were on red. She didn't see the overzealous range rover hurtling towards her. She didn't hear her scream escape her throat as the sound crushing metal and shattered glass devoured her.

# Chapter Forty-Three
# Catherine

Catherine eyed the phone confused.

"Who was that?" A voice came from behind her. Catherine's body flushed with heat. She turned slowly to meet the accusing eye of the Superintendent, Catherine looking like a deer trapped in headlights.

"Errmm…" Catherine said, her mouth falling open. "It was Jason from counter corruption. Just asking about some enquiry into the inspector. I said I would sort it."

Mary Dutton eyed her with contempt like observing a worm dying in the sun. Her face like stone.

"You wouldn't lie to me, would you?" Catherine shook her head.

"No Ma'am," she snapped. "I'm just a little uncomfortable with all this because I'm helping the investigation into my supervisor."

"Old supervisor," Dutton bit. Catherine regarded her and nodded.

"Old supervisor."

"Well," Dutton said after another moment. "Chop chop. Don't leave them waiting. I want her out the door before the end of the week." Dutton slipped away like a cold night when the dawn broke. Catherine let herself breathe. Her phone pinged. She eyed the message. It was an address. Catherine opened up google. An old warehouse. WELCH MILL. It hadn't been used in years. It was a mail depot before it was bought out and turned into an abattoir. What the hell was the inspector going there for?

Catherine checked the open incident logs. She couldn't find anything. Why was she going there so urgently? Checking the corridor was clear, she called Laura back. It went to voicemail.

"Ma'am call me back please," she said in a hushed whisper. She ended the call and sat there alone in the quiet office, wondering what web she had found herself caught in.

# Chapter Forty-Four
# Laura

The range rover slammed into the back of the Audi, exploding the rear window and showering her in a rain of glass and metal. She banked hard, narrowly missing oncoming traffic. She couldn't stop. Desperation wrapping its cold hands around her heart. Her colleagues' lives were in danger.

She drove on, the sight of furious motorists disappearing in her rear-view mirror. People got out of their cars and stood with their heads in their hands on a littering of glass that looked like jagged marbles. Someone would call that in. Something else to add to her resignation letter.

Laura arrived at the warehouse a few minutes later. It was similar to the place where she had found the body of Olivia Murray, or as the press had named her 'The Blood Angel.'

The night bled across a cloudless sky. The midnight sun hung over her like a ghostly hollow. A Black BMW sat empty in the courtyard.

*Craig's.*

No other cars met her eye. Where was Dennis? Where was her backup? The boys in blue should be here by now. Dennis should have called them. The more she thought about this, the less any of it made sense.

Why was Dutton speaking to the press? Why was she trying to derail the investigation? Just to discredit Laura? No. It had to be something deeper than that.

She would find Craig and Jeremy and then go after the super. She was going to blow the lid off this whole thing.

Crush her nightmares into the spiralling black whirlpool for good.

She reached for her phone but found it smashed under the passenger seat. She let out a frustrated scream behind her teeth. She pressed the side buttons on the iPhone. The screen blinked to life in a shattered rainbow of colours. She held the side button to speak to Siri, to ask the little machine to call Catherine back.

*Siri unavailable. Connect to the internet.*

No signal. No internet. No backup. She played with the screen as best she could and managed to get the torch going. Her heart lit up. At least if she was stumbling around in the dark, she would be able to see the monsters coming for her.

The gate was unlocked when Laura pressed against it. Her eye caught something above her. She shone her light on it and pressed her hand to her mouth. The barbed wire was coated in dried blood, and a hell of a lot of it too like a painter had had enough and tossed the whole tin of vermillion at the canvas and gone for a beer.

The warehouse stood tall like a monolith of darkness, resembling some kind of crypt. She pushed through the gate with a creaking that cut through the silence. Not even the crows nested in this place.

The air felt heavy, sick. Something bad had happened here. She could feel it. The crunching of the gravel under her feet was like loose bones. She approached the main entrance. Two heavy doors that had been chained together.

"Hello?" She called out. Her voice echoed around the courtyard of ghosts. Empty machines with smashed windows that sat long forsaken. Hidden in between the machines was another vehicle covered with a layer of tarp.

She lifted it and saw the vehicle. Laura didn't recognise the make, like something you might see at some kind of antique show. She eyed the reg plate.

It was the same as the Mondeo the first victim was found in. Someone had planted it here knowing Laura would find it. But why?

*Ghosts are playing games, my dear. You have unfinished business. Go inside. Go see him. He'll be so happy to see you again.*

She eyed old trowels stained with decayed feed. Straw and hay bales sodden with rain and mold.

*Straw.* The realisation slammed into Laura's mind. This was it. This was where it all ended. Laura pushed the heavy doors open and stepped inside.

# Chapter Forty-Five
# Sheree

Sheree screamed as loud as she could, tearing her throat like she was having acid poured down her gullet. He grabbed her thighs and dug his huge fingers into them like the jaws of a horse were digging into her, the knife dancing around her eyes.

"Good!" He said gleefully. "Keep shouting! Keep screaming! There's no one around for miles! Only her. She'll be here soon. But for now, it's just me and you." Spittle flew from his lips and slapped Sheree on the face. His eyes were mad like a wild animal. He looked like someone having the time of their life, and Sheree was the entertainment.

"Let me go…" She sobbed, snot running down her into her mouth. Her eyes red, tears salty on her tongue.

"You don't get it do you?" He said, leaning in closer. "What have you done with your life? Hmmm? How many family members have you stolen from to fill your veins with shit? How many lives have you impacted with your lifestyle? Wouldn't you rather die as something that benefits society rather than living as something that destroys it?" He wiped his mouth, a long sneer boring into her eyes. "You are but a rat in a world of lions. Society would be so much better without vermin like you."

"I have a daughter," Sheree cried. "I… I can't be without my daughter, you have to let me go!" Sheree slammed her eyes closed, falling into silent sobs.

"Your daughter?" He said, righting himself, a cackling laugh filling the room like an excited hyena. "You haven't seen your daughter since the social services took her from you when she was three months old, and that was four years ago!" Sheree felt a wave of pain slam into her chest.

"How do you know that?" She croaked.

"Because," he said, tapping his temple. "I know everything," he hissed. He slammed his hands onto the chair. Sheree recoiled. He swayed like a dancing cobra under the spell of a snake charmer. "I know that you were taken into care as a child because your drug-addicted mother didn't care about you." He leaned in closer. "And now, your child has been taken into care." He circled his finger around her face. "The wheel continues to spin." His face turned hard. "And it will continue to spin until someone breaks it."

His face was cruel, and she eyed him like he had the face of every lover that beat her. Every client that raped her. Every service that failed her. Every dealer that kept her hooked. He was the embodiment of all the wrong in her life, and in those dark eyes, she knew they knew each other.

"I know you…" She whispered. He nodded.

"Took you long enough." He righted himself, a long smile etched across his face. He moved back into the shadows. "I have something to show you," he said, calling back to her casually like he was asking if she needed something from the kitchen. The sound of a lock unlatching and the creaking of a door. Then the sound of wheels squeaking cut through the sound of her heartbeat in her head. She waited, staring into the dark.

The body emerged from the blackness on a wheelchair. Her skin a dulled yellow like marred brass. Hair roughly stitched to her scalp like hanging spider's legs. Her eyes sewn shut. Mouth stitched into a stretching smile. Straw breaking through the gaps like withered fingers.

Sheree's mind couldn't comprehend what she was seeing. Her mind fractured, the pieces disappearing down a black abyss. No words could invoke what she felt staring at that *doll*. It was beyond fear. Beyond terror. Beyond comprehension. He stood staring at the corpse, marvelling at it like a sculptor lavishes their fine work before the opening night at a museum.

"I'm going to take your fingers first," he said. "I learned that from the last one. Then, I'm going to take your toes, then your tongue, then your eyes. And then, I'm going to stuff you. Make you perfect. Make you pure." His words vanished into the air. She couldn't make sense of them. The sack of stuffed meat sitting opposite her. What she was to become. What he was going to do to her. "Beautiful, isn't it?" He said. He traced his fingers over the stitching. "Finally, you will be able to turn your life into something great." He stood silently, breathing long and deep. The air rattling out his lungs. "I have something else to show you." He wheeled the grim display back into the dark. Sheree wondered what else he would emerge with. Something that would firmly cement her mind in the barren plains of insanity.

She didn't know how long she sat there staring into the hungry blackness. Seconds? Minutes? Days? Time seemed to stand still. Suspended in a hellish dreamscape she couldn't escape from. Urine ran down her leg. Hot and potent. She held her breath. The trickling tapping on the inside of the wooden bowl under her.

He emerged again from the dark. Another wheelchair.

A man was bound unconscious and bloodied. He was wearing a suit, his head slumped against his shoulder like he had fallen to sleep in a drunken stupor.

"You know who this is?" The man said. Sheree stared at him vacantly. He snapped his fingers, waving at her. "Hey!" His voice reached that faraway place. She snapped to attention. "Do you know who this is?" He repeated. She eyed the bound man. She knew who that was. She hadn't seen him in years. Blocked out the memory with brown euphoria. But his face burst from her mind's eye. She swallowed dryly.

"Yes," she croaked. "He's the Sargent in the police. He's the one that took my child off me."

# Chapter Forty-Six
# Catherine

Catherine moved through the offices like her heels were on fire. A call blared through the radio of the uniformed cops of a car pileup on the A180 and was caused by an unmarked car driving erratically.

*Laura,* Catherine's mind snapped. *What the hell are you doing?* Officers jumped from their half-eaten food and darted out of the office. The radio went nuts with senior officers in the control room trying to find out what car it was and who the hell was going to get their ass handed to them. She needed to find where the rest of her team was. She had tried to call them but all went to voicemail. Her heart was in her throat. *Laura. She sounded in trouble.* Forgoing all preservation of her career, she marched to the superintendent's office.

She knocked on the door. Dutton answered quickly, pulling a face of war.

"Detective," she said.

"Ma'am," Catherine brushed past Dutton and moved into her office. Dutton closed the door. "Something's going on," she said breathlessly. "I can't get a hold of any of my team." She sat down with her hands in her hair, staring at the floor.

"What do you mean?"

"I can't raise them." She licked her lips, ready to kiss her career goodbye. "Laura called me. When I told you it was the counter-corruption unit… I lied." The air seemed to leave the room. "I lied to you and I'm sorry but I didn't know what to do. Laura was driving to the old abattoir on the outskirts of town. Saying she was meeting the Sargent and

Craig there. She sounded panicked and scared, but she didn't tell me why they were going there, but I think it's something serious. Something bad is happening."

"Slow down Catherine, slow down," Dutton said, her voice softening. She moved to her, putting a hand on her shoulder. "Let me make you a tea." She slipped behind her desk and Catherine heard the sound of a drawer opening. "Have you raised the alarm to anyone?"

Catherine shook her head. "No. I don't know if there's an operation going on or anything. I'm sorry I lied to you, ma'am."

"We can talk about that later," she said, putting tea bags in a mug. "Does anyone know?"

Catherine again shook her head. "No. I can't raise an incident. No one has said anything. I just don't want anything to happen to them."

Dutton nestled the tea in Catherine's hands.

"Good," Dutton said. She gripped the back of Catherine's head and forced the soaking rag over her mouth, smothering her nostrils. The hot tea fell to the floor and Catherine scratched at Dutton's fingers. The chloroform found its way into her bloodstream and her cries and whimpers became lighter, her arms growing heavy, and the world faded away.

# Chapter Forty-Seven
# Laura

Laura stalked through the empty space of the warehouse, tracing her torch along the disused machinery, milking racks and chains that hung from the ceiling and swayed gently as if swung by an invisible child. She called out in a harsh whisper into the foreboding silence.

"Hello?" Her voice flat in the dead air. She stepped further, the shards of glass and sand crunching under her feet. All of the windows were boarded up, the only slither of daylight from the dying sun.

She moved deeper into the belly of the beast. The door slammed shut behind her, the rattling of metal shuddering her bones. She turned on her heel and pointed the torchlight to the closed door. The chains swayed ominously. The darkness was suffocating, forcing its way down her throat, so thick she was almost choking on it. She fought every urge in her body to not bolt for the door and run into the night. Who had closed it? Was it the wind? Or was she not alone?

"Hello?" The word slipped from her trembling lips.

Footsteps.

Footsteps getting closer.

*Behind you!*

Laura turned sharply, dousing the darkness in light. Particles of dust filled the bright beam of the torch. Nothing faced her, only dead machinery that sat forgotten and rusted.

A door scraped open in the distance. Up ahead standing on the top of a staircase, she saw a shadowy figure slipping through a doorway that flickered with golden light. Laura's feet were nailed to the ground. She knew what she had to do. She had to go after them.

"Hey!" She called. Was it Craig? Jeremy? Even Dennis? Or was it *him*. Was this a trap? A rat in a hole?

*I should turn back. I should go and find a phone and wait for backup. I'm in over my head here. In way too deep.*

It was the ear shattering scream of a man that made her high tail it up those stairs. Rough, agonising. *Familiar.*

Laura burst through the door. What met her eye stopped her in her tracks like hitting an invisible wall. A long corridor flickering with the light of hundreds of candles that were placed along the floor, their flames dancing excitedly. Suspended from the ceiling were photos that spun slowly on thin thread. Hundreds of them. All of her. All of her and Ron.

Laura moved through them, trying not to touch them like they were doused in acid. Photos of them on their trip. The day they first met on the job. Cutouts of newspaper articles when they discovered the death house of Alex Thompson. Photos of them on holiday. Photos of Laura in lingerie. Pictures of Ron with his shirt off. Christmases. Birthdays. Weddings. A history of her life for her to see. She felt bile bubbling up inside her.

A door, heavy and thick stood open. The stench that emanated from it made her stomach dance even more. She peered inside it. A sodden mattress and a bucket filled with God knew what. A broken syringe on the floor. Dried blood pooled on the ground like someone had butchered a pig. The walls were marred with dirtied handprints.

Foregoing all preservation, she stepped inside. She touched the dirtied wall. Her fingertips marked with mould. She saw part of the wallpaper coming away by her feet.

Laura pinched it and pulled it away. On the underside of the fragment, was a word.

RAW

Laura peeled more of the wallpaper away. It crumbled in her fingers like overdone lamb. She discarded the sodden paper like bloodied bandages off a patient. Patchy plastering on brick came through. She eyed the underside of the paper, and she felt that train of bile hurtling to her throat. The words on the paper were a backwards imprint of the writing on the wall.

WARBURTON

Written over and over again, etched onto the walls as if by a madman.

WARBURTON. LAURA WARBURTON. LAURA WARBURTON.

Words and thoughts made no sense anymore. What she was feeling was beyond language. How long had this been here? Years? Decades?

She heard another scream. A woman. She tore away from the abominable shrine and raced out of the room.

At the hallway stood a closed door. Her mouth ran dry. This was it. Everything she needed to see. It was all behind that door. She moved closer. On the door a piece of paper. Laura's trembling hands touched the note.

*Ready to face your past Laura?*
*Kiss Kiss.*

# Chapter Forty-Eight
# Laura

The door scraped along the concrete floor as she heaved it open. The room was edged with darkness, only a single bulb of light illuminated against the grey floor and walls. In the corners, Laura could make out stacks of wood and crates. On the ceiling, butcher's hooks hung freely, and chains wrapped around the hooks and rungs. Rusted pipes pushed from the ceiling like old veins. The stench of chemicals burned her nostrils, like stepping into a mortuary. On the ground, flecks of dried blood met her eye, along with it on the walls. The ground was coated with plastic that reflected the bulb harshly. A woman faced away from her bound to an old wooden chair.

*Sheree. It had to be.*

She wasn't moving, and Laura worried it may be too late. Her body upright. She must be awake, but lord only knew what horrors she had been subjected to. Her hair was missing in clumps and her bloodied scalp wrapped what little strands she had left in bloodied piles.

In front of her sat Jeremy. His face bloodied. His eyes closed. What had happened to him? She went to rush to him, but something held her into place.

Jeremy creaked his eyes open.

"Laura! Oh, thank God. Come, get me out of here!" He pulled on his restraints harshly. Laura could see the raw friction burns on his wrists. How long had he been here? Where were Craig and Dennis?

He came into focus then. The sound of clinking and tinkering with metal in the dark.

*This is it. The face of the ghost.* The figure moved along the darkness. Her past misery coming to reap her and finish what he started. To fulfil his murderous promise that he made to her all that time ago.

"Ron?" Laura said, the world slipping from between her teeth, like she was speaking to the dead. Her heart fell into her stomach. She felt what little resolve she had begun to crumble as he stepped into the light. He was tall. Built. A large wound on his neck and a cut across his eye. She didn't recognise him at first. But that was for good reason.

It wasn't Ron.

"I've been waiting for this moment for so long," Craig said, caressing the handle of the knife.

# Chapter Forty-Nine
# Laura

When you believe something to be real: a faithful spouse. A secure job. A reliable car. The world has a habit of turning things on its head and dunking you inside black water that fills your lungs. She had been wrong all this time. It wasn't her past coming to claw its way back into her life. The monsters were much closer than that. Right under her nose. She had been consumed with her past traumas that she had ignored the earthquake erupting around her feet.

She had been holding onto the sick wish that she could see *him* again. Even though it was the last thing on earth she would ever want. To admit that to someone, that you missed the man that made your life a living hell, was insanity. But there was comfort in misery. At least with Ron, it was familiar agony. But now, she was lost completely.

"Craig…" She said his name repeatedly, trying to get her mind to turn over like a car with a dead battery. "What…" That came next. She couldn't think of words. Sentences made no sense anymore. Everything around her collapsing like a cannonball through a hall of mirrors. The shattered remnants of her mind, her life, stared back up at her in jagged shards.

"I was wondering how long it would take you to get here."

"Get him, Laura!" Jeremy screamed and squirmed in his chair, his face flushing with red. "Call for backup! Get me out of here!" Craig backhanded Jeremy across his face, sending those flabby cheeks hurtling west like he was sat on a motorcycle that had just cranked a hard turn. Jeremy crashed to the floor, still strapped to the chair, his face leaking red onto the plastic.

"Craig," Laura repeated. "I…" She pointed her phone to the floor. "What are you doing?"

"Isn't it obvious?" He said, holding up the knife. "I'm cleaning up!" He said this with a menacing glee, like a fairground operator who had installed daggers into the sides of the waltzers. "Did you know that 97% of resources are used up by just 3% of the population? Police assaults are going through the roof. Assaults on paramedics, doctors, and prison officers. The hard-working people of this country that give their sweat and blood every single mother fucking day to the likes of these wretches," he pointed the blade to Sheree who squirmed at the sight of it. "For them to suck the system dry."

"The system isn't perfect Craig," Laura said, her voice trembling. "We know that. We know there is evil in the world. But we can't –"

"Ah! Wrong!" He laughed, dragging out the last word. "The system is fucked. That's true, but… that's because no one has made a stand yet. A drug addict that beat and robbed a helpless old lady was found dead in a warehouse today. Nobody would even give a shit. Nobody cares about these scum bags. And good and evil? Ha! Just two sides of the same coin. It's all flawed. Who decides the rules? God? The government?" Craig looked at the glint of the bulb light dance along the edge of the knife. "Or do we make our own rules in this world? Maybe the system has gone soft? Oh, just give them another chance," he mocked. "Tougher sentences for knife crime. Tougher sentences for domestic abusers. Tougher this, tougher that. And guess where tougher has gotten us? More prisoners. More debt. More lives ruined.

Higher crime rates. Higher suicide and mental health issues. The system is broken Laura. You know it in your heart."

Laura looked around the room. A bale of straw sat on the table next to an assortment of cutting instruments.

"Are you going to gut me like you did those other women?" Laura spat. "The victims. Are you going to do to me what you did to them?" Craig paused, and both locked eyes.

"No," he said, lowering the knife. "You're too *pure* for that." Sheree's eyes widened.

"Pure?" She whispered. Her head craned back to Laura. "You're Laura Warburton, aren't you?" Laura swallowed hard.

"How do you know that?" Sheree reset her eyes and then glanced at Craig.

"It makes so much sense now…"

"What makes sense?" Laura coughed. "What the hell are you talking about?"

"What she means is, Laura," Craig said, taking a step towards her. "Is she found my old scribblings. The notes, the writing under the paint that I had done for you. When I met you all those years ago. Sheree stayed in my old room." Laura's brain began to squeeze.

"I… I don't understand."

"Sure you do," he said. He winked and mouthed to her. *Kiss, kiss.*

"Those days when my father would lock me away in this very warehouse, in those rooms when I was misbehaving. When you solved his case. Found his house of specimens. *Alex Thompson.* When he was out completing his work to save society. Getting the rats off the streets. You stopped him. Left me and my mother to fend for ourselves. "He was a cruel man," he continued. "He locked me in that room when I misbehaved, leaving me nothing but straw dolls to play with, telling me to make a *perfect* world with them. Then you and my brother ruined it. Ruined all of it!"

Laura didn't want to ask. The insect of truth and realisation burrowing into her mind. She didn't want to say it, but she couldn't help it.

"Who was your brother?" She whispered.

"You should know," he seethed. "You murdered him."

# Chapter Fifty
# Laura

"What…" All of Laura's limbs went numb. Her phone slid out of her hand, the torch light projecting her head into a distorted silhouette in a dull halo on the high leaking ceiling.

"I saw him with you. The way you both were together, and I thought, why can't I have that? Don't I deserve some level of happiness? After you put my father away…"

"Ron didn't have any family…"

"But he did Laura! That's the best part! He did have family. A loving family that needed his help and he abandoned us." Laura could feel the rawness of the emotions grating along her bones like someone was feeding chicken wire through her muscles and tying "My father beat my mother. Raped her most nights. But she couldn't let appearances slip. She *had* to keep going. Keep working. Do you know how embarrassing it would have been for her? The shame it would have brought on the family if she, after climbing the corporate ladder with blood, sweat and tears in a male dominated world like the police, that if she would have said that her husband was beating her and locking her son away for nights on end? Do you know what it's like to see your mother with vacant eyes that constantly hold a deafening scream behind them just begging to get out?" Craig slammed his fists against the tray containing the torture utensils. One fell to the floor and rattled on the ground. His eyes were reddening like a boy that had cried a thousand nights to the empty wind.

"And then my cock sucking brother found his happiness. Left us and spat in the face of what my father was trying to create. A better world for children to grow up in. Ron saw an easy road to success. He knew what our father was doing and let him continue until the time was right.

"When the case broke and we were rescued from here, mine and my mother's names and identities were kept out of the media. We were given new identities. Our old lives wiped clean from any records, and we were free to start fresh. I joined the police. To know my enemy. To get closer to my prey. To continue my father's work and exorcise my hatred for mankind's scourges that crawl along the ground like bottom feeders, sucking the life out of everything they touch."

"What does this have to do with me?" Laura croaked.

"He was avid on social media. I would look at your face on those long nights when I was trapped alone. I saw you both together, standing and looking so happy. It corroded what little bit of a soul I had left. I wanted that. I wanted *you.* I tried to craft you. To make you out of spare parts." He eyed Sheree. "But I couldn't. So, I found you instead."

"The photos at the crime scenes. My ankle bracelet. The message in my home. The anonymous tip offs. They were from you?" Craig nodded.

"Every single one." Laura swallowed dryly.

*Where is Dennis?* She thought. *Where is the backup?*

Jeremy moaned lowly on the ground, him coming round following the blow to the head. His eyes blinked the lights in his head back into existence.

"What the…" He groaned, flopping his head like a fish out of water.

"I knew you couldn't resist the case," Craig continued. "After the discovery of what my father did to those people in that barn. After Ron *solved* the case and took the glory for himself and propelled you to live in his shadow forever." He began to stalk around the room, stepping over Jeremy and tracing the knife blade along Sheree's shoulders who recoiled in harrow. "Living under the shadow of the man that abused you. Invisible to everyone but him. Sounds familiar to my situation, don't you think?"

"Ron was a monster."

"Apple doesn't fall far from the tree, does it?" He snorted a laugh. "I knew that I had to bring something to your attention. To draw you closer to me. Following the death of my brother, I knew that you needed something to prove yourself. That you didn't just earn your promotions because of how good you were at throating my brother's cock." Laura's skin crawled at the thought. But something in her mind scratched against the back of her skull like an insect.

*He was right.*

"I can make my own life," Laura croaked. "I *have* made my own life. Your brother... The things he did to me. The things he made me do. Every day I lived under his reign I felt I was drowning." Tears were gathering in her eyes. "The day your brother went overboard was the happiest day of my life. The day I could finally shed his cruel gaze from my back and I could start my own life again." Craig nodded.

"Of course. And you have done so well. I laid the bait, and you followed it, sniffing the air like a hungry dog for a chance at becoming your own person again. Your cunt dripping at the thought of getting that good hard case solved."

Laura heard footsteps encroaching behind the door to her back. They were here. Finally. A bolt of hope shot through her. Laura turned quickly and pulled the door open, ready for the boys in blue to charge into the room.

Dennis stood facing her. He smiled.

"Ma'am." He said as he casually sauntered past her like she was nothing more than a discarded bag of dog shit on the floor. What little feeling Laura had left was receding like a stagnant bog, revealing the bones of the dead that had been eaten to the marrow by fatty crayfish.

"Dennis," Laura croaked.

"Yes?" He said as he stood next to Craig.

"Where is the backup, Dennis?" She stammered vacantly. "Where are the others?"

"Hmm…" He said, putting his hands on his hips like a teacher who had just been given the third stupid answer of the day. He gave an exaggerated shrug. "Guess they aren't coming after all."

# Chapter Fifty-One
# Catherine

Catherine awoke with her hands bound and a gag in her mouth. She was hot. Practically boiling from the inside out. Her hair sticking to her head. Her eyes opened and blackness welcomed her. Contact on all sides. She was trapped.

*Am I dead...* She thought. She kicked out the best she could. Tracing the walls with her fingers.

*No, not walls, she thought. It was wood.* Her vision adjusted and she could make out a break in the dark. A slither of change. Doors. She was inside something with doors. She pressed her tied hands against the gap. It didn't budge. Claustrophobia ran through her. Trapped in an airless tomb.

She pressed her shoulder against the wood and pushed. It didn't budge. She inched for space. The back of whatever the hell she was in pressing against her.

*I can't move. I can't breathe. I can't move. I can't —*

With another hard slam, Catherine broke free and landed face-first on the carpet. The room was empty and dark. Catherine crawled along the ground like a caterpillar, pulling herself to her feet that were bound together with rolls of thick tape. She fingered the desk phone which fell and dangled from its handset.

She pressed her ear to it. No dial tone. Fear ravaged her. She clambered to her feet, using the desk for leverage. She was still in Dutton's office. Locked away in the dark. She felt woozy and caught herself on the desk before she said goodnight on the carpet.

*Laura.* The name slammed into her mind like a home run at the baseball landing in the mouth of a drunk punter. She needed to get help before Dutton came back. Catherine tried to find anything she could to cut herself free but drew nothing. No scissors. Pens. No staplers. Nothing to cut herself free with.

It was night, and nobody would come to check this office until the morning. She had to get free. She had to get help for Laura. Catherine shuffled herself to the door. With sweating palms, she loosely tried to turn the door handle. Locked. Her mouth, arms and legs bound, she desperately searched for something to cut her loose. Finally, she saw something. She had an idea. It was crazy, but it could work.

She worked herself up the desk and pulled open one of the draws and pinched a bundle of paper in her fingers. She dropped them on the floor, the chloroform still running through her veins. She took a moment and breathed deeply, before grabbing the discarded sheets off the ground and placing them roughly into the waste bin under the desk.

She gripped the neck of the desk lamp and flicked it on. A few seconds passed and she tapped the lamp to her skin and felt it was hot. She fumbled and pulled the lampshade off, the bright orb burning into her eyes. The tape around her mouth began to move towards her nose, constricting what little airflow she had left. She smashed the glass around the bulb, careful to keep the filament intact. It was hot, like a firefly burning through the night air. She pulled the lamp down and pushed it into the paper bin. It began to smoulder, then flames began to emerge like a golden spirit from dead ashes. Catherine placed her tape-bound hands over the flames. She could feel the heat eating away at her skin, bubbling the plastic that bound her arms.

A scream of pain erupted behind her gag as the flames cooked her wrists. Finally, they came away with a snap. She pulled the gag from her mouth and let herself cough onto the ground. Then, she unwound and peeled off the tape around her legs.

The room was filling with smoke fast. She raced to the door and tried the handle again. It was locked.

Flames leapt out of the bin and fell onto the carpet and began to smoulder. The fire alarm burst into life, blaring in her ears. Catharine banged on the door as hard as she could, screaming, inhaling thick smoke. The flames began to spread like flaming hands up the walls. The paint bubbling and popping like swollen boils. The flames ate the carpet like a river and yellow dancers. She ran, picking up a chair and hurled it against the office window but it bounced back at her, falling to the flames that devoured it hungrily. She screamed more, her lungs burning. She was trapped, and the flames were going to eat her alive.

# Chapter Fifty-Two
# Laura

"You were in on this the whole time…" Laura croaked, glaring at Dennis. He nodded.

"Of course!" He said. "It was quite simple really. I have premium access to the systems. I'm the *data guy*, remember? I was able to put it all together for you to find like a trail of breadcrumbs leading straight to us and the work we have been doing!"

"I'm going to be sick…" Laura said breathlessly, flushes of heat running through her. "Dennis. Why?"

"They are rats ma'am," he said. "Nothing but rats, the lot of them. My mother. She was robbed a few months back by these scourges. We couldn't find who did it. Took everything from her. She killed herself. Jumped from a bridge." His voice changed. It was hard. Words laced with potent venom. "I saw what Craig was doing. I had the chance to report it. But then I saw the long list of violent crimes coming in. I wanted to be part of solving the solution, and not just throwing a bandage over it and hoping it didn't bleed right through."

Laura could see it all now. The trail. The motivation. The power of a mother high up in the force. Even the bodies filled with straw in Craig's warped childhood trauma-ridden mind. The way his father killed those people. She could only imagine what it must have been like living with such a monster. She didn't need to think too hard.

"Does Mary know?"

"Of course," Craig said. "She knows I won't stop, and she won't see me in prison. And she also knows that the reduced crime rate will get her higher up the ladder."

"Explains why she doesn't want me here…"

Dennis quickly moved to Sheree. "Don't you see?" He erupted. "We gut this bitch, let her bleed out onto the ground. We clean up our DNA, and then we cut the spinal cord of the piggy in the suit and let him take the rap for it all. He's the reason the MIU was going to shit. He didn't give a fuck about the lives of the people that were being ruined. Only about getting through the day doing as little as possible. We get to be a part of history and you get to have your time in the spotlight again." He eyed Jeremy who was blubbering like an idiot, drowning in a pool of his own blood, snot and tears.

"You want me to help you…" Laura gasped, the air barely leaving her lungs. Craig stepped forward, moving towards her.

"We can actually make a difference here Laura. Truly, we can. We can be famous and rid the world of these people for good. My mother raised media attention. The force will take anyone as their scapegoat. Our unit will be hailed as being the best." He stared into her eyes. She had never noticed it before, but they were just like Ron's. Maybe that's why she thought she recognised him the day she met him? Or why when she had destroyed her home in a drunken stupor she fell into his arms and let herself be held by him? They were all damaged. Just some found it easier to hide than others. In this *Cutting Room,* all of you is stripped back to the bone and everything flows out.

Craig placed his hands on her shoulders. She could smell the death emanating from him.

"Let us help each other. Let us change the world. You came to me, Laura. Call it crazy, call it fate, but something led us here to be together right now. A million other things could have happened to us along the way, but here we are now. I want us to be together. To be the team you and Ron were. To bask in the glory of the world."

Laura turned her face away. She couldn't look into those eyes. But then, something awoke from inside her. Something primal. Something deadly.

"You're insane," she bit. "You deserve to be in the hospital with your demented father."

The back knuckles of Craig's hand slammed into Laura's face, throwing her to the floor, filling it with the familiar taste of copper. She looked up to him, him towering over her. Like she was on the boat again. She spat crimson onto the ground.

"You're just like your fucking brother," she hissed. He smiled.

"Love makes you do crazy things. You'll come to my way of thinking. You're off the case. No one knows you're here. You have no one around you to miss you. Who will come looking for you? Nobody Laura. And I will keep you here, just like I have the others. Until the day you love me."

"You're never going to get away with this," she hissed through a bloodied mouth.

"And that," Craig said, moving towards Dennis who was staring at Sheree like a dog eyeing a fresh piece of meat. "Is where you're wrong." Craig pulled his hand back, grabbed Dennis by the collar and drove the knife into his neck. Blood spurted out in a bright bubbling fountain onto Sheree's face. She shrieked a banshee's wail. The blood drained from Laura's face. Dennis contorted and twisted. Craig yanked the dripping knife free, Dennis' mouth bubbling with thick blood. Craig drove the knife into Dennis' back again and again. Blood splashed his face and it rained onto the floor. Flesh carving clean from bone. Clothing tearing and ripping. Laura wailed. Sheree screamed and Jeremy sat wide-eyed, trying to comprehend what was happening.

Dennis collapsed to the ground, a guttural rasp escaping his lungs. His life force pooling around him, soaking the plastic sheeting as the thick murk coated Laura's hands like a red tide. Craig remaining stoic. Nothing behind those menacing eyes like he had simply dumped a bag of trash in the waste bin. Killing was nothing to him. Dennis. Laura. The world. They meant nothing to him. They were as disposable as the air he exhaled from his sickened body.

Dennis stopped twitching. Sheree's screams escaped her mouth like sharp sporadic hiccups. Craig righted himself, wiping the knife on his trousers, running his bloodied hands through his hair like hair gel.

"I never liked him anyway," he said. "Creeped me out." He pulled out a pack of cigarettes and lit one, walking bloodied footprints around the room like he was taking a dog for a walk or going to the kitchen to fetch another beer before the big game starts.

"Why Craig?!" Laura screamed, pressing against the floor. "You monster! What did he do?"

"Nothing!" He said, taking a long drag. "But I don't need dead weight in my life. He could have talked. Dead men don't talk Laura. What's the saying? Two men can keep a secret as long as one of them is dead?" Laura began to sob. Her tears mixed with the still pool of red that soaked into her. Craig shook his head disapprovingly. "I killed him to protect *us*. Don't you see that? He knew! And he would have talked Laura. He would have torn us apart."

"Fucking die..." Laura hissed. "And what if I tell? What about that? When I go and tell the world about your sick experiment?" He burst out laughing, chuckling to himself like a mad schoolboy. "What's so funny?" She blurted, rage gripping her. Those evil eyes flashed to hers.

"What makes you think you'll ever leave?" He laughed sinisterly. "You're going to stay here where I can be with you forever. Maybe we'll even have kids? Maybe a family. Just the lot of us, tucked into our perfect life. The way I have always wanted. The press will ask where you are of course, but mother will sort that. Maybe tell them that you're pregnant. Get a real love story for them to talk about. And then, in a few weeks, some celebrity will leak a sex tape or some politician will be caught hanging out the back of an underage girl, and the world will move on. They will forget your name. Just like they forgot about me. And I will have you all to myself. Finally. My perfect woman. My perfect life." He stabbed the knife into the air. He moved to the rickety tool trolley and pulled out a leathery mask of a mutilated woman and donned it on his head. Laura looked into those zombified drooping sockets. A sight that would haunt her every time she closed her eyes. He turned to Sheree. "Let's begin, shall we?"

# Chapter Fifty-Three
# Laura

Craig taunted the knife edge around Sheree's face. Then without a word, he buried the knife into Sheree's thigh down to the handle. She wailed. Oh, how she wailed. An ear-shattering pitch Laura didn't know that the human body was capable of hitting. Something exploded inside Laura's body, and she found herself charging toward Craig. He yanked the knife out, a flow of red gushed from the wound.

"Stop it!" Laura screamed, rushing for the knife. Craig parried, driving a fist into her jaw.

"I don't want to hurt you, Laura!" He panted, his shirt sticky with sweat. "But this is the way it has to be. It makes sense!" He turned back to Sheree and grabbed a fistful of her remaining hair. She howled once more. A hand coiled around his ankle. He turned to see Laura bloodied and enraged, pulling him away. He kicked out, colliding with her shoulder. A sharp pain erupted in his fingers. He screamed and turned to see Sheree clamping down on his index and middle finger with her teeth. He tried to pull them free, but they wouldn't give. His world turned into an inferno of agony as he heard the crunching of his bone, and then finally the release as he fell backwards. Bloodied stumps where his fingers once were. He fell to his back, gripping his hand. The knife clattering to the floor. Screams muffled by the dead leather mask. Sheree worked at the binds quickly, pulling and kicking like she was about to slowly be descended into acid. Her face bloodied, strands of flesh and bone nestled between her teeth. She drove those bloodied gnashers into the binds and tore through them like a hungry rat. One arm free, she pulled at the other. Laura clambered to her feet. Craig stood, moving for the knife. Another wail of pain left his mouth as Sheree drove her heel into his palm. He gripped her ankle and thrust her into the air, tipping her strapped to the chair on her back. He straddled her.

"You have been a pain in my ass since I picked you up," he hissed, bringing his huge hands over her face. "I'm really going to enjoy this." Laura crawled on her hands and knees. Slipping along Dennis' blood. Gasping for air. Inching towards the knife. Jeremy's face met her eye. He wasn't moving. Was he breathing? His body bathed in the blood that flowed from Dennis.

Craig drove his palm into Sheree's face, dislodging two of her teeth. His fat fingers crawled along her cheeks towards her bulging wild eyes like a hungry spider. She bucked and writhed, slapping, grabbing, and kicking the ground. She couldn't move. That dead woman's face all she could see, before he jammed his thumbs into her eyes.

Agony. Searing hot agony consumed every inch of her. Nothing else existed but pain and the scream that exploded from her mouth. She clawed at his hands in vain. She kicked and writhed and screamed as blood began to pool around his fingers from the bursting of jelly balls in her head. He was laughing. Screaming in glee so hard he was close to ejaculating.

Laura drove the knife into his back. He erected, the wind blasting out of his lungs. He clambered, falling to the ground. Laura pulled the knife free then grabbed Sheree's broken body. Her eyes pits of bruised and congealed red.

"Come on," Laura croaked, pulling her free from the chair. They hobbled to the door. Sheree was silent, touching her face. The door burst open. Red dots danced around her and Sheree's body like a kid with a laser pen playing with the pet cat.

Cops clad in black body armour and helmets aimed their HK53 rifles at them.

"Armed police!" One screamed. "Get on the fucking floor now!" Sheree waved her hands out, blinded and frightened. Laura held her hand out screaming for them, trying to get them to listen to her. Adrenaline red lining, the bloodied knife still in her hand.

A rifle cocked.

"Drop the weapon! Put it down or we will shoot!" A cacophony of explosive voices bombarded them. Laura stared into the blinding lights mounted on the weapons.

"Shoot them!" Craig screamed, tearing the mask from his face and tossing it to the ground. "They've stabbed me! Shoot them! Don't let them escape!"

"Put your weapons down!" Laura screamed. They couldn't hear her.

"Drop the knife!"

More screaming. More reasoning. Sheree rushed forwards. Laura grabbed out at her.

A weapon fired.

# Chapter Fifty-Four
# Laura

Laura dove to the floor as the gunshot rung out. Feet rushed past her, the knife on the floor and kicked away into a corner by a heavy boot. Sheree lay in front of her. Laura moved to touch her, but hands gripped her under her arm and hauled her away. She turned. Craig was standing there with his arms outspread, the mask covering his face. The depiction of terror in human form. In his hands were two bloodied knives.

He rushed them and they opened fire. His body exploded in all directions. The sound of the gunfire rattling through the hallway. The photographs of her old life dangling around her, she traced her fingers over them as she was carried away by a brute in black, letting her bloodied fingerprints mark the end to them all.

Craig fell to the floor. She could hear Jeremy screaming and calling out. Sheree was carried out of the hallway, her head falling back like a broken doll.

The midnight air hit her face. She would cry, but she had done enough of that. An ambulance was in the courtyard. Laura was placed on a gurney and paramedics poked and prodded her. Sheree was piled into an ambulance. The light strip flickered through the night. Sirens blared as it sped out of the compound. More squad cars arrived. Dog handlers. CSI vans. PSU and a helicopter hovered overhead.

Another ambulance was idling in the courtyard. Light spilling out onto the gravel. Inside, a familiar face sat in a blanket blackened and covered in soot. Catherine sat sipping a cup of coffee. When the medics were done, Laura sat with Catherine on the edge of the ambulance.

Firearms officers walked out with Jeremy, who was placed into another ambulance. Then the body bags soon followed.

Her eyes met Catherine's.

"You saved my life." She whispered. Catherine placed a hand on Laura's shoulder.

"Just doing my job," she said.

"You deserve a promotion." They shared a beat of silence. An alarm struck her. "Mary Dutton," Laura went to continue but Catherine hushed her.

"She's fled the area. She won't get far. We've got a PNC circulation. She's on every news channel. Even Interpol have been made aware in case she tries to flee the country." Laura let the news settle in, then felt a wave of admiration creep into her stomach.

"I shouldn't have given you such a hard time Catherine. You did real good."

"Stop," she said. "You'll give me a big head."

A moment later, Laura rode in the ambulance and was checked over at the hospital. In the bed across the ward, she saw Sheree with bandages around her face and her leg with IV drips attached to her like she was some kind of science experiment.

Jeremy was quickly discharged after an MRI scan and some medication and follow-up appointments for counselling. Celine visited and Laura gave her her house keys to check on Bagpipe. Finally, she let herself fall to sleep, and for the first time in years, nightmares of the ocean didn't visit her.

# XXX

I tried. Please know that I tried. All this was for you. I was searching for perfection. Isn't that what we all want in our lives? Love? Happiness? Purpose? Perfection?

My reasons for doing all of this. I knew you wouldn't understand. But I believed in you. I believed in us.

Please don't hate me. I'm in pain. I'm always in pain. It never ends.

I feel cold. It's turning dark around me. Please don't hate me for what I am. But love me for what I wanted for us. That's all I ask.

# Chapter Fifty-Five
# Laura

The news story broke and there was around-the-clock coverage for three weeks solid. Candle-lit eulogies. Midnight marches. Investment into drug and rehab facilities from the lottery fund to get people off the streets and into work. Investment into deprived areas. School talks. Apprenticeships for released prisoners. Domestic violence refuges set up.

Despite the methodology, Craig had made a difference in the world after all, and in a way, Laura had a shred of respect for that. And just as he said, a new scandal broke, and the story was thrown onto the pile of washed-up news.

Eight more bodies were recovered from the bowels of the warehouse. Each of them was preserved and disfigured. The infamous *Straw Man* killings. Officers that had made the grim discoveries went off with stress and were booked a long string of counselling sessions. Laura doubted they would ever return to work.

The bodies were identified, and a further three were found in abandoned buildings all over Wigtown, each in varying states of decomposition. Some with their hair dyed the same colour as Laura's. One or two were found wearing some of her clothes. That explained the empty hangers in the wardrobe.

Dutton had been arrested for trying to board a ferry at Dover using a fake name. The trial was in a few weeks, but Laura didn't care. She would hear about it sure, but the less time she spent thinking about it the better.

The police family liaison officer tracked down each of the victim's families to give them closure. Some slammed the door on them, their children's choices and lifestyles rendering them dead to the family long ago. Some cried. Some stayed silent. Grief affects people in many ways. But it always hurt, no matter how hard you tried to bury it. It always came out in some way or another. You had to feel it, to let it heal, and then you can truly move on with your life.

The day Laura got home from the hospital, Celine had had the locks changed and she offered her a celebratory drink. Laura turned it down.

"None for me," she said, then took Celine to bed where they fucked until the sun rose in the morning.

With the golden dawn caressing her face, Laura slipped from her warm sheets and into her work clothes. She kissed Celine's rouge lips and traced her bronze skin. She was so beautiful. Even first thing in the morning.

She stepped into the station and was greeted with a barrage of claps and cheers as her name and huge 'WELCOME BACK' banners were draped on every wall. She said her thanks, gave a little speech, then said that she needed to get back to work.

In the office, Jeremy was typing away on his computer, his eyes still a little dark around the edges. Catherine was sitting with a bunch of files on the desk and gave her a silent nod as she slipped into her chair. Two new recruits were sitting at the once vacant desks. Laura nodded them a hello, and they both sprang to their feet, fighting over who would get to make her coffee. Laura held up her Starbucks, and then the conversation moulded to if she wanted biscuits to go with it.

She opened up her inbox and began cycling through the emails. Her curser stopped over one. She clicked it.

*Detective Inspector Laura Warburton.*

*I would like to thank you for everything you did for me. I'm doing okay. My eyes were saved but I'll walk with a limp now for a little while. After what happened I checked myself into one of the new rehab centres. I'm a month clean now and living somewhere new away from my old triggers. That's something the therapist told me. I need to watch for 'triggers,' and that included people.*

*I've been working closely with the social services and I'm going to see my daughter in a week. I can't wait. It's been so long. I hope she recognises me.*

*How do you cope with your demons? Mine won't go away no matter how much I try. But then again, maybe after I have finished my course and gotten the hell out of Wigtown for good, I'll be able to sort that too. One thing at a time.*

*One thing that all of this has taught me is that what we have isn't forever. We think it is, but it can be easily taken away. We can blame the world for our own circumstances, but it comes down to making the right choices. Something I am trying to do.*

*Life is for living, not just surviving. And I have been just surviving for so long I have forgotten what it feels like to be really happy.*

*Anyway, that's enough from me.*

*Take care of yourself. Keep up the good work, which is something I never thought I would say to a fucking cop.*

- *Sheree*

Laura leant back in her chair, sitting for a moment, contemplating the email before opening a reply.

*You're amazing Sheree. Don't let anyone ever dampen that spirit you have inside you.*

*Until we meet again –*

*Det. Insp Laura. W*
*M.I.U*

A knock came at the door. One of the helpdesk officers.

"Ma'am," she said. Laura looked up from her computer.

"Hi, how are you?"

"There's someone at the helpdesk wishing to report a crime."

"Is everyone out *there* busy?" She said, scanning the room with a slight smile. The helpdesk officer didn't share the joke.

"He asked for you personally," the officer thumbed the door frame. "He's in a bad way." Laura closed the computer and got up from the chair.

"I'll be right there."

She moved through the office and as always, cops were running around like frenzied flies trying to stop the world from falling apart. Moving along the station to the front desk, she saw a man standing there who looked like he hadn't slept in a month, chewing on his nails and fidgeting.

"Good morning, sir," she said. "I'm DI Warburton. How can I help?"

His eyes fell into hers and she saw desperation spiralling in those bloodshot eyes.

"I need your help," he sniffled and pulled out his phone, a picture of a young boy maybe around age six, on a big beach with a bigger smile. "My son," he said, fighting back the tears. "My son is missing."

For the exciting next book in the series, head to Amazon – Jay Darkmoore..

If you enjoyed this title, please leave a review. Reviews are how indie authors make a name for themselves and are able to keep releasing content for you hungry readers to eat up.

Thank you for taking the time and spending it reading my work. I thoroughly hoped you enjoyed it.

Join my newsletter and receive a free story and news about new books!

www.jaydarkmooreauthor.com

Follow me on social media –

TikTok - @jaydarkmoore
Instagram – Jay_Darkmoore_Author
Facebook – Jay Darkmoore

## Thanks for stopping by!

o        J

Jay Darkmoore is a UK-based author with a background in crime and investigation. He is a huge fan of all things dark - exploring the macabre, demonic and darker aspects of the human psyche.

Jay likes putting his characters in terrible situations and then turning out all the lights. To date, he has self-published novels of horror, crime and dark fantasy dystopia. His inspirations are Stephen King, Keith C Blackmore and Nick Cutter.

When not at his desk, Jay spends his free time making YouTube videos to help writers in their craft, promoting other books he has enjoyed, as well as hitting the gym and taking wild cold plunges with ducks.

He is a single parent to his son Joe who is his biggest fan.

Printed in Great Britain
by Amazon